KNOX'S WIFE

Janet Walkinshaw

By the same author

Long Road to Iona & other stories

KNOX'S WIFE

Marjorie Bowes was six years old when England rose in revolt against the religious reforms of Henry VIII . . .

Chapter 1

For Marjorie, God was her Grandfather Aske. He lay, long and thin, on the daybed in his bookroom surrounded by warriors and writhing monsters waiting to be vanquished.

'What's that?' he would ask, pointing his stick. Marjorie put her hands behind her back. She'd been warned not to touch the tapestries in Grandfather's room because they were precious.

'A unicorn, Sir.'

'What does it mean, the unicorn?'

'A virtuous woman.'

'What does virtuous mean?'

'Sir, a good woman who loves God and obeys her husband.'

The unicorn became entangled in rosebriars and was shot by the huntsmen and carried to the king. Marjorie couldn't see the point of being virtuous if you were going to be killed and eaten. She said so.

Her grandfather guffawed, his wheezy laugh turning into a choking cough that brought the servant running.

Then her mother hurried Marjorie from the room and scolded her for being insolent.

The person Marjorie loved most after her mother was Annie the nursemaid. Annie was fat and squashy and smelt of the caraway seeds she was always chewing for her stomach. Annie had nursed all the Bowes children. Marjorie was the eighth and there would be more. Some nights Annie ate too much sweet pastry and couldn't sleep and sat up in bed burping and sighing. She would wake Marjorie and take her into bed and cuddle her until eventually Annie fell asleep, snoring noisily with her head thrown back and Marjorie would slip back to her own cot.

*

Back in those days of rebellion, there were tenants in dispute with their landlords, and men escaping retribution for their crimes, and some who just wanted excitement. There were many who were angry, or hungry, or both. But for most the uprising was in defence of their God. They called themselves the Pilgrims.

Marjorie learned the facts and the legends from her mother and servants as she was growing up.

But she had one memory she never spoke to her mother about, not even in the years when they were friends, before they both fell in love with the same man.

*

The rebellion started in October, 1536. It had been raining for days and the leaves which had been bright orange only a week before lay in heaps on the paths and were turning black and slimy. The back way between Aske Manor and the village lay across the meadow shorn of hay, through the coppice, and over the bridge which met the high road leading north to Scotland and south to London where Good King Henry lived. They said prayers for him every night.

They were going to the village to visit Annie's sisters. They had reached the high road and paused while Annie stood panting with a hand at her chest, for the last bit of the path was steep, when they heard a noise, the sound of singing and shouting. Annie shrank down below the level of the road and pulled Marjorie down with her. First along came some men on horseback. Then there were two men carrying a red banner slung on poles above their heads.

The banner had five hands painted on it. Marjorie thought they were badly done. She could paint better than that and she knew that hands were pink and not white.

These two were followed by some men on mules and then a lot of boys and men on foot. There were women running alongside them, laughing and singing as well. The singing was ragged, the words whipped away on the wind. Now and then there was a splatter of raindrops from the overhanging trees and the men shook it off and swore. Some of the men were marching in step, like soldiers. Marjorie knew about soldiers. Her father was one.

'Is it the war, Annie?' she whispered.

'Sssh.'

Some carried muskets. Most carried staves, with here and there a long pike. Some had bows slung over their shoulders and a holster of arrows. More horses followed, great beasts that looked as if they should be pulling a plough, not carrying three or four men on their backs. The men paid little attention to the woman and child crouching beyond the ditch, though some of the boys shouted at Annie, words that drew her snorting laugh.

The last of the procession passed, several carts laden with barrels and boxes, and pulled by poor-looking mules.

When the noise was fading, Annie and Marjorie cautiously picked their way along the verge of the mud-clogged road. The strangers stopped in the village and Annie, holding tight to Marjorie's hand, skirted round the backs of the cottages till they came to the one where her sisters lived. The two women were already out in the front, from where they had a view of the green. Annie lifted Marjorie up to stand on the roof of the chicken coop so that she could see.

The singing and cheering had stopped. The strangers were settling themselves on the grass. Those that had boots were pulling them off and easing their toes. A passage was made so that the horses and mules could drink at the pond.

'Would you look at that,' said Annie's big sister.

They watched the innkeeper wave away payment for the cups of ale he was handing out to those nearest him. 'Well,' said Annie. 'That's never been known before.'

And then, over their heads, the bells of the church began to clamour, and the whole green fell silent. The bells were ringing backwards, the lighter voices of Paul and Simon and then the deep voice of Gabriel. The bells had been a gift to the church from Marjorie's family to give thanks for the victory over the Scots at Flodden, when Grandfather had come home safely. When Marjorie was little she thought the angels lived in the church tower and this truly was their voices. Now she knew better. She knew they were rung by men and that ringing them backwards was the signal for danger.

The women left their houses, and the men who had begun the winter work of repairing walls and animal shelters ran down from the fields. When everyone was gathered the church bells stopped. Marjorie, clinging harder to Annie, felt her skin prickle. She'd had little to fear in her life, but there had been plenty of tales of horror from Annie and the other servants.

'Are they Scotsmen?' she whispered.

'Ssh.'

A man was hoisted up onto one of the benches outside the inn. He wore a black patch over one eye. All the time he was speaking he turned his head from side to side so that his one uncovered eye could look all round and see the people.

Annie and her sisters were nodding and hissing. Beside them Tom, who was Annie's uncle, kept repeating 'What's he saying?'

'The King has killed the Pope,' said Annie.

The speaker's next words raised a howl of anger from the assembled villagers and cheers from his own followers. Marjorie, in fright, dug her fingers into Annie's scalp and she yelped.

Tom shouted 'Nay, nay. They'll not close our church.'

This cry was taken up by others. The man with the eyepatch was speaking again. Around him the village men were standing up straighter and easing their way forward, while the women pulled at their clothes to hold them back. Most of the women were crying. Marjorie started crying too.

Tom dashed into his shed and came out with his scythe. It was clean and shiny, already put away for the winter.

'What you doing with that?' asked Annie sharply.

'Defend the church.'

'Old fool.'

The man with the eyepatch leapt down from the bench. The village men and boys crowded round him, old Tom pushing his way to the front, his shiny scythe waving over their heads.

Annie pulled Marjorie down and they stumbled round to the back of the house, over the roots of cabbages and turnip peelings, sending the scratching hens squawking and scurrying, and headed for the path to home and safety, away from the clamour.

Chapter 2

Marjorie was woken by a noise. It was dark. She could make out the faint glow of embers in the fireplace. She lay quietly with her heart beating. The priest said dreams were sent by the devil to tempt children to mischief. Whatever she had been dreaming, it wasn't that which woke her.

She heard the noise again, the faint whinnying of a horse. But that wasn't right, for the men never took the horses out after dark. She nudged Catherine, who grunted and turned over.

'I heard a noise.'

'Mice. Go back to sleep.'

She padded over to the bed being shared by Philippa and Margaret and shook them, but they were sound asleep, Philippa snoring slightly for she had a cold. In the anteroom she shook Annie, but last night Annie had sat up late in the kitchen talking over the day's wonders with the cook, and was too tired to wake properly.

'Go back to bed. No honey for you tomorrow.'

Marjorie crept to the window and opened the shutter. On the horizon, where the dark land showed against the lighter sky, she could see the glow of a fire. She knew what that was, for she had been told about it often enough. It was the beacon on the hill, which was only ever lit when there was danger. In fine weather Annie would walk her and her sisters up the hill, to stand at the foot of it and hear tales of marauding Scotsmen.

Down below her she could see a small glow of light in the stable. Marjorie was the daughter of a soldier. If the house was in danger, and she was the only one who knew, she had to rouse the household and warn them.

She pulled a shawl round her shoulders and crept from the room. The staircase was dark and she had to feel her way down. Near the kitchen she paused by the little window in the wall, like the squint in the church which was used by lepers to watch the mass because they couldn't come into the church.

This window looked down into the kitchen. She saw two men, strangers, crouched over the cooking range, with bowls and spoons in their hands. They ate as if they were starving. They didn't look like ruffians, but then they didn't quite look like gentlemen either. She had to tell someone.

She tiptoed along the passage that led to her mother's room. The room was empty. Down another flight of stairs and to her grandfather's library. The door was ajar. She heard her mother's low voice. She stopped and listened. Perhaps her mother was being held prisoner and it would be up to her, Marjorie, to rescue her.

Then there was another voice she didn't recognise, and then her grandfather's voice. Relief flooded through her. It was all right. They were safe. She could see the flicker of firelight, and the shimmer of the unicorn tapestry. It was trembling slightly in the draught, and the light glinted on the shiny arrows of the huntsmen. She crept closer.

'You can't stay here,' said her grandfather.

'I don't want to,' came a strange voice, the voice of a man. 'We're moving south. The west is rising. Cumberland, Westmorland. Within days I'll have forty thousand men who will fight. Will you join us?'

'No,' said Grandfather. 'I will not raise arms against the King.'

'It is not against the King. It is to warn the King against his advisers.'

'You are being specious.'

Her mother said, 'Oh, Cousin, why do you do this thing?'

She called him cousin. He was family.

'How can I not? I tell you, the whole of the north is rising. Commons, gentry, nobles. Every right-thinking Englishman. You see what the King is doing to the

13

monasteries. The brothers are being turned out and the gold and silver plate sent to London. The plate from the parish churches will be next. Do you think they will overlook the silver chalices and cups, all the sacred vessels that were given to the Church by good Christian families? Families like ours. Sent to London to be melted down to pay for the greed of the King and his court, to pay for his fine palace and the clothes of his whore.'

'Sir, you forget yourself,' snapped Grandfather.

'Is everything to be destroyed? Are we to stand by and see this happen?'

'No doubt the King has his reasons.'

'You are too far from London here, you don't know what goes on. There's talk next of taxing the sacraments, did you hear that? Taxing baptism and marriage. Yes, I know we can afford a little bit of extra tax, but the poor people cannot. Ask the people in your village how much tax they can pay, else their children will go unbaptised. But it's not just money. He thinks he can interfere with the will of God. He thinks to crush everything we have always believed in. He has abolished all the holy saints' days. And there are to be no more prayers for the dead.'

Her mother's voice was hesitant. 'He could not do that, surely. Surely he cannot forbid prayers for the dead?'

'He can, and he has.' The speaker's voice was low and grim. 'He has said it.'

There was a silence then.

'What of the souls of the dead in purgatory?' Her mother's voice was low and sad. Every night family prayers included those who had died.

'The King says there is no purgatory. He thinks by his word he can abolish it. Are you with me?'

'I am not, Sir.' The voice of her grandfather, was cold.

'Our banner displays the five wounds of Christ,' the man went on, as if he hadn't heard. 'We have sworn an oath to uphold God's faith and the Church, for the restitution of Christ's Church and for the suppression of heresy.'

Heresy. Marjorie shivered. She knew about heresy. People who spoke heresy were burned. And then they burned again forever in the flames of Hell. There was no peace for them. It was right that there should be no heresy. She wanted to rush into the room and say to this cousin she had never seen that yes, she would join him and kill heresy.

'It is easy to swear. Not so easy to do.' Grandfather's voice was calm.

'We plan to march to London. York and Doncaster are with us. Our men are besieging Pontefract.'

'Civil war,' said Grandfather.

'No, not civil war. The voice of the people will be heard.'

'Civil war,' said Grandfather again, flatly. 'England has been laid waste before by civil war. My father fought on the side of the house of York in those wars. Henry Tudor was the enemy but he brought peace and now his son rules. Are we to unseat another king? Who will take his place?'

'We have nothing against the King personally. He has fallen into the hands of evil advisers. The worst of them, Cromwell, is a common upstart, an adventurer, and the Archbishop of Canterbury, who should be defending the Church, he is the biggest heretic of all.'

'And do you think those men will stand by and see the country rise? Do you think when you reach London, if you reach London, they will open the gates and welcome you in? Do you think the King will say to you, I am sorry, gentlemen, of course you are right, I will abandon my plans?'

'We have force of numbers.'

'They have trained soldiers, and the money to pay for mercenaries. What are you? A rabble of countrymen, farmers, millers. I hear our blacksmith has joined you.'

'Most of the gentry and many of the nobility. Are you with us, Grandfather?'

15

'No,' was the answer. 'You and your companions can sleep here tonight, but you must be on your way at dawn. I want no trace of your passing to remain. My house will not rise in revolt against the King.'

Marjorie heard the scrape of her grandfather's chair being pushed back.

'I am sorry for you. I am sorry you have become involved in this.'

'We will die for the cause if need be.'

Grandfather's voice was rueful. 'That is one of the follies of men, my boy.'

Marjorie realised she needed to pee. She was shivering and frightened. She gave a sob. There was silence inside the room. Her grandfather said 'Elizabeth? It's the child.'

The door opened and her mother came out and saw her, and gathered Marjorie into her arms. She peed then, but her mother just wrapped her shawl tighter round her and kissed her. Marjorie saw at her back the other man in the room. It was the man who had been leading the crowd, who'd spoken to the villagers, the man who had a black patch where his right eye should be. Grandfather took up his candle.

'I wish you goodnight, and goodbye. Elizabeth will see to your needs. I would like you to be gone in the morning. After this night you are no longer one of my family.'

They listened to Grandfather's steps walking slowly along the passage to his private chamber.

'This is my youngest, Marjorie.'

He came forward and laid a cold finger on her cheek. 'It is for the children we do it,' he said. 'Will you support us, Elizabeth?'

'Give me your oath,' she said. 'I will swear it.'

Marjorie twisted round to see what was happening. He took a bible from the inside of his jacket and held it out to her mother. Marjorie always remembered that moment. She could recall the glow on her mother's face as she put her hand on the holy book and swore the oath.

The oath of the Pilgrimage of Grace was copied and preserved many times. Marjorie saw a copy of it in her uncle's library in London many years later, and recognised it for the words her mother spoke then.

'I swear by this holy book to maintain the Holy Church militant, the preservation of the King's person and his issue, nor to do any displeasure to any private person, but by counsel of the commonwealth, nor slay nor murder for no envy, but in my heart put away all fear and dread, and take afore me the cross of Christ and in my heart His faith, the restitution of the church, the suppression of these heretics and their opinions, by all the holy contents of this book.'

Her face was alight with joy as she repeated the words. Then there was a silence. She leaned forward and kissed him gently on the cheek.

'God's blessings on you. Speed you well in your good purpose.'

Her mother took Marjorie into her bed and held her tight. She must forget what she had seen. She must not tell anyone, not her sisters, not even Annie.

They marched out the next day, in orderly lines, the men and boys of the village, carrying cudgels and billhooks, scythes and pitchforks.

'Where are they going?'

'To London. To tell the King to give us back our saints.'

The road was deeply rutted and the men were sliding and slipping in the mud. At the very end, as fast as he could, came Shortie Willie, struggling to keep up with them, falling further and further behind. He must have caught up eventually. He never came home again.

The men marched away and as they marched they sang, the thumping rhythm in time with their feet.

Christ crucified
For thy wounds wide,

17

> *Us commons guide*
> *Which pilgrims be*
> *Through God's grace.*

Marjorie heard that song again in Berwick, many years later, sung by a young washerwoman as she thumped her dolly into the vat of clothes. She sang it mindlessly, as a child will chant with his play, not thinking of the words, but Marjorie felt an icy fist in the pit of her belly at the sound.

Chapter 3

It rained for weeks. The servants built huge fires in every room and squabbled endlessly. Two of the stable boys had gone, disappeared with the pilgrims. Elizabeth Bowes spent a great deal of her time in her room, on her knees at her prie dieu, and had little time for her children.

When Marjorie wanted to go with Annie to the village she was told abruptly that it was not possible. It was too wet. It was too far. There was trouble. Annie pinned a shawl round the child and took her out to wander in the potager, which was as far as they were allowed to go. Annie huddled in the doorway to the dairy gossiping with the wheelwright while Marjorie walked round and round the paths, poking at black slugs with a stick, turning them over to see their white undersides and lifting them onto the muddy vegetable beds. Annie told her in foreign countries the people ate the slugs when they were hungry.

She used the excuse of a sudden squall of rain to run and crouch at Annie's feet, where she hummed gently to herself, pretending to be lost in her own thoughts, but listening hard to the conversation going on over her head.

'The King has sent guns to defend Hull.'

'Where's Hull?'

'South.'

'Will there be fighting?'

'Oh aye.'

Once she heard the family name mentioned and Annie made a shushing sound. Marjorie leaned out of the doorway and banked up some stones to make a river. Satisfied the child wasn't listening Annie returned to the discussion.

'Go on,' she said.

'Well,' said the wheelwright. 'I did hear as how Robert Bowes, the mistress's brother–in–law, had all his cattle driven off.'

'Why was that?'

'Why? Because there were doubts he was loyal to the cause, though he commands the men in the East Riding.'

'Is he true to the cause?'

'He is now,' said the man. 'Else he'll lose his cattle again.'

In the kitchen a traveller held up his boots for inspection.

'Mended in London,' he said. 'And you know what, the cobbler charged me a sixpence, only sixpence. And you know why? Because it is a great thing we men of the north do for the Lord. That's what he said, a great thing. And wished us joy. What do you think of that, then?'

'And what are the folk of London doing? Apart from standing by and admiring?' asked the cook, slapping the skivvy to get back to work and not stand around gossiping.

Then one day the first of the village men came drifting back. There was talk of a truce. Captain Aske, who saw more with one eye than other men see with two, had gone to London to talk to the King. Marjorie's heart swelled. Captain Aske. Cousin Aske. Talking to the King himself.

'Aye,' said the men. 'And he'll stop there and forget us in the north. The King will make him rich.'

'No, he won't,' Marjorie cried. 'For he is a good man.'

Annie, horrified, snatched her up and hurried her from the kitchen.

'Forget what you heard,' she hissed. 'You shouldn't be in the kitchen at all. Some lady you're going to grow up to be. You want to be like your mother don't you?'

'Yes, Annie,' said Marjorie. It was true. She wanted to be a great and beautiful lady like her mother.

But her mother was preoccupied, and her grandfather confined to bed with an ague, and her sisters were too busy at their lessons to be interested in someone they regarded as still a baby. Annie dozed a lot in the afternoon. Marjorie continued to haunt the kitchen.

She crouched by the fire eating gingerbread and watched a cloak steaming in the heat. It belonged to a messenger who could not stop the night for he had to carry word further west.

'This blasted rain,' he said, his mouth full of game pie. 'It makes for slow travelling. I'm a day behind as it is.'

He was a grumpy man, and tired, and told them that men were wandering throughout the north looking for a leader to follow.

'Aye,' said the gamekeeper. 'You can let the pheasants out of the pen, but it's hard to get them back in again.'

'The gentlemen want peace with the King,' said the messenger. 'See, it's not in their interest to stir up trouble. The poor people will be the ones that suffer. Again.'

Yuletide came and went. But that year no one was jolly, for no one knew what would happen. Nor were the church bells rung, for the priest did not know whether it was allowed or not. It was the second year of bad harvests, and there wasn't enough to eat. More and more food was going from the manor house to the tenants in the village, and still there was not enough. Always in the air was the fear of more trouble.

The house was quiet. The servants were intent on looking after Grandfather Aske above everything else, for he was very old. When he died there would be many changes, and servants do not like change.

Marjorie slipped into the great hall by the little door that led from the kitchens, a door which was only ever used by the servants, and which opened silently in a dark corner. Her mother was standing by the window on the far side of the room. At first Marjorie thought the man with her was the doctor, come to talk about Grandfather, but when he turned she saw that it was the man with the eyepatch, Cousin Robert Aske.

21

She was about to run forward to greet him, but paused by the door, in shadow. She saw Cousin Aske put his arms round her mother and kiss her full on the mouth. Elizabeth Bowes clung to him with a sob. Then he released her and turned away and walked out of the room.

Marjorie wept into her pillow that night, with anger and anguish.

She carried that memory with her always. It was one of the memories of the time of the Pilgrimage of Grace which she never discussed with her mother.

Chapter 4

Although the King had promised a pardon, they took Robert Aske to York and hanged him, and disembowelled him while still alive, and when he was finally dead, they hung him in chains from Clifford's Tower.

Throughout the north they chose men at random and hanged them. They used chains, for ropes rotted too quickly and the King wanted his vengeance to be visible for a long, long time, and never to be forgotten. At Eastertide when the flesh had fallen off the bones and the bones had slipped out of their bonds, the women crept out at night and gathered up what remained of their husbands and brothers and sons, though that too had been forbidden. When frightened priests refused to allow burial in the churchyards the women defied the priests and did it anyway, and no one had the heart to stop them.

Marjorie heard these things from the servants, when the softly murmuring women forgot she was there. She grew up knowing that men will defy their King and willingly die for a God and for a way of worship. But as she saw more of the world she wondered which God? And which way of worship? And who is to decide?

Chapter 5

Marjorie stood by the open window of the long gallery with her mother and sisters, listening to the sound of the passing bell carrying to them on the wind.

Then suddenly there were joyful peals, a cacophony of tuneless sound, and then as suddenly it stopped and the doleful pealing began again. It went on all day. The King was dead. The maids told them, giggling, that some of the village men forced their way into the bell tower and rang the bells for joy, till the constable turned them out.

There was not much mourning in the north for King Henry. For many his death was like a woman unlaced from her gown at the end of a long, long day who sighs with relief and slides her hands easefully over her waist and belly.

By then Grandfather Aske had also died.

Aske Manor and most of the estates that went with it were inherited by Marjorie's mother, and therefore now belonged to Marjorie's father. It was for that, said the servants, that he had been wed to Elizabeth Aske when they were both no more than children. But Elizabeth's daughters, avid readers of romances, knew that it was a love match.

Soon after Grandfather Aske died, Captain Bowes came home from the wars, and there was a new baby every year, and Marjorie was no longer Annie's pet.

With her sisters she learned her numbers. She learned to read and write, and learned simple Latin and some serviceable French. She learned how to run a large household, how to draw honey from the hives, how to brew ale, how to make cheese, how to make sweetmeats.

She learned to be a virtuous woman.

It was a matter of pride to Elizabeth Bowes that her daughters were brought up using the same manual of advice that the Queen had decreed should be used to teach the Princess Mary to be a good Christian woman.

The girls spent a lot of their time sewing shirts for their father and brothers, and embroidering shifts for their wedding nights. And one by one her sisters reached marriageable age, were found husbands, and were gone.

What had it all been about, Marjorie sometimes wondered, all that with the Church. She tried to talk to her sisters and their tutor about this, but they weren't interested. Long before the King's death the people slid back into their old ways as if there had been no upset, no Pilgrimage, no retaliation. Once the King had taken all the wealth from the monasteries he lost interest in how the people worshipped.

Now the new King Edward, the sixth of that name, changed things again. He took his duties as head of the Church seriously. His commissioners spread out over the country and eventually reached the north. They brought orders that the pictures painted on the walls of churches should be whitewashed over, and statues removed, for these were idolatrous.

They explained, less than patiently, that the King was a Protestant, and so should everyone else be.

Where once people had been angered by any threat to the church, now they could only look on sadly. There was no one to lead a resistance, no passionate, driven man with an eyepatch.

One of the things the new learning that came from Germany and the Low Countries taught was that the dead are dead and nothing done on earth can affect the way they are treated in Heaven or Hell. King Henry had decreed this too, but it seemed he was less concerned with the theology and more interested in the money paid to the church to buy indulgences for the dead soul. The money he could confiscate. The prayers weren't much use to him.

Marjorie's father and her brothers, soldiers all of them, could see the truth of this. They talked as they took their

25

ease in Elizabeth's parlour, before courteously excusing themselves to return to the stables. The girls sat silently, stitching and listening.

It meant little to them that King Edward had turned his attention to the priests who were paid to say prayers in perpetuity for the souls of the dead. This had to stop, apparently. The endowments which paid them were to be given up and used to set up schools.

In the church in the village there was a corner closed off behind a wooden door with a grille in it. It made a room no bigger than a closet. There was a tiny stone altar on which a candle was kept constantly burning and a stone bench.

This was the chantry set up a long time ago by Elizabeth's family, the Askes, and sometimes when the church was quiet if you went close you could hear Father Edmund singing softly his litany of names. Margaret and Elizabeth, George, Richard, Robert. Marjorie's great great grandfather had given the money to pay the priest. Father Edmund was the fifth priest to hold this position.

He spent most of every day, and for all anyone knew part of the night at prayer in the chantry. The children of the village laughed at him, openly; the children at the Manor secretly, for discourtesy would be punished. He wrapped himself in layer upon layer of clothing, and why not? He needed it, kneeling or sitting all day in that little stone closet with only the warmth of the candle. Underneath all the clothing he was thin and the village children laughed at his stick legs.

The village priest mostly ignored him. In his eyes Father Edmund was a failed priest in the service of the manor house. The village priest had more learning and was in the service of God.

Sometimes Father Edmund came to the manor and ate with the family when there were no other guests. He paid little attention to the conversation round the table. He lived most of the time in a kind of trance. He spent so much time alone with only the dead for company that he had forgotten how to converse with the living.

'Father' was only a courtesy title, Elizabeth told the girls. He was not fully ordained by a bishop, and was not allowed to say a mass.

When the King's new law came through, the constable locked the door to the chantry. After that Father Edmund would be found sitting beside the locked door. He sat silently till someone approached and then he would start up and ask that the door be opened. They could only shake their heads and lead him away to sit in a kindly housewife's kitchen for a while. The villagers gave him food, and a basket went to him regularly from the big house, as it had always done, but he gave most of it to the village children, or they stole it anyway.

One day Marjorie blundered into her mother's room, not realising he was there. Her mother was kneeling at her prie dieu and Father Edmund was kneeling on the floor by her side and they were reciting the litany of saints. *Saint Agnes, Saint Gregory, Saint Augustine, Saint Athanasius, pray for us.* This was forbidden. This was now the heresy.

Her presence stopped them. Father Edmund left then, following Marjorie down the stairs and out through the servants' hall. As he took his leave of her at the door he looked at her quite sensibly.

'All my life I have been wasting my time,' he said.

Soon after that he was found drowned in the river. It was thought he had slipped on the wet bridge and fallen in.

Captain Bowes wrote many letters to his brother in London about the chantry endowment fund. His brother made enquiries of the bishops, and of the King's almoner. No one was ever able to trace what happened to the money. It never went to a school or any other good purpose that they knew of.

Chapter 6

Whitsuntide came. It was a fine spring, and there was a feeling of holiday in the air. It was the time of waiting between the sowing of the grain and its ripening. There was little to be done on the land, and people relaxed. Their bellies were empty for there was not much food about at this time of year, save for greens and pigeons and rabbits, but it was the hunger that precedes the feast and the lengthening days made people optimistic.

Spirits are high and hopeful in springtime. The roads were dry and people travelled round neighbouring villages, gossiping and wooing. When Marjorie passed near the kitchen she would hear the voice of at least one strange man there, flirting with one or other of the maids.

Her sisters were no better, whispering together in corners and falling silent as she approached, for she was still too young. They chattered about the new boy King. It was said he was handsome. And clever. 'He has written the new Book of Common Prayer which we are all to use in the Church from now on. It is in English. I would love to read his poetry,' said her sister Catherine, and losing concentration, pricked her finger which bled onto her sewing. Supposing . . . well, supposing they could go to London, and supposing they were to meet him . . . . Their mother scolded them but smiled too. It was all nonsense of course, but had not the late King married a commoner? And times were changing.

When she went into the village, Marjorie heard different talk. People were complaining about what was happening in the churches. The water in the stoup at the church door wasn't holy any more. And priests could marry. As if they didn't already have their women but now they could have the benefit of clergy like everyone else. Now the villagers had time to think and time to stand around and talk, and grieve for the dead wandering in a purgatory that the King said didn't exist, but how could he know?

One day as she sat quietly on a bench outside a cottage in which her mother was murmuring words of encouragement to an old servant who was dying, she heard two men pass by on the road and heard what they said.

'The North rose before. It can rise again.'

'Mother,' walking back up through the meadow home. 'Are the people very angry? Will there be fighting again?'

They were almost at the stable block before her mother answered her. 'No,' she said. 'No. There is not the heart for it.'

Some people said it wasn't the King for he was only a boy, it was his advisers. Marjorie's father laughed when he heard this.

'That was what they said of the old King, didn't they? And what happened? His advisers all lost their heads, one after the other. Then only the King was left, and did anything change? Did the King give back the gold to the Church? Tell me, are the monks back in their monasteries?'

When on that Sunday of Whitsuntide, the village priest stood facing the congregation instead of facing God at the altar, anger ran through the church. Marjorie, hidden from view in the high sided family pew, could feel it. The priest had the new Book of Common Prayer in his hand and he started to read from it. It was in English, as people had said it would be. He was barely given a chance to go beyond the first few words. Some of the women at the back of the church began to howl, drowning out his voice. He paused.

'Say the mass, Father,' someone shouted. 'Say it right.'

'Where are your vestments?' The cry was taken up. 'Why are you standing in front of God half naked?'

Some women – peering round the edge of the pew Marjorie saw Annie's oldest sister among them - rushed past the priest into his vestry and dragged out the box in which the beautiful sacred vestments were kept and pulled them out. The stole and the blue and green cope with its shimmering embroidery were tumbled on the floor and pulled at by many hands. The women shook them all out and approached the priest. He backed off round the church, stumbling over his feet, with the people making way for him and laughing and shouting encouragement.

Marjorie's little sisters, one on either side of her, gripped her hands tight. The youngest one started to cry and Elizabeth Bowes reached over and took the child onto her lap. Captain Bowes sat straight and stiff and kept his gaze on the further corner of the ceiling.

The priest became trapped in the corner by the locked chantry. The women bundled him into the vestments as if he was a child, and threw the cope over his head, everyone cheering, and they pulled him to the front of the church again.

'Please,' he kept saying. 'Please.' There were beads of blood on his cheek where someone had scratched him.

'Say the mass as we're used to it,' said the women.

He was pushed up to the altar where he began to gabble the Latin words. Everyone in the church knelt down, even the village constable who stood at the door, not daring to interfere. Captain Bowes knelt, and gestured to his family to do the same.

Chapter 7

Marjorie was summoned to her father's room, the room where once her grandfather seemed to her to be God.

She curtseyed to the uncle she had rarely seen, but had heard much talked about. Sir Robert Bowes had been forgiven for taking part in the Pilgrimage of Grace. Perhaps he pleaded he had done so under coercion. Perhaps it was true. Marjorie was beginning to understand that men were forced to do things they might or might not believe in, but that belief might come and go as a matter of expediency. Robert Bowes was said to have skill in his tongue, for he was a lawyer, and it had no doubt been put to good use. He was now one of King Edward's Council of the North.

In the face the two brothers were very alike, but whereas her father was lean and sinewy, his older brother had lost whatever fitness he had had as a soldier and grown heavy in the body and flabby round his neck.

'This is Marjorie,' said her father.

'How old is she?'

'How old are you now?'

'Sixteen, Sir. Nearly seventeen.'

'Why has she not been married already?'

'Her mother clings to her. Besides, she's bookish.'

Her uncle smiled. 'Nothing wrong with some learning in a woman. I could ask round my colleagues in Gray's Inn.'

'Lawyers.' Did Robert detect the sneer in his brother's voice? Marjorie, standing submissively as she had been taught to do, hands clasped in front of her, saw his mouth twitch.

'Rising men.'

'We saw what happened when the old King gathered rising men round him.'

'Times are changing, Richard. Just owning land isn't enough any more. It's all trade now. It's knowing the right people. That's what's important. I'll find you someone. Why in God's name did you have to have so many daughters?'

'Go back to your sewing, Marjorie,' said her father.

Marjorie did not return to her mother's room immediately. Instead she slipped up to the attic room where she had been accustomed, as a child, to hide with a book. She sat for a while on a stool covered with a faded wool tapestry worked by some long-dead Aske ancestor and tried to work out what it was she was feeling.

She had seen her sisters married off, one by one, to men they barely knew. This one's land marched with theirs, that one had property in Dorset that could be exchanged for land in Yorkshire, the other was the son of someone who was owed a favour from the past. Alliances were made, deals were done, and whenever was the girl consulted? It appeared they were running out of marriageable options. She was destined to give some veneer of breeding to a merchant family whose only virtue was that they had money.

She sighed with exasperation. She knew she was not being entirely fair. Her parents did think of each daughter's welfare. None of the husbands was excessively old, or ugly, or vicious in his habits, so far as anyone knew. And her sisters derived excessive pleasure from the marriage preparations. She had sat with them many boring evenings listening to their talk. After marriage their letters to their mother talked happily of portraits sat for, and recipes to cure aches, and loyal villagers, and most of all beautiful babies. Marjorie thought she would prefer to live her life peacefully with books.

There had already been a few young men brought to Aske with a view to marrying her off, but nothing had come of any of these visits. Perhaps her conversation put them off. She hoped so.

Sir Robert had not come north only to deal with family matters. He had been appointed Depute Warden of the East and Middle Marches. It was his job to make sure the border was strongly defended against the Scots. What better way than to appoint his brother Richard to the command of Norham Castle, the biggest and strongest of the border defences?

Hadn't England always depended on the Bowes family? They fought at Flodden Field, and at Solway Moss, and the two brothers had been taken prisoners together after the battle of Haddonrig, almost within sight of the town of Berwick itself. Fortunately the family could afford the ransom. If Richard Bowes was beginning to think he was growing too old for soldiering, he could not argue with a commission from the King, but could only stipulate that on this posting he wanted his wife with him.

Elizabeth, distressed to be leaving her comfortable home, chose Marjorie to be her companion.

*

Richard Bowes went on ahead, to relieve the retiring captain. Marjorie and her mother travelled more slowly under escort to the nearby town of Berwick where they stayed a night as the guests of the captain of the garrison there, and then the next day turned westward towards Norham.

They could see the great towers for miles. The castle was built on a hill in a bend of the River Tweed which surged and foamed at the foot of the cliff forming the hill's northern flank. In was thought to be virtually impregnable. It had withstood many sieges. Their retinue circled the hill, passing a cluster of cottages that formed the village of Norham, and approached the castle's southern gateway.

They had been seen and the drawbridge was down. They rode over it across the wide moat, and under the gatehouse and into the outer bailey. Marjorie gasped at the sheer size of the place. Beyond the rising ground of the outer bailey was another moat and a wall surrounding the inner bailey. In the inner bailey were two great towers of many storeys – she counted them – six, seven rows of windows on the highest, each tower topped with battlements. Round everything were high curtain walls of stone with their arrow slits and battlements.

The outer bailey itself was crowded with workshops and stables, and the men's quarters. Norham housed a sizeable garrison. The bailey was probably more crowded than usual, for the men were anxious to catch a glimpse of their new commander's lady and daughter. Men peered from the windows of the gatehouse and on the battlements they paused in their sentry duty. The smith shoeing a horse and the wheelwright mending a cart straightened up and looked at them with open curiosity. From the brewhouse over on the far wall, the brewer and his boy emerged to study them.

They were doubly welcome, for they had come accompanied by a new contingent of men to garrison the castle, men who last week had been following the plough and now would have to be trained to soldiering. Many of those who now paused to watch their arrival would be able to go home, their stint of duty done.

There was a moment's pause, and then all was activity as men hurried forward to take the horses - and there was her father striding across the bailey to welcome them. His greeting was affectionate but brief. He wanted to inspect the new men who were standing back, looking bewildered as well they might. Some of them had never been away from their village before.

He introduced the steward who was to look after them. The Captain and his family were to live in the gatehouse, the steward explained as he led them through a door in a circular tower and up the stairs. They were on the third floor. Captain Bowes had his office on the floor below.

'If an attack comes you run fast as you can to the inner bailey.'

'Are we likely to be attacked?' asked Elizabeth.

He smirked knowingly, as one privy to great secrets. 'There's a truce. But you never know. The bastard Scotsmen will break their fast with you in the morning and dine off your corpse at night.'

He was a small man, and the wrists poking out from his tunic were thin and bony with thick blue veins. He was old, his fighting days done. He hardly looked at them.

He said, 'You'll be safe enough. If they come I can handle a hot tar barrel.'

He pointed out the bedrooms, one for Elizabeth, next door to her husband's, and one for Marjorie to share with Sarie, the maid they had brought with them from Aske.

'Been no family here for years. Last captain and the one before kept their women at home.'

There was no need of more servants. They would be looked after by the steward. But since it was not seemly for the women to have their laundry done in the castle, to be seen by soldiers, it would be sent out to a woman in the village.

'It's a lot different from home,' said Marjorie.

'A soldier's wife should be accustomed to some hardship,' said her mother reprovingly.

The rooms were small and sparsely furnished, but clean. They had been swept out and fresh rushes strewn on the floor. Rushes! At Aske they had woven mats. Although it was nearly midsummer there was a chill in the rooms. Men bringing up scuttles of coal and wood for the braziers tangled on the narrow staircase with the men bringing up their mattresses and bedhangings, which they had brought from home. The parlour had wainscotting but it was a poor sort of wood, not the oak they had at Aske. Marjorie ran her hand over it and could feel it dry and splitting.

From the window she had a clear view of the tall towers.

35

'Who lives there?' she asked.

'That one on the left is the palace of the Bishop of Durham,' the steward replied.

It was a long time since the bishop had been here, apparently. He was old now. He lived in his palace at Bishop Auckland. The last time he was here was when he took refuge during the Pilgrimage of Grace.

'Of lamentable memory,' said the steward. And no one said anything, too careful to ask on which side his sympathies lay.

'And the other?' asked Elizabeth.

'The keep. If there's a siege you'll be safe there. It has guest rooms for visitors. For the King if he comes, or the Duke of Somerset his uncle. Or anyone from London. The rooms there are as fine as the Bishop's.'

'I am arranging for tapestries to be brought from our home,' said Elizabeth, who was clearly wondering why they could not be housed in those fine rooms.

The wall hangings were a long time coming. There was much correspondence to and fro about sizes and fixings. Marjorie had hoped for the unicorn tapestry from her grandfather's study, but eventually those that came were smaller and poorer, the ones which had hung in the parlour that was allocated to minor visitors to Aske.

Her father was always on call, and spent long hours in the administration of the castle. He was frequently absent, for there were patrols of miles of border. Although there was ostensible peace with the Scots, the reivers were active and the soldiers had their hands full following up reports of looting and burnings of farmsteads. Richard would have supper with them as often as he could and then stay on, dozing by the fire while his wife and the maid sewed, and Marjorie read aloud to them.

The first few nights their sleep was disturbed by the stamp, stamp of the soldiers' boots as they patrolled the walkway above their heads, but soon they were used to it.

Sarie was jittery and jumpy for a while. All her life she had been fed tales of the brutality of the Scots on their border raids, and how they rampaged over England, killing and raping and burning. She was frightened to be so near, to be able to see that terrifying country, though in fact the heathland to the north looked no different from that to the south. After a while a sufficient number of young men bragging about their courage in battle reassured her that she would be well protected if the Scots attacked. She soon forgot the sturdy blacksmith's journeyman she was keeping company with back home, and began to dream of marrying a soldier.

Apart from the reivers, who never came near any of the castles, the border was quiet. If there had been danger, Captain Bowes had to keep reassuring Elizabeth, he would never have asked for his family to be with him. He inherited from the previous captain a good intelligence network which would give sufficient warning of trouble. Trouble would depend on the diplomacy of London, and for now it suited the King and his advisers to be at peace with Scotland.

Marjorie had brought books from Aske and was content enough, but her mother had too much time on her hands. At Aske she had the management and supervision of the house, and her days were busy in the dairy or in the stillroom, supervising the care of the babies, organising the provisioning of the household. Here there was nothing for her to do. The domestic management of their quarters was in the care of the steward. When Mistress Bowes asked for something to be done differently, he would nod and show his gums, and nothing would change. Even the cook who had been assigned to them took his orders from the steward. They could not make any decisions which were independent of the greater world of the castle.

It was with relief that Elizabeth Bowes found herself being useful sometimes. Every important person who came to the north had to call in at Norham, ostensibly to pay their respects, and no doubt, as Captain Bowes remarked to his wife, report back to London that the Captain of Norham was doing his duty. She would then be the hostess, and preside as she had been used to doing, but these occasions were not many, and only reminded her of what had been lost in agreeing to come here.

Marjorie watched anxiously as melancholy began to overtake her mother, who spent more and more time kneeling at her prie dieu.

Chapter 8

As a good servant of the crown, Captain Bowes made sure his men followed the new ways of worshipping. The castle had its own chapel, a small building in a corner of the outer bailey. Every Sunday the garrison chaplain read from the new Book of Common Prayer, and the soldiers who were off duty and obliged to attend gabbled the responses as best they could. No one expected the Captain's wife and daughter to squeeze into the small chapel with the common soldiers, so no one knew that every Sunday they held a private service in their own quarters.

Elizabeth Bowes had sworn an oath to uphold the true religion, and she would keep that oath, no matter what the King said. When the King was a grown man and could use his own judgment instead of depending on advisers, he would see the error of his ways and all would be as it was before.

She had no difficulty in remembering the form of it. They prayed to the Virgin Mary and the saints as they had used to do. Only the sacrament was missing, for they could not ask the priest. And although the priest was supposed to ensure attendance at church, he did not dare challenge the Captain's lady.

And what man pays any attention to what a woman is stitching? There was no need now to embroider altar cloths, so they embroidered cushions instead. For just as a unicorn can be a virtuous woman, and a pomegranate can be a fruitful womb, a lily can be the Virgin Mary, or it can be just a lily. Who is to say what is in the mind of the person creating it if the creator chooses not to speak?

Captain Bowes kept well away from their private quarters on a Sunday. He cared little one way or another, true faith or new learning were all the same to him. His only interests lay in soldiering.

The garrison priest was a sour middle-aged man who had been for a time in the household of the Bishop of Durham at Bishop Auckland. He resented being consigned to Norham and grumbled continually about it. His duties included the pastoral care of the village of Norham and he did not bother to hide the fact he despised them. Neither Scotch nor English, ignorant halfbreeds, was his opinion.

He was a Londoner, and unlike the priests Marjorie had known before, he was an educated man. He had read Augustine and Anselm, and could quote from them. He sprinkled his conversation with Latin words and rapidly lost the attention of Captain Bowes, though Marjorie could just about understand him, once she had attuned her ear to his accent.

They had him to dinner. They understood why the Bishop had chosen to deprive himself of the company of such a learned man. He had dirty fingernails and was unfastidious in his table manners. Her mother shuddered at the thought of such dirty hands holding the blood and body of our Lord.

'I would just prefer it if he could consume the bread and wine at our table with less noise,' said Marjorie.

He talked continually of his grievances. He disliked the new religion and the new order of service in the Church, but even so they guarded their speech when in conversation with him. Not by word or deed could they betray that they too wanted a return to the old ways and the Latin mass. It was better that the discretion of the man was never tested. He was continually writing to the Bishop to ask to be transferred away from Norham, back to Durham and the cathedral where he could tend the books in the library instead of the souls of ignorant soldiers.

One day he came rushing over to Marjorie and her mother as they sauntered in the sunshine on the wall walk. He waved a letter at them. He was almost weeping for joy.

'At last, I have been rewarded. I am to be set free.'

'Is our company so uncongenial?' asked Marjorie.

He ignored her.

'The Bishop is to come, and take me back with him.'

Chapter 9

'I intend,' said Captain Bowes. 'To invite the new priest at Berwick to be garrison chaplain.'

Bishop Tunstall stopped chewing.

'He is not suitable.'

'It was Protector Somerset who sent him here.'

'If I had any say in the matter I would not have chosen to welcome him in my diocese. But he is outside my jurisdiction.'

'My brother, Robert Bowes, writes to me that this man Knox is held in high regard in London.'

'In what way is he not suitable, Bishop?' asked Elizabeth.

Marjorie watched the Bishop as he hesitated in his answer. Clearly he didn't yet have the measure of his hosts. They were known for being staunch supporters of the Church. Had some of them not, after all, taken part in the Pilgrimage of Grace, that abortive attempt to protect the Church? One of the leaders, wasn't he a cousin, twice or thrice removed?

However, they were equally staunch in their support of the new protestant King, and were clearly favourites with the Protector, my lord Somerset who was said to make all the decisions while the King was underage.

'He's Scotch. The town is full of the Scotch and the worse for it. Renegades from the law, most of them. They needed someone who could speak their language. That was what I was told. But I have also been told he is a troublemaker with extreme ideas.'

'God knows they need controlling,' said her father. 'I had one of my men with a smashed arm last week after a stramash in the town.'

Marjorie had heard something of the new priest from the talk in Norham when she visited the cottagers.

'Perhaps he was sent to Berwick to be as far away from London as possible.'

The Bishop seized on this.

'You have the right of it, Miss Marjorie. He attracted large crowds at St Paul's when he preached there.'

He took a sip of wine, and went on.

'Before that he was involved in the murder of the senior prelate in Scotland.'

'Murder?' Elizabeth drew in her breath.

'Cold-blooded murder,' said the Bishop. 'Cardinal Beaton. A vicious and cruel act. As a result he spent time as a prisoner in the French galleys. That is why he is now in exile from his own country.'

The Bishop talked on, in his soft voice, musingly.

'It is not clear why he was released from the galleys. Perhaps he offered his services to the French.'

'In what way, Bishop?'

'Perhaps he is a spy. That may have been the price of his freedom. I speculate of course, but I am an old man and have seen men change their allegiance many times. It might be unwise to have this man infiltrate your border defences here.'

Captain Bowes laughed at that. 'If he is such, then admitting him to the castle would be the best thing I could do. He can report back to his masters that we are well armed, and ready for anything.'

Bishop Tunstall was President of the Council of the North, but his main power was as Bishop of the vast See of Durham, a position that gave him sovereignty over the north, greater even than that exercised by any King. For, after all, a bishop could speak directly to God.

'He has to preach the new religion, as he is ordered to do,' Elizabeth told Marjorie later when they were preparing for bed. 'He obeys the King, as we all have to do. But they say in his heart he still adheres to the true church. Poor man, I pity him.'

'Would it not be better,' asked Marjorie. 'For him to give up his position as bishop and live quietly with his beliefs?'

But Elizabeth thought this was not possible. And anyway, he had plenty of quiet support in the north. Here they had never taken to the new religion as they had in London, where they seized on new ideas and new ways with unsettling eagerness. There were stories of persecution of Catholics in the south, those unwise enough to be too vehement in their opposition to the King's innovations, but it was not my Lord Somerset's policy to be too harsh with the north and its bishop. The memories of the Pilgrimage of Grace were still fresh. And besides the Duke was said to be working towards permanent peace with Scotland along the debatable lands of the border. The north needed to be kept strong and united.

Everyone who lived near the border never forgot that the Queen Mother in Scotland was Catholic. She was of the powerful Guise family of France. England sat poised between two enemies. The Protector was not going to add religious quarrels as tinder to a situation which could flare up into war.

Bishop Tunstall, to appease the Catholics, was kept in his post, as long as he appeared to conform to the King's reformation of the church.

He stayed at the castle for four weeks, sometimes going out with his entourage to visit various parts of his diocese, sometimes holding court in the vast hall of his part of the castle. There were banquets to be given for those powerful local men who must be kept sweet if they were to support the King. At these, dressed in his gold and silver robes heavy with jewels, he looked stern and lordly.

Once, after yet another evening of noise and argument and overeating, he invited Elizabeth and Marjorie to stay behind and sit awhile with him before he retired for the night. He joined them in his private parlour. He came wrapped up in his house gown of silk lined with fur. He sank into the comfortable chair by the fire, a chair which his servant had piled with cushions. The servant was dismissed.

'This is restful,' said the Bishop. He toasted his feet at the fire and sighed. He felt the cold and his rooms were always kept hot.

Marjorie surreptitiously eased the armpit of her gown away from her body. She was sweating. And she was tired. It had been a long evening.

'I am an old man,' he said. And indeed he was just a thin old man, with wispy white hair and hands corded with veins and slightly twisted. Marjorie found it difficult to believe that such a very old man could still be alive and still be so active. He looked as if the first strong wind would blow him over.

'I've passed my life's allotted span. But I still go on, in the service of God. I wish the King would release me from my duties. I would spend the little time left to me in prayer, and perhaps commit to print my thoughts on the new religion.'

He failed to look at either of the women when he said this.

'The new religion is an abomination,' said Elizabeth.

There was an exhalation in the room, like the sigh of a fresh breeze on a clammy day.

'That is what I think too,' said the Bishop.

Nothing more was said, but after that night the Captain's lady and daughter would regularly receive a message from the Bishop that they were welcome to join him in his private room. They talked of nothing of consequence. They talked as old people do, though the Bishop was a generation older than Elizabeth. They talked about how the world was changing, and never for the better. Then Marjorie, bored, and given permission to go through to the Bishop's library in the next room, would pause in her browsing to catch a phrase in Latin and, alert, begin to pay attention.

She could not say exactly when the conversation changed and the platitudes were left behind and the talk turned to religion. But why shouldn't it? He was a bishop after all. It was his life. He had the care of their souls. The Bishop would murmur in Latin the words which he had been accustomed to say all his life as he mediated between man and God at the altar. He and Elizabeth talked softly of the miracles wrought by saints. They talked of the pilgrimages they had both made, the Bishop all his life and Elizabeth in her youth, pilgrimages now forbidden, to shrines now dilapidated from neglect.

This talk made Marjorie uncomfortable, for she knew it bordered on the dangerous. If challenged, could the Bishop and her mother claim they were only reminiscing, and there was no harm in it?

But there was harm. If someone, her father say... no not her father, he would never ask. But if her uncle, or someone from London wanted to know what they talked about, she did not want to be able to say. So she would quietly settle herself in a window seat in the far corner of the library, out of earshot, and read determinedly until her mother came to find her to walk back across the bailey to the gatehouse.

And then one morning her mother shook her awake while it was still dark.

'What is it? Is it danger?'

'No. Get dressed. Keep silence. Don't wake Sarie.'

Marjorie rapidly pulled on her gown and shoes and followed her mother down and out across the bailey to the chapel.

As soon as the door was closed tight behind them, a flint was struck and the Bishop was there, lighting candles. He was wearing his cope and while Elizabeth knelt with Marjorie reluctantly crouched by her side, he swiftly and quietly said the mass as it used to be said, drinking the wine himself and serving the wafers to the two women, all the time murmuring quietly in Latin, while Elizabeth made the responses.

Marjorie was shivering. She did not want to be doing this. She was terrified someone would see the light and investigate, and find them, and tell her father, or worse, spread it around that the Captain's lady was a papist. For the bishop's reputation she cared nothing, though she quite liked the old man. For herself, she would happily have denied the validity of the whole masquerade, given the opportunity.

But she trembled for her mother.

'Missa est,' said the Bishop.

And between them they hastily packed away the remains of the candles, and the chalice and pyx, and removed all trace of their presence.

Soldiers on guard up on the battlements were silhouetted against the dawn as they left the chapel. If they were seen, nothing was ever said about it.

'I leave tomorrow,' said the Bishop. 'Hold fast in the truth. Do not let the heretic Knox lead you into sin.'

Chapter 10

The Bishop left, and took with him the garrison priest, who wept no tears to be leaving. The dust of their passing hovered over the road for hours afterwards. The men of the garrison cleaned up the detritus of their visit, the great Palace Tower was closed up once more and life settled back to normal.

'Richard, I will not have that man from Berwick as a guest in my house. Have him as your garrison priest if you must, but we need not be friendly.'

'We needs must, my dear,' said her husband.

'He is a criminal. A convicted felon.'

'He was a prisoner of war, as I was.'

'I am not well enough to entertain guests.'

'Then Marjorie will take your place.'

'Does he speak English, Father?'

'They say he has a glib tongue. He will make himself understood.'

'I cannot understand, Richard, how you can entertain the idea of a foreigner, possibly a foreign spy, at our table.'

'We entertained foreigners at Aske.'

'They were gentlemen.'

*

He came on foot. Marjorie stood on the wall walk above the gatehouse and saw a man in black striding along the road from Berwick. He did not turn up the hill to the castle but turned instead towards Norham village, where he knocked on the door of one of the cottages, and bending under the low lintel, went in.

Marjorie continued her vigil. Presently the man emerged from the cottage and turned up the hill. It was a warm day.

He had been wearing a black cloak when he started out but now it was wrapped round his arm. His movements were vigorous. Young, thought Marjorie. She ran rapidly down the steps and into the gatehouse to take her place beside her mother to welcome their guest.

Soon he was there, shaking out the cloak and talking to the steward, and Marjorie learned for the first time that the dour steward had family south of Berwick, and John Knox could pass on news of them. Marjorie saw that she had been wrong in her first assessment. He was not as young as his brisk movements suggested. Probably near the age of her mother. Not a tall man, not as tall as her father. Dark eyes under heavy black brows, greying. Clean-shaven, with the grooves curving from his nose to his chin deepening as he smiled, greeting his hostess.

The talk at dinner limped for a while.

'You will know the border well, Master Knox,' said Elizabeth.

'This part of it. I am charged with the pastoral care of the folk that canna get to Berwick for the services.'

'And do you also visit on the north side of the border?'

'No,' Knox was sober in his reply. 'Set foot in Scotland, I dare not.'

'What would happen if you did?' asked Marjorie.

'I would be burned at the stake as a heretic,' he said.

They ate in silence. Her mother was pushing the food round her plate, not looking at anyone.

'I've fought the Scots many a time,' said Captain Bowes. Perhaps he thought to lighten the atmosphere.

Knox took it up instantly.

'You were taken prisoner at Haddonrig, I have heard.'

'That's right.'

'That was a battle that need not have happened. Your King Henry over-reacted.'

'Indeed, sir, he responded to treachery and double-dealing.'

49

'Nay. He was too hot-blooded.'

'There was to be a peace treaty.'

'Your King broke it.'

'Your King James promised to meet our King at York. He never turned up.'

'Would it have been safe for him if he had?'

'Do you know, Sir, the insult to our King?'

'It was none of King James's doing.'

'Who else then? For offence there was.'

'Cardinal Beaton was at fault. Like all treacherous churchmen.'

'The one who was murdered,' said Elizabeth Bowes.

'Aye,' Knox looked at her. 'Aye, that one.'

'Were you there, sir?'

'No. No, I was not.'

'We heard you were.'

'I wish I had been.'

'To kill a good man?'

'He deserved to die. He bled Scotland dry to keep himself and his whores in luxury. Ah my friends, can you picture the cruelty of his church and the greed of his churchmen taking food from the very mouths of infants. Any dissent was met by cruelty and killing. Aye, women and children were destroyed to feed his lust for power.'

Knox swept his hand out and knocked over his wine beaker. Absently he waved aside the steward's help and wiped it up with his kerchief. Elizabeth murmured something. Knox paused in his actions.

'I regret,' he said. 'My tongue carries me away. I forget I am in the home of a gentlewoman. I am not accustomed. I beg your pardon, Mistress.'

But she would not leave it alone.

'Master Knox,' she said. 'Have you always been a priest?'

'Until now I never had a parish, Mistress. I worked for many happy years as tutor to the boys of various lairds.'

'But you were ordained?'

'By the Bishop of Dunblane.'

'So you have sworn allegiance to Holy Mother Church, and the Holy Father in Rome.'

'So did we all in those days. We knew no better.'

'But now you have broken those oaths.'

'Elizabeth,' said Captain Bowes, rising to his feet. 'You will excuse us. I will take Master Knox and show him over the castle. He will be interested to meet the men.'

'I've met some already,' said Knox. 'They come to Berwick, to my church.'

Marjorie and her mother helped the steward clear away the table.

'Father has the right of it,' said Marjorie. 'A glib tongue.'

The steward scowled at her.

Chapter 11

Berwick could never forget it was a frontier town.

The border between the two nations had wavered backwards and forwards over the debatable lands for centuries and each shift led to more slaughter. The border lands were vast tracts of mountain and forest, wilderness inhabited by a few violent families. It was not an area in which it was wise to settle, for at any time a marauding army could come from north or south to burn and rape. The town itself had been pillaged times without number.

But now the border for two generations had been firmly settled to the north of the town, and Berwick was English. The burghers sat snug inside their mighty defensive walls, walls which kept the masons of the town in constant work as they were continually being rebuilt, higher and stronger as the cannon of the enemies became bigger and more powerful.

The river flowed on the west flank of the town, and the sea lay to the east, so that the town sat on its isthmus, well protected from attack.

There were some six hundred soldiers garrisoned in Berwick. Some were Englishmen, commissioned by the garrison commander. Most were mercenaries of half a dozen nationalities, from the German states, from Flanders, from every country in the Holy Roman Empire, all in the pay of the King, attracted as always to the flashpoints between nations. When their pay came late they could be vicious.

Most troublesome to civic peace were the Scots mercenaries who chose to fight for the English King, perhaps just for money or just as likely because they were sought for some crime and could not go home. Some perhaps placed their loyalty from religious conviction. The Scottish Regent was in thrall, as they saw it, to the French and worst of all, to Rome. All the soldiers were ill paid and idle for want of occupation, at this time when the policy of both the Crowns was cautious amity.

It was a town where fights broke out spontaneously, with or without drink taken, a town where women shut their doors against men crippled in past wars, refusing alms even when politely asked, and where merchants would step indifferently over bodies in the street. A trading town with a busy harbour. A town full of spies, English, Scottish, French, Spanish, Dutch and for all anybody knew from the Holy See itself. A bitter town. Within walking distance lay the battlefields of recent memory, Flodden, Pinkie, Haddonrig. A frontier town. A town neither Scottish nor English, both Scottish and English.

Marjorie and her mother had stayed there for one night on their way north, but they had arrived and left in semi-darkness. Now they were seeing the town properly for the first time.

Outside the walls spilled a floating, fluctuating population living in shacks of wood, many of which looked as if the first strong wind would blow them down. Here and there the shelter was no more than lengths of torn canvas, bleached by the sun, stretched over branches. It was a seagoing town, there were old sails aplenty. Children ran about shrieking, while their mothers stood and gossiped.

The stink as they approached told them why these had been banished from within the walls. The stench from vats of the urine used by the fullers of cloth drifted towards them and Elizabeth and Marjorie drew their capes over their faces and clutched pomanders closer. There was continual hammering, on metal, on wood. Here were the markets for traders denied a permit to enter the town. There were vegetables and cheeses, hares strung up, fish drying in the sun. A few scraggy chickens scratched at the earth and scattered from under the horses' hooves.

53

In front of Marjorie the hoof of one of their escorting soldiers' horses caught a squawking chicken which tumbled away in the dust. An old woman came running at them, screaming, silenced when she caught sight of the livery of Norham. A child took advantage of her lack of attention to grab the still flapping chicken and run off. No one else took much notice.

Further on, word of their coming must have gone ahead for in the road there was a child with a jug of ale, lifting it up to offer it to them, spilling most of it. Their soldier escort waved him away, but Marjorie paused and gave the child a penny, for the rags barely covered his nakedness.

'They're better off than they look, Miss,' said the soldier disapprovingly. 'Don't encourage beggars.'

On her grandfather's estate no servant would have spoken to her like that, but she was finding that soldiers, particularly soldiers here on the border, did not hesitate to speak their minds, no matter whom they were with.

The soldier went on contemptuously. 'First sign of any disturbance and these shacks are abandoned and they crowd inside the walls. Glad enough then of the shelter of the town, though they won't pay their taxes like good Englishmen.'

They were admitted through the gate. The town seemed quiet after the pandemonium outside. It was Sunday, and the people were gathering to attend the church.

As Elizabeth and Marjorie entered the Parish Church heads turned. Sarie slipped in among the crowd already gathered in the middle of the church, but their guards stayed at the door, with men from the Berwick garrison whom they knew, judging by the gruff greetings Marjorie heard as they entered.

Captain Bowes had sent word ahead, and space had been left for them in the closed pews of the gentry, where the mayor and his wife waited to welcome them. Once seated and conscious of being no longer the centre of attention, Marjorie looked round. There was no rood screen, only the

54

scar on the walls on either side where it had been fitted. All looked bare, empty of colour, and dim, without the votive candles which used to light up every church. The old altar was gone. She saw it later in the graveyard, like a dead thing, in a corner by the well, tucked half out of sight. There was nothing in its place, only a lighter patch on the wooden floor to show where it had been. Some weak attempt had been made to paint over the floorboards to try and blend in the light patch with the darker area surrounding it. Against the wall there was a raised platform with a lectern in front of it, on which was perched a copy of the Great Bible.

She could make out faintly on the walls the pictures which had once been there, now whitewashed over. On one panel over to her right, someone had started to paint on the white panels the words of the ten commandments. The first three had been scribed and the panel was already full, so big were the letters, and the words stopped half way through, so that the last two lines read 3. *Thou shalt not.* Perhaps they found it a laborious job. Perhaps it needed two of them, one to scribe the letters and one to apply the black paint.

The next panel would, no doubt in due course, remind the people what they should not. And so on and so on, till the wall was full of thou shalt nots, and the people would have only this to look at on a Sunday and could no longer gaze on the pictures of the Holy Family and the saints. Few people could read, but all could understand pictures of fields of sheaves and mice in the shelter of a wall, and squirrels with their little hoards of nuts.

When the noise had quietened and all were waiting, Master Knox came into the church. He was wearing his gown now, and looked altogether bigger and darker, almost fierce. He walked up to the platform, nodding to left and right as he was greeted by the people.

He read quickly through the service for the day in the new Book of Common Prayer as prescribed by the King's bishops. He doesn't like it, thought Marjorie. I wonder why.

The congregation here were evidently becoming familiar with it, for when the responses had to be given they spoke up with little hesitation. He opened the Great Bible and read a passage from it. Then there was a kind of sigh in the church, and a rustling and fidgeting. Clearly they were settling down to enjoy the part they had been waiting for.

What the reading was and what sermon he drew from it Marjorie could not afterwards recall. But she never forgot the sense she had of everyone being totally absorbed in his words and being carried away with the emotion in them. He spoke to the people as if he were a voice inside their head. He moved about as he spoke, addressing people, looking at them, smiling at children, clasping his hand in the air as if drawing down power from above.

He pondered the meaning of the words. He drew from the text parallels with other texts. He talked of the love of God. He talked of the love of Jesus. He talked of sacrifices, in this town which had sacrificed so much to power-hungry kings. He talked of the harvest soon to come. He talked of the fish in the sea and the birds in the air. He promised – what did he promise exactly? What was it he promised that caused hearts to beat faster and spirits to lift? He was winding up. He stopped speaking and said a brief prayer, and there was a collective sigh, as of satisfaction, throughout the congregation.

Knox said, 'Let us now break bread in memory of our Lord's sacrifice.'

There was a general movement: the men carried in trestles and boards and set them up the length of the church, and those that had stools brought them and sat down, and the others crowded round.

'Are you comfortable at Norham Castle?' asked the mayor's wife while they waited. Elizabeth replied, and they talked, Marjorie only half listening to them.

Master Knox was helping move benches into place and handing the very old people into them with a smile and a pat on the shoulder. Now he came to the pew in which they were sitting and offered his arm to Elizabeth, and led her, silent and bemused, to the table. He placed her between an elderly woman in grey serge and a young man in sailor's clothes. Marjorie was put between two little maids who looked at her shyly, and one of them surreptitiously rubbed her finger over the material of Marjorie's gown, and whispered behind Marjorie's back to the other, giggling.

The other gentry followed from the pews and took seats where they could find them. They seemed to be familiar with this, and to find nothing odd about seating themselves without any hierarchy. As the mayor explained to Marjorie much later, it was either that or not take part at all, for Master Knox declared all were equal in the sight of God, so for the sake of their salvation they could not refuse.

The men brought flagons of wine and women brought loaves of bread and Master Knox placed his hands on both and said 'Eat in memory of me, drink in memory of me.'

The bread and the wine were passed down the table and each man and woman tore off a piece of bread and poured a spoonful of wine into their own individual bowls which they produced from pockets in their clothing. From where she sat Marjorie could see her mother, looking horrified. When the bread reached Elizabeth she passed it on to her neighbour without taking any. With a puzzled look on his face he held it out to her, then when she still did nothing, tore off a piece and took her hand, actually laid his hand on hers, and placed the bread in it.

Marjorie froze, waiting for her mother to do something to offend the man. But she did not. She ate it. When the wine came she could do nothing for she had no cup with her. The neighbour offered his cup to her. When she shook her head he indicated the side of the cup out of which he had not drunk and pressed it into her hand. She took a sip and handed it back.

When the bread reached Marjorie, down her side of the table, she tore off a piece and ate it, and likewise took a sip of the wine offered in the coarse pottery cup of the maidservant. It was hedgerow wine, elderberry perhaps, rich and deep in colour. Marjorie had never thought before about the wine which the priest had turned into the blood of Christ. She assumed it had always been something special, made for the purpose in some holy place.

All this was done quietly, with murmured courtesies as people passed the flagons of wine and the bread. Marjorie felt she was being watched and looked up to find John Knox looking at her. He smiled, and she smiled back. It wasn't so bad, this new way of communion. Then, as quickly, the tables were cleared and the boards put back against the walls, the people stood quietly and Master Knox pronounced the benediction.

He stood at the door of the church shaking hands with the congregation as they streamed out. Elizabeth passed him without acknowledgment and hurried away into the graveyard. Marjorie curtseyed and ran after her mother.

Elizabeth was crouched in a corner of the graveyard behind some high tombstones, vomiting. She brought up the bread dyed red with the wine. But since they had eaten nothing since early morning her stomach was empty and after she had cleared out the small offering, she retched emptily. Marjorie and Sarie held her and rubbed her back. Two other women, glimpsing what was happening, came over and formed a shield so that others might not see.

'Pregnant?' one of them mouthed the word to Marjorie, who shook her head, blushing for her mother.

Elizabeth straightened up, her face white and her brow glistening with sweat. When she was steady they supported her back to where they had left the horses.

58

Chapter 12

'It was obscene.'

'It was only ordinary wine. Hedgerow wine.'

Her mother was sleeping now. It was three weeks since the day they went to the church in Berwick. Marjorie sat at the window and looked down into the inner bailey. Darkness was already settling over the land. Away to the northeast she could see the faintest reflection in the pale gold clouds of the sunset there must be to the west out of her sight. Down below the linkboy was moving from sconce to sconce, firing the torches. At the forge the glow of the furnace died as it was damped down.

Soon the smith and his boy left the building, pulling on their jerkins against the night. It was only September and not yet particularly cold but they would feel it more than most. The torches flickered as men passed underneath, as they came from their various workshops. Soldiers began to muster in the yard, and she watched her father emerge from the gatehouse below and inspect them. They were ordered to their posts, at the gate of the compound, at the main gate, climbing up the narrow steps to the battlements. The men they replaced assembled in the yard, were dismissed and drifted away to their quarters. There floated up to her the melancholic sound of a man singing in a language she did not understand. There was a shout and the singing stopped. She closed the shutter and wrapped the shawl tighter round her shoulders.

Since the Sunday when they went to Berwick and shared in the communion in John Knox's church, her mother had fasted. At first they did not realise what was happening. Her mother played with the food on her plate like a child forced to eat something it did not like.

'What's the matter?'

'Nothing. I'm not hungry.'

Then she stopped even pretending to eat. She had no energy except to sit at the fire, which now had to be lit every day because she had no strength to keep herself warm. She was obviously ill. Her cheeks were sunken and her skin dry and rasping to the touch. Now she had taken to her bed. She lay twisted towards the wall. She had been picking at the plaster, scraping it with her thumbnail, scrape, scrape. Her hand was so thin Marjorie fancied she could see the whiteness of the plaster through it, between the bones. She feared for her mother's reason.

Every now and again she would moisten her mother's lips with water. She had heard it said that a person may live for a month without food but only for a week without water. Her mother was turned in on herself, caring nothing for husband or daughter, or the babies left at Aske in the care of their nurses.

Jesus, Maria, miserere mei. Miserere mei. Over and over. Lost in grief for the death of her soul. And sometimes she would mutter words that they could barely make out. *He died for the truth.* Sarie, sharing the vigil with Marjorie, thought she was talking about Jesus. Marjorie wondered.

Captain Bowes was becoming frantic. He who had seen death so often on the battlefield, could not now bear to be in the same room as his weak, muttering wife. It had never struck Marjorie before how much her father loved her mother. They had been married, these two, when barely more than children for the advancement of both families. A lifetime and fifteen children together had forged bonds so close that Elizabeth had abandoned the comfort of Aske to live here in this cold place, and he now became unmanly at the thought of losing her.

The doctor from Berwick came, but he wanted to bleed the patient and Marjorie resisted this. She might not know as much as a doctor who had studied medicine for so many years but this she did know, that if he drew blood from

Elizabeth, the sight of it would cause her surely to lose her mind completely.

Marjorie tried to explain it to her father.

'She believed herself to be committing a heresy in attending a service that was so obviously Protestant.'

'Nonsense, girl. It was no more than decreed by the King. Where is the heresy in that?'

It went further than that, beyond what the King ordered, but she could not say so. If the people in Berwick liked the form of John Knox's service, she did not want to draw official attention to it. Her father had no interest anyway. He was a soldier. He had given his whole life to the service of the King, without question, whoever he might be, whether King Henry or King Edward. His life revolved round weapons, cannon and horses, scouting rotas and the disciplining of men inclined to fight each other when there was no obvious enemy in front of them. Where men's motives were concerned, he assumed they centred round wealth and power and greed for both. The form a religious service took was a matter of indifference to him. He had not the language to talk about the things of the soul.

Marjorie did not dare tell him that his wife's thoughts now dwelt on a man with one eye who was not a soldier, but who had led an insurrection against the King because the King threatened to destroy the true religion. A man to whom her mother had clung in the quiet night and who went from her arms to a terrible death.

'She believes that in drinking the communion wine at Berwick she was drinking the real blood of Jesus.'

'It was just wine,' he shouted.

'I know that,' she shouted back. He was startled. Daughters did not raise their voices, never to their father.

'It was just wine,' she went on, more quietly. 'But it had been blessed by John Knox and he is a priest. So it became the blood of Jesus. And she drank it, and she thinks she had no right to do that.'

'Then get him here. Get him here to tell her it was just wine. Dear God in Heaven is the man as much a charlatan as the old priests were?'

Every day Sarie went to the kitchen to prepare little dishes of bread and milk, flavoured with honey and spices. The first time the cook and his men tried to tell her she had no business there, and insulted her in a way she had never heard in her life, short of actually laying hands on her. When they heard the captain's lady was ill, though, they gave Sarie a corner of the table and the fire, and a dish to prepare food in. But to no purpose. Elizabeth Bowes would not eat.

'Cinnamon,' said Sarie.   'She's always loved cinnamon.' This was true. Even though it was one of the most expensive of spices she would have a little dish of it beside her in the evenings, and dip slices of apple in it. But there was none in the kitchen.

'I'll ask in Berwick,' said Marjorie. She went herself as soon as it was light to fetch John Knox, not trusting anyone with a message. She took with her only one soldier.

'Do you know where he lives?' she asked, as their beasts jogged gently towards the town.

'Down by the harbour. Anyone can direct us.'

They were through the town gates as soon as they opened. They were directed down a narrow lane lined with warehouses, inside which carts were being loaded with sacks and boxes. They could hear the horses shifting restlessly, waiting their turn to be harnessed. The air was full of the smell of dung and fish, spices and fruit.

They made their way slowly along to the harbour. Laden carts pulled out from the warehouses and lumbered past them. At the end of the road they came out into sudden bright light and there in front of them was the jetty, lined with ships, their masts taller than the warehouses and rigging like cat's cradles forming a pattern against the sky. Beyond them, standing out in the mouth of the broad river, were more ships at anchor, rising and falling gently on the tide.

From portholes in the sides of the ships, ladders came out and rested on the ground and men, and some women too, were toiling up and down, with sacks and crates, loading woollen cloth, bringing off barrels of wine, and more bales of cloth wrapped in hessian. Every now and then a merchant or his clerk would pull open the wrapping to check the contents, exposing fine silks and brocades. All over the place children were nipping in among the adults, picking up what was dropped, sweeping up what was spilled, and making off with it.

While Marjorie stared around, the soldier dismounted and was asking directions. He came back to her.

'Master Knox lodges with his brother, the merchant William Knox. At the far end there.'

They led their horses along the crowded quay. There were few curious glances. In this town people were used to strangers and most of them were too busy working to care. When they reached the house that was pointed out to them she sent the soldier away to rest and water the horses.

She considered the house. This end of the street where the river narrowed was quieter. It was not a big house, three storeys merely. She knocked. The door was answered by a girl in an apron.

'Master's out.'

'It is Master Knox the preacher I seek,' said Marjorie.

The room she was shown into was panelled and furnished with some fine carved oak chairs by the fire which burned in a tiled grate. She caught a glimpse of a room beyond, furnished with a desk and shelves on which were rolls of parchment and some books in fine bindings. John Knox's? Or his brother's? The woman who now came into the room was short and plump, with a round face. Marjorie had seen her in the church.

'It's John you're looking for? I'm sorry you can't see him. This is one of his quiet days. He does his reading and writing today.'

Marjorie was still standing in the middle of the room. 'My father is Captain of Norham Castle.'

'Oh I ken fine who you are, but he still willna be disturbed.'

Marjorie felt her cheeks grow hot. She shouldn't have to explain. Was her mother's illness to be common gossip among the fishwives of Berwick? For in truth there was a faint smell of fish in the house. In her agitation to control herself she must have sniffed, for the woman in front of her suddenly lifted her hands to her nose and sniffed, and smiled.

'You'll have to thole the smell, for I've been teaching a new lassie in the kitchen how to gut the trout for the dinner.'

'My mother is dying,' said Marjorie.

'John's not the man you want then. He'll not be doing any of your papist last rites.'

Marjorie sank down onto a bench by the window.

'It's not for that,' she said. 'He caused it. He must heal her.'

'He's a clever man but he's no doctor.'

'We have a doctor. Please.'

Without thinking she had lifted her hands in supplication. Now she lowered them and clasped them across her chest. Mistress Knox considered, then nodded.

'I'll go and speak to him.'

She went out of the room and Marjorie sank back against the cushions, closing her eyes. Then she felt a gentle hand on her shoulder. Mistress Knox was standing beside her with a beaker of ale in her hand. Marjorie drank it gratefully.

'I'm sorry if I was short with you, lassie, but you see we're plagued with women coming to the house looking for John. Any excuse will do. And he hates to be disturbed at his writing.'

Presently John Knox appeared at the parlour door. His sister-in-law left them. He closed the door behind her and sat down opposite Marjorie.

'My mother is starving herself to death. Will you come?'

'Why does she want me?'

'She doesn't. I'm asking you because you caused it.'

'I? What did I do?'

'She was sick after taking the bread and wine in church that day.'

'Nobody else was. The bread was wholesome. There was nothing wrong with the wine.'

'It's not that. It's just that she believes it was blasphemy.'

'What was blasphemy?'

'She believes she was drinking the blood of Christ. Truly that it was his blood.'

He groaned and shook his head. 'We have been teaching people not to believe that nonsense.'

'She has not heard enough of your teachings. She has believed all her life that the priest can drink the wine because he is a special person.'

His expression was bleak. 'There is nothing special about a priest. He is a man, like any other man.'

'Will you come and talk to her? Explain that.'

In reply he went out into the lobby of the house and pulled a cloak from the hooks on the wall. He shouted something through to the kitchen, in his Scotch tongue, and then led Marjorie from the house.

'Sir, can we stop in the town. I must purchase some cinnamon. It might tempt her to eat.'

'Wait,' he said and went back into the house. He came out in a few minutes with a small package which he dropped into her hand.

'With the compliments of Ellen, my guid-sister.'

Chapter 13

'We came to your church because my father insisted. The new learning is heresy. And now my mother will die because of it.'

'No one died of a theory yet.'

She had sent the soldier on ahead. He could not overhear.

'Sir, what of the people who have been burnt? We hear stories from London. Good Catholics, dying. What of the ....' She was about to say, what about the Pilgrimage of Grace, and the leader with one eye who was hanged, but she stopped herself. This man probably considered that rising to be folly. It was still too dangerous to talk about that time.

'They died because they opposed the will of the King.'

'And is my mother to die because she believes she is opposing the will of God?'

'And you, Miss Marjorie. You do not look as if you are dying for a belief.'

'I am not such a fool.'

'So drinking the wine did not offend you?'

'It was just elderberry wine.'

'Yes, it was. The shipment of wine from France we had been expecting had been held up in heavy seas, so we substituted a few bottles of my guid-sister's excellent hedgerow wine and what odds? Do you despise, Miss Marjorie, the product of honest toil by common people?'

'I did not mean that. We used to make such at Aske.'

'But perhaps it did not find its way to the altar. Well, Miss Marjorie, the next time you come to break bread in my church you will find some fine French wine. The delayed shipment has been with us for a week, and I declare it excellent.'

'Master Knox. It is hard for old people to change their ways.'

'Your mother is not so very old,' he said, mildly. 'I begin to approach that age myself.'

'You are a man. You have been out in the world. You have seen many things which my mother has not.'

They rode on in silence.

'You look tired, Miss Marjorie, if I may make a personal comment. It must be lonely for you at Norham Castle. Do you have a woman friend? I have never seen you with one.'

'I have Sarie.'

'No companion?'

'I have mother. I have no need of anyone else.'

'Have you no sister or aunt who could come?'

'The life here is not as comfortable as they are accustomed to.'

She sensed his smile without looking at him.

'It is a question of what they are used to,' she repeated.

'There are women, respectable merchants' widows in Berwick. With your father's leave I could ask one to be a companion to you. You should not have the whole burden of your mother's illness.'

'No.' She raised her voice. 'I have Sarie. We will manage. Besides, it is none of your business.'

The soldier, riding on ahead, turned at the sound of her shout and made to pull up his horse, but Marjorie waved him on.

'It is the law now that everyone must take communion in the new way at least twice a year,' said John Knox. 'I will be offering it in my church in Berwick and in the chapel at Norham. Perhaps if she were to plead illness on those days, I could omit to notice she was not there.'

'Can you tell her that?'

'Yes.'

But it would not totally answer. That was for the future. If her mother lived.

67

They were back at the castle by mid-afternoon. John Knox went to pay his respects to Captain Bowes while Marjorie went up to her mother's room. Elizabeth was still lying in bed with her eyes closed. Marjorie gave the cinnamon to Sarie and sent her away.

'Mother,' she said. 'Mother, Master Knox is here.'

She gave no sign that she had heard.

Marjorie tidied up the bedclothes and made sure Elizabeth was decently covered and waited. She waited, while beyond the window the dusk gathered round the castle. She looked out over the moorland beyond which lay Scotland. John Knox could not return there. His own country was closed to him. She wondered what family he had left there. Presently, she heard him climbing the stairs and went to meet him. She took him into her mother's bedroom.

'Mistress Bowes,' he said in a soft voice. Again, she gave no sign that she had heard. He reached out and took the hand which lay lifelessly on the bedcover. He closed his eyes and bent his head and began to pray. His voice was soft and persuasive. Then the prayer slid into inconsequential talk, the life going on outside, the harvest, the doings of the people of Berwick. He talked and talked. Sometimes he was talking to the sick woman in the bed, sometimes he seemed to be talking to himself, sometimes he was talking to God. Marjorie slid a stool forward so that he could sit.

He talked of the people in Berwick known to her and unknown, of babies born and new houses built. He talked of the grace of God and asked God to give back to Elizabeth Bowes a life worth living. His voice went on, murmuring. Marjorie leaned back against the wall and fell asleep.

She woke with a start to silence in the room. Sarie must have brought in candles for they flickered now in the sconces. She was alone with her mother. She looked wearily at the bed and started up. Her mother was awake. Elizabeth tried to speak, but her lips were dry and cracked and it was obviously painful.

Just then Knox came back into the room, followed by Sarie. He was holding a bowl. He sat by the bed and held the bowl to Elizabeth's lips, and she drank. She twisted her face.

'It's only water,' he said. 'And a little salt and honey. We have flavoured it with cinnamon, haven't we Sarie?'

'A magic potion,' Sarie giggled, very likely with nervousness.

He said sharply. 'There is no magic. This is a mixture will help a body deprived of nourishment.'

He carefully withdrew the cup. 'You will eat something now?'

'No.' The word was faint.

'Then I will have to return tomorrow and we will talk some more.'

He stood looking down at her.

'God is not angry with you. He will not let you go.'

His face was grey with exhaustion. Marjorie offered him a bed for the night. He told her Captain Bowes had already offered, but he preferred to go to the soldiers' quarters and find a pallet there.

'Your mother and I will break our fast together in the morning.'

He was back at daybreak. At midday raised voices could be heard from the room, his voice deep and slow, hers querulous and shaky.

'What it was about I don't know,' Sarie told Marjorie afterwards. 'I just sat in the corner like a mouse.'

Captain Bowes heard them too.

'Good,' he said. 'An angry soldier is a fighting soldier. An angry man doesn't want to die.'

He went back to his duties. Towards afternoon Knox left Elizabeth in the care of Sarie.

'I think she will eat something now,' he said. He sat down on the settle by the fire and covered his eyes with his hands. Marjorie saw moisture on his cheeks.

Whether in cool reason or hot anger no one could be sure, but Elizabeth Knox was persuaded to eat. It was slow at first. She could not keep down much solid food, but gradually the colour came back to her cheeks and each day she had the strength to walk a few more paces round the room.

Every day Knox stayed with her for hours, talking. When she was asleep he would sit with Marjorie in the parlour. Sometimes when the light was good enough he read, sometimes to himself, but sometimes by invitation aloud to Sarie and Marjorie, sitting sewing. His voice was deep and musical, and very comforting. Her father would put his head in, and go away again, satisfied that all was peaceful.

John Knox left them only once. He was duty-bound to take the three Sunday services at Berwick, and he left early in the morning, returning late, riding with the moonlight to be back with them.

And then the last day came.

'I have started your mother on a course of reading.'

He paused, and stood awkwardly.

'Thank you for all you have done,' said Marjorie.

'Thank you for making me welcome in your home.'

On a sudden impulse Marjorie reached out her hand and took his. His palm was all calloused, all along the cushions of flesh round the palms and along every finger.

'Those calluses never came from turning the pages of a bible.'

'No. They came from my time when I was a French prisoner, rowing in the galleys.'

'Oh.' She dropped his hand.

'I do not talk about it.'

'Were they so cruel?'

'It was cold.'

70

'And hungry?'

'Not very hungry. A hungry oarsman is a weak oarsman. They needed us strong.'

After he had gone, the place felt empty.

Chapter 14

This is the story which John Knox told Elizabeth and Marjorie and Sarie one wet afternoon as they sat after dinner by the fire.

'Let me tell you what it was like for us in Scotland. You'll understand that bibles in the English tongue were coming into the country, smuggled in over the border, and across the sea from the Low Countries. But it suited Cardinal Beaton to keep the common man in ignorance. He made parliament pass a law that the scriptures could only be read in Hebrew, or in Greek or in Latin, though even the men who claimed to be churchmen could read none of those languages. Some of them could barely read their own.

'There were a lot of good people then. Many people were already meeting in each other's houses, to read the bible and discuss it and talk of the ideas coming from the continent. Men and women in every walk of life, from the common labourer to the lawyer and the merchant, the laird, aye, and some of them the highest in the land. All over the country from the Mearns to Galloway and from Argyll to the borders here. They were men of solid judgment and their voices were heard.

'The Commissioners of the Burghs and some of the nobility put pressure on the Cardinal and he was forced to retract, and the scriptures became available for all to read. Ladies, you should have seen the brave men then who walked around with the English bible openly in their hands and boasting they had been reading it in secret these long years.' Knox laughed. 'And when they opened it they had to blow the dust off from its long years hidden at the foot of a kist. Such brave creatures.

'Howsoever, in retaliation the Cardinal took his church court to the fine town of Perth and held an inquisition there.

Four men were hanged and a woman drowned, and what was their sin? No more than it was alleged they ate goose on a Friday.

'That was the nature of Cardinal Beaton. There was a lot more of that.'

Knox paused, lost in thought, lost in memory. The women quietly stitched.

He sighed, and went on. 'The Regent was James Hamilton, the Earl of Arran, a soft man, easily swayed by whoever he was having words with at the time. He had been persuaded that our little Queen Mary had best be betrothed to your Prince Edward, as he then was. Had that happened our two countries might now be united and at peace.

'But the Cardinal did not want that. He was in thrall, you understand, to the Queen Dowager who was set on an alliance with her native France. And of course your King Henry had turned his back on the Pope and was thought of by Beaton and our Queen Mother as a heretic. Cardinal Beaton threatened my Lord Arran, and held his son hostage, and prevailed on him to repudiate the contract with England. We know what happened then.

'Beaton's treachery unleashed the anger of King Henry against the Scots. Henry took our ships as prizes, and imprisoned merchants and mariners. This caused a lot of hardship to our people. But that was not enough. The English fleet landed thousands of soldiers, who ravaged the countryside. They swept north, destroying the crops, killing and raping. I weep now for the suffering my people endured.

'Beaton made no move to aid his countrymen. He fled to his castle of St. Andrews and fortified it. He never came within twenty miles of the fighting.

'Instead he called on the French. They came in their thousands. They came expecting the Cardinal to fight with them, for it was in the same cause after all, the cause of

Rome against the heretic Henry. They were to be disillusioned. His banner was unfurled alongside the French, and he and his men were called on to muster. Coward that he was, he did not answer, and damn few of his men did, so his banner was folded up again and put back in its bag, while he lurked in his castle, well away from any danger.

'English and French fought one another on Scottish soil, destroying crops and dwellings, and the people who starved and died were the Scots with no one to defend them. And Cardinal Beaton, leader of the church, who had the ear of the Queen Mother and control of the Regent, sat in his castle of St. Andrews in luxury with his woman and did nothing. Do you wonder he was hated?

'When George Wishart, that good gentle man, came from the continent to preach the word of God to his fellow Scots, Beaton had him arrested and burnt at the stake while Beaton himself watched from his castle ramparts.

'Is it any wonder that when the time came he was dragged from his lair and murdered and his body exhibited to the people?

'I was not there,' continued Knox. 'I had followed Wishart. I loved him for I knew he spoke the truth. I travelled with him round Scotland while he preached. God help me, I carried a sword to defend him. But when the time came I was not there. I was not there.'

He paused and Marjorie, looking at him, thought for a moment the firelight gleamed on a tear on his cheek.

He went on. 'When someone you love dies for the cause you both believe in, you feel you should have died too. You feel guilt because you are alive. Was his belief stronger than mine? Wishart was a braver and a better man than I will ever be. I should have been by his side, fighting. But I was not. He said to me, one life is enough for a sacrifice – gang back to your bairns.

'I obeyed. I went back to my duties as a tutor, and a fine man died, and I lived.'

74

Marjorie's mother was weeping. Marjorie pondered the words. When someone you love dies. Had her mother confided in Knox? Had she talked to him of things she never talked to her daughter about? She had no right, Marjorie thought. It is in the past. It is a shameful episode. It should not be talked about.

'I was but a dominie teaching the sons of lairds their numbers and a little Latin to no great purpose. One of the lairds had joined the rebels now holding the castle in St. Andrews. He wanted his boys with him. I delivered the boys to their father and stayed on in the town.

'And there I found my voice. The Church was leaderless. Beaton's castle was occupied by men who defied the law, such as it was. The people were bewildered and in bad need of guidance. I taught the bairns of the town first and the people heard me and elected me their preacher. George Wishart gave me the substance and God gave me the voice and there I stayed till the French fleet sailed into the bay and we were taken prisoner. And so I was sent to the galleys.'

Elizabeth Bowes asked. 'How could you bear it? A freeborn man, to be a slave?'

'Slavery is a state of mind. Prisoner I might have been, slave never.'

And then he shook his head.

'I'll speak no more of it, save to say it ended when your King Edward arranged for all the prisoners to be released. I was brought to England and sent here to Berwick.

'For your King has need of preachers who know their bible and can spread the word. He is done with ignorance and superstition.'

Chapter 15

Marjorie sat on the bench outside the Bishop's Hall and watched her mother and John Knox walking on the battlements.

They paced the walkway along the curtain wall above the keep. In the low afternoon sunshine their shadows spilled over the walls, and now stretched ahead of them as they turned east. They were of a height, and they faced ahead while they talked, except now and then her mother turned to glance at her companion, but from this distance Marjorie could not see her expression.

Her mother today was wrapped in a heavy cloak, not because she needed it in this unseasonably warm autumn weather, but because she was conscious of how thin she had become when fasting, and tried to hide it. Even now Sarie ought to have been upstairs stitching at her mother's skirts, tightening up the waists so that the hems no longer drooped and trailed. Except she was over by the stables, giggling with her soldier lover.

Every now and then the couple up above passed one of the guards, who stood straighter as the walkers approached, drooping when the captain's lady and her companion had passed by. What were they hearing? What would be reported back to Uncle Robert Bowes, who was bound to have spies even in his brother's household?

They talked of raising people from the dead, Sir.

Black magic?

Jesus did it. Sir.

What else?

Whether charity was the same as love, Sir.

Love? They talked of love?

They passed on, Sir. I heard no more.

Was the preacher assessing the strength of the guard?

I couldn't say, Sir. He seemed absorbed in the lady.

They came down from the wall, Knox turning to hand Elizabeth down the last few deeper steps, and then he strode away across the bailey, to where the guard opened the picket gate for him, and with a slap on the man's shoulder, he was gone. Men were always doing that, slapping each other on shoulder and back, a thump in the ribs. Marjorie remembered her brothers doing it all the time, so much energy to throw around, so much exuberance.

She felt the beginnings of the drag in her belly that warned her of the start of her monthlies. Her mother was free of all that now.

*

'Mother, when can we go back to Aske?'

'Norham is our home now.'

'It was only meant to be for a short time, surely?'

'My place is beside your father. Aren't you happy here?'

Her mother sat with her hands folded in her lap, idle. Marjorie was stitching at a woolwork tapestry, a small one, intended for a firescreen. The central motif was a unicorn. She had written to her sister Jacintha, who was now ten. A preening child, Marjorie thought, overhearing too often remarks by older women who should have known better that she, Jacintha, would turn out to be the beauty of the family. But she was clever with a quill and Marjorie had asked her to sketch out a small copy of the unicorn on the tapestry in grandfather's bookroom. The unicorn free and proud, not the unicorn defeated and captured. Now she was trying to stitch this, a creamy unicorn surrounded by guelder roses, but her skill with wools was less than Jacintha's with her inks.

'Perhaps it's time you had your own household. Maybe I have been selfish in keeping you with me.'

Marjorie thought of her sisters, the married ones secure and comfortable in their own households, gradually filling up the nurseries. Did they ever feel this restlessness, this dissatisfaction? Of course it could be done. If she wanted to leave Norham they would not force her to stay. She could go back to Aske. A husband would be found for her.

A new sensation, a lurching as if her insides had turned over. She wanted to cry. She threaded more wool into her bodkin. Her hands began to sweat. She gripped the bodkin more tightly. Suddenly it snapped in two. Carefully wrapping up her work in its silk cloth and dropping the pieces of the broken bodkin into her workbasket, she said, 'I think I will lie down. I have a headache.'

'Yes. Rest.' Her mother, leaning back in her chair, her hands idle in her lap, a faint smile on her lips, had not noticed anything.

*

Marjorie and Sarie were sorting through a kist of winter clothes which had come from Aske. John Knox was with Elizabeth in her parlour.

'Mother will be glad of these. Now she has hardly any flesh on her to keep her warm.'

'She's putting it back on, now she's content.'

Marjorie listened for sounds from the next room. A chair was scraped over the floor and a door opened. There were the murmured words of farewell. Telling Sarie to carry on without her, she quickly threw on a cloak and ran down the back stairs, so that she reached the main door before him. She waited. A light step and there he was.

'Miss Marjorie,' he said.

'Master Knox. May I walk some of the way with you?'

He nodded and together they were let out of the postern gate, and walked down the steep track which led off the hill. The undergrowth here was never allowed to grow, in case it hid enemies. Puffs of dust eddied round their feet and little stones skittered away. Knox reached out a hand to steady her, but she ignored it.

They turned round the foot of the hill and began on the road towards Berwick. This track could be seen from the castle walls. There was a point by the river where she would have to turn back, because the road there passed out of sight of the guards on the battlements, and she was forbidden to go beyond it unaccompanied by a soldier. Up to that point she could be seen by the guards on the walls, and was safe. It was one of the restrictions that irked her most.

She walked without speaking till they reached this spot. She stopped.

'I must go back.'

'Yes. I thank you for your company.'

'Master Knox. I have something to say to you.'

'Miss Marjorie?'

'My father should say it.'

'Why can he not speak for himself?'

'Because he is,' she hesitated, 'he is unaware. Master Knox. I think you should not come so often to Norham.'

He looked away from her over the river, towards the moorlands of Scotland.

'Am I no longer welcome? Why is that?'

What could she say? Because my mother has become too fond of you? Because we no longer live in the days of romance where a man could be a friend of a married woman and no one think it more than courtly dalliance? Because perhaps there is danger here for my mother, for all of us?

'My mother . . . ' she began, and stopped.

She could no longer see his face, just the set of his shoulders, tense under his cloak.

'There will be talk,' she said awkwardly.

'I'm sorry for it.'

This was harder than she had expected. Then she felt her temper rise. She should not have been put in this position.

'Master Knox. I am grateful to you for the help you gave my mother when she was ill. She is not ill any longer. I

79

would not like to see her caused any pain. Some friendships are not suitable.'

'I hadna understood the peril.'

'My mother is weak.'

'I minister to your mother's soul. She is greatly troubled. What else do you suspect?'

He sounded angry now. There were some low sharp gorse bushes growing here, and she reached out and pulled off one of the yellow blossoms and crushed it between her fingers. The honey scent rose to her nostrils. She was aware that Knox had turned and was now watching her.

'You do well to protect your mother. But there is no need. She is safe enough with me. I wouldna covet another man's wife.'

She dropped the petals into the river and watched them swirl for a moment in the water and then disappear. When the gorse is in flower, love is in bloom. So went the old country saying. The gorse was always in flower, summer and winter. Furiously she turned away and dashed at the tears that were starting in her eyes. This was horrible.

'Your mother is clever. She analyses what she reads in the Bible and wants to talk about it. I can render her that service. But no other. Do you understand, Marjorie? She thinks ower much on past actions and the fate of her soul. She sees guilt where there is none. I can talk her out of it. I canna stop now.'

'I understand.'

'You dinna understand Marjorie. It's you.'

'What?'

'Marjorie. It is not your mother who has become dear to me.'

She gulped and turned back along the path towards the castle. He reached out a hand to stop her, then mindful of being seen, he dropped it.

'I am not a poet to say fine words. I am a simple man. And I am not a fool. Here stands a priest with no means and

80

little future. If you told your father what I have said I would be banished. I know that. I won't speak of it again. I will make some excuse to your mother. I will not come again.'

She turned and ran back to the castle. At the gate she turned and caught a last glimpse of him, as he pulled his cloak round himself and turned back onto the road to Berwick, beyond the point where Marjorie could not go.

Chapter 16

The Privy Council sent Sir Robert Bowes north again to report on the defences along the border, and to do a thorough survey of Norham Castle. He brought with him news and gossip from the south. There had been risings, it seemed, among the Cornishmen and in Kent, protests against the new Book of Common Prayer.

'Of course, English is as much a foreign language to them as Latin.'

One group of rebels almost reached London. The risings had been brutally suppressed by John Dudley, Earl of Warwick.

'He's the coming man. My God, we thought Edward Seymour hard but he's a new-born babe compared with Dudley.'

'Where do we stand?' Captain Bowes meant the family. Where are the Bowes family in these movements of the influential and powerful?

'I question whether Seymour will last, King's uncle or no,' said Sir Robert. 'He lets in too many refugees from Spain. Dissenters and Jews. Londoners don't take kindly to these incomers. They blame Seymour. And he favours the tenants against landlords when it comes to enclosures. He has the sense to see that a contented people make good soldiers if they're needed. They have something to defend. But it's made him too many enemies.'

'What happens if he falls?'

'He'll pull down plenty more. Your Bishop Tunstall, for one. He's on shaky ground. He still favours the old religion and only lightly disguises it. I hope you stood no nonsense when he came here.'

'The Bishop is a good man,' said Elizabeth Bowes.

'No doubt,' said Sir Robert drily. 'But a good man would do well to keep his head down if he wishes to retain it.'

'We have no particular sympathy for the old man,' said Captain Bowes. He frowned at his wife.

'I cannot pretend to dislike him, just because the King's advisers say I must.'

With the coming of Sir Robert the castle was activated into greater activity and the men who thought themselves well drilled under their captain were sent out on exhausting manoeuvres to demonstrate their readiness for war. Sarie repeated to Marjorie and her mother rumours picked up from Sir Robert's servants, some of them Londoners unhappy to be this far north. The King was looking once more at war with France and Scotland. Sir Robert's presence travelling along the border with his surveyors did nothing to dispel these rumours.

But gossip works in both directions, and Marjorie began to fret that it would not take long for a suggestion to reach the ears of her uncle that the regular visits of John Knox to Norham Castle were not just as spiritual adviser, but held a deeper purpose. For John Knox had been unable to stick to his resolution not to come to Norham. He had written to Elizabeth to say he was ill and would not see her for some weeks. She had immediately gone to visit him in Berwick.

'It's a kidney stone,' she told Marjorie. 'He's had it since he was in the galleys. Poor dear man.'

'I expect his sister-in-law looks after him well.'

'No doubt,' said her mother. 'But Mistress Ellen Knox cannot talk with him the way I can.'

Knox pleaded pressure of work and said he would come only if sent for. He was sent for often. Elizabeth's growing bodily health seemed to be matched by increasing mental anguish. She was still not convinced, it seemed, that God wanted her to follow the ways of the new religion. Her conscience still troubled her. When he came he spent more time with the soldiers of the garrison and less with the family. But Marjorie would be walking through the bailey, or taking the air on the wall walk, and look up and find his eyes on her.

Her father, trusting as he was and knowing John Knox for a true friend, would have disregarded any talk, but his brother was a man of the world, and would have a greater awareness of the damage that could be done to a family's reputation if there was a hint of an unsuitable alliance. And so more than anyone she fretted for her uncle to be gone.

John Knox was asked to dine. Meals were uncomfortable. The two men, strong-minded and wilful as they both were, found they disliked one another. How could they understand each other? Her uncle was the head of the family, instinctively Catholic despite the political necessity, wealthy, trained as a lawyer with a rich London practice, polished in his speech, careful of his opinion, influential at court, ready to serve with his wits and his estates in the north anyone who was in power.

How could he find anything in common with such a man as John Knox, a famously renegade priest, austere in his living, comfortable with the poor and the dispossessed, he who had been both, obsessed with his mission, and outspoken in his opinions?

The men were courteous to one another when the women were present, but when Elizabeth and Marjorie retired to their parlour they could hear the raised voices as the men continued to sit over their wine. Marjorie was sorry for it. She wanted everyone to think well of John Knox.

At last Sir Robert took his leave, fussing with his secretary over boxes of lists and maps.

Whether it was coincidence, or whether it was the outcome of that visit, Knox was summoned to appear before the authorities.

Bishop Tunstall required Master Knox to hold a special public preachment at Newcastle. His congregation would be the Council of the North, which included the Earls of

84

Westmorland and Cumberland, the Lord Mayor of Newcastle and many important knights and their ladies. The Bishop and Sir Robert Bowes would also be there.

The charge was that he preached too vigorously against the new English form of the mass, and that in his church he was not using Archbishop Cranmer's new Book of Common Prayer. All preachers were supposed to follow this each Sunday, reading the prayers and the liturgy for the day as laid out in that book.

'A mingle mangle of a liturgy,' he told Marjorie. 'Better to preach the word of God as it's written in the scriptures, not words put into my mouth by a committee in London. Why do these people think they can improve on the bible? And too many people here still wallow in idolatry. Soft words dinna gather in the flock. Better to speak plainly and be heard clearly.'

The consequence if he were found guilty would be the loss of his licence to preach. Without that, he would have to be silent. When she thought of John Knox silent, Marjorie could as soon imagine the moon to fall from the sky. But preaching without a licence could lead to a lifetime's imprisonment, or worse.

In the event, he returned to them within the fortnight, having routed, he said, his enemies.

'They sat there with their mouths agape. I told them, I told them the truth in good plain language, and none could deny it.'

'You must have sounded like an Old Testament prophet,' said Marjorie.

'That I did,' he said, then paused in his stride, for when he was excited he could not stay still. He looked at her keenly. 'I think you do not mean that for a compliment, Miss Marjorie.'

'What will they do?' asked her mother.

'Nothing. Bishop Tunstall, Dreaming Durham whose day is past, realised he could do nothing. I spake no more than the same that the King believes.'

Such hubris, thought Marjorie, such conceit, and yet ... And yet she knew that the relief she felt for his return among them was more than just happiness for a family friend.

Chapter 17

The year turned. They continued to live quietly at Norham. Marjorie sent for more books from Aske, but even these had lost their savour.

The couriers who came regularly brought news from London. After they had given their messages to Captain Bowes they sat in the kitchen over hot bowls of broth, and relayed the gossip, which Sarie brought to the two women, sitting aloft in their parlour. Edward Seymour, my lord Somerset, uncle of the King, had been removed from his position, and the King had a new adviser, John Dudley, now calling himself Duke of Northumberland, to the growling fury of many in the north, for this was the title that rightly belonged to the Percy family, who had been tricked, everyone said, into relinquishing their lands to King Henry. King Edward appointed him Lord Protector, and they said he was all but King himself.

As the summer wore on the news the messengers brought became more alarming. There was considerable unrest in the south. The sweating sickness was back in London. Thousands were dying, even friends of the King. But that wasn't the worst of it. After all, sickness and death were in God's hands and there was not much anyone could do.

It was a declaration from the King's council that was causing the anger.

'It's the coinage, see,' they said. They soon found out what the changes meant.

John Knox had come to dine.

Since his declaration of love to Marjorie, there had never been an occasion when they were alone together. She had made sure of that, but she suspected that John Knox himself was being similarly careful.

When it became evident that neither by word or deed would he reveal his feelings, she began to relax, and in relaxing enjoyed his company. She had never been the friend of a man before. The only men she knew as she was growing up were her father and brothers, and the servants and villagers at Aske. Now here was someone she could talk to, and sometimes forget that he was a man and she was a woman and he had declared his love for her.

But not quite. There were times when she felt the oddest sensation in her body. I am blushing inwardly, she thought. It was the only way she could explain it to herself. She longed to ask someone what it meant, but she could not talk to her mother, and it seemed to have little to do with Sarie's chatter about the rude behaviour of her soldier sweetheart.

It could not go on, she decided. The matter lying between them had to be spoken about. She chose a day when John Knox was dining with them, and her mother expressed a wish to have some new embroidery silks from Berwick, Marjorie declared she wanted some materials for her woolwork.

'Perhaps Master Knox could escort me?'

He had his head turned away from her. 'Yes,' he said, and it was almost inaudible.

'Ask your father for a soldier escort to bring you back,' said Elizabeth.

At the stables where the horses were being made ready they found a group of the men with their voices raised in argument.

'Excuse me, Master Knox,' said the groom who was holding Marjorie's horse. 'The men would like to ask you something.'

'Aye,' said the farrier, touching his cap to Marjorie. 'It's about our pay, Sir. We don't rightly like to ask the Captain. He says there's a new order come from London. The Captain said that this shilling will only be worth ninepence in August, and every groat will then be worth threepence where now it is worth fourpence.'

'That's right,' said Knox, cautiously. 'That is what the proclamation says.'

'We can understand what's said. We're not stupid. But cannot see the hows of it, if you see what I mean. See re. I have this shilling, which I have worked hard to earn d save. If I was to buy something with a shilling now, I uld receive a shilling's worth. But if I wait to August to buy the same thing I would only receive ninepence worth. Is that right, Master?'

'That's right,' he said. 'That's the way I understand it.'

'But the problem is,' said the farrier, persisting. 'That if I go into Berwick just now and offer the tavern this shilling and ask for a shilling's worth of ale,' he paused and a voice from the back said 'We'd all be your friends, Harry!'

He continued. 'And I offer the tavern keeper this shilling, he would be daft to take it from me, and he won't.'

'And you'll have to stay sober, Harry,' said the voice at the back.

The farrier went on. 'Because, if he still has this shilling in August, it won't be a shilling any more, but only ninepence. And he'll be the poorer.'

They rode off, accompanied by the soldier, leaving the men still muttering among themselves. Their escort rode ahead to make sure the road was safe, for the reivers had no regard for the border and were as dangerous to the English as to Scots.

'Marjorie?'

'John.'

It was all they needed. They smiled openly and joyously at one another.

'When did your feelings for me soften?' he asked.

'I think it was when my uncle most obviously did not like you.'

'I think you have the heart of a rebel.'

89

'It matches yours.'

'Nay, lass.' He was serious. 'No more troublesome priest. I will conform. I will be above criticism. None will find fault with me. And I will come courting you.'

'I think my father would not allow it.'

They fell silent then and jogged quietly towards Berwick. After she took her leave of him with a cool nod for the benefit of the protective soldier she found at the haberdashers that what went for ale went for wool also. The haberdasher said apologetically that he could only give her ninepence worth of wool, instead of the shilling she offered, for the shilling would lose its value soon.

'And they say, Mistress, that after August the value could be reduced some more, and soon the coinage will be worthless.'

It was true. In August there was a further reduction, and the old shilling coin became worth only sixpence. Word spread that the lords and landowners close to the court, who had had plenty of warning of what was to happen, had paid off all the debts they owed early in the spring in the old coinage before the pronouncement was made. The vintners, tailors and book printers who had been pleased to have long-standing accounts settled, now found themselves in possession of these all but worthless coins.

The tenant farmers who proffered the coinage in rent at the Martinmas term had to pay twice the amount to satisfy the obligation. Many did not have enough money and had to promise away next year's crops in order to stay on their farms.

There was a great deal of murmuring against the Privy Council in London, and word came of riots in many towns, where the hardship was greatest. The country people who took their vegetables and chickens and cheeses into the markets in the towns had the upper hand. They could fix the price for their produce, and the townspeople had to pay it if

90

they wanted to eat. They had little to give in return that the country people wanted.

All over the country there was uneasiness.

Chapter 18

'I have been ordered to Newcastle.'

'Again?' asked Ellzabeth.

'Not accused this time. Sent to take charge of the parish there. Though I am surprised they want me. Or perhaps they do not want me but I am being forced upon them.'

Elizabeth sank back into her chair. 'You're leaving us?'

'I have no choice.'

'What are we to do?'

'There's a good man taking my place.'

'I cannot talk to anyone else the way I can talk to you.'

'You can write to me, write to me with your thoughts, and I will reply. It will be as if I were in Berwick and the snow prevented you coming to see me.'

She burst into tears. 'How can I manage without you?' she asked. She rose and left the room. John and Marjorie looked at each other. In truth she was as distressed as her mother but determined not to show it.

'Well,' she said. 'You will be missed.'

'It is no wish of mine to go.'

'Mother is being over-emotional. It's only forty miles. No distance at all for a strong man on a good horse. And as you say, you can write. I am sure my mother will keep you busy answering her letters.'

'Marjorie.'

'And no doubt we will have word of you regularly. You will keep in touch with your congregation in Berwick, won't you?'

'Marjorie.'

She looked up at that. Their eyes met. He must have seen in her expression something of his own longing, for he moved forward and put his arms round her.

'Marjorie,' he said again.

She lifted her face to his, and he kissed her, a gentle kiss at first, and then more fiercely, with nothing of brotherly friendship in it. She felt her stomach flipping over.

'I dream sometimes of a peaceful life with you by my side. A peaceful parish where we can content ourselves with our bairns and our livestock, ignored by the wide world.'

'Is it only a dream?'

'Would you make it real?'

'I would if I were given the chance.'

'You would wed a poor preacher with no money and little future?'

'Yes.'

'I could maybe earn a bit tutoring as I did before.'

'It doesn't matter.'

'That's as much as I can offer you.'

'It's enough.'

'And maybe one day I could take you to my own country. I still have cousins there. You would be made welcome. But I fear... ' he stopped.

'What do you fear?'

'I fear I have been noticed. The best any of us can hope for in these troubled times is that we are invisible.'

'We could be handfasted,' she said.

He caught his breath. 'I will speak to your father.'

She pulled away from him.

'No, no. Whatever you do, you must not speak to my father.'

'Why not? We cannot be wed without his consent.'

'He would never agree.'

'Your mother then.'

'No. You must not. She would tell my father. She would be angry.'

'I can see I am not a suitable person to wed his daughter. But I think I can marshal arguments enough.'

'He believes priests may not marry.'

'The King says priests may marry. It is good enough for me.'

'And for me.'

A handfasting was binding. Not yet a marriage, but a commitment to marry. He would be bound to her as she would be bound to him. None could separate them, though marriage might lie some distance in the future.

'Please don't speak to him. He would send me away. I would be forbidden to see you again.'

'A secret handfasting,' he said slowly. 'I do not like it. I would have the whole world know.'

But in the end it was Marjorie's will that prevailed.

*

Marjorie and Sarie left their horses in the care of their escorting soldier. He lounged against the seawall, flirting with the fishergirls awaiting the arrival of the herring boats.

Ellen Knox was expecting them.

'Sarie, lass, would you like to stay here while I take Marjorie to meet a friend of mine? You can make yourself comfortable in the kitchen.'

This Sarie was always happy to do, for there was a new young man living in the house, apprentice to William Knox. Their voices could be heard in the next room, where William was teaching the lad the science of accounting. At some stage the young man would be released from his studies and make his way to the kitchen to be cosseted by the cook. Sarie had found herself in his company before.

'We won't be long,' said Ellen. But Sarie had no interest in where they were going.

Ellen led Marjorie out through the kitchen and scullery, and they passed along the path between the vegetable rows and into the lane at the back, and along to a pend. The pend smelled of horsedung, for the building next door was an inn, and sometimes the ostler used this pend as a shortcut when

94

the main entrance was mobbed with travellers. But it was clean enough underfoot, and the cobbles were dry, for it had not rained for over a week.

'It's here,' said Ellen, and led the way up a narrow outside wooden staircase to the small lodging above.

John Knox heard them coming and opened the door before they had reached the top of the stair, and moved aside to let them in. Marjorie paused for a moment, letting her eyes adjust to the poor light. The room had very small windows, and a low ceiling. Books were piled neatly on the trunk which stood under the window, and there was an ink pot and several quills lying on the window ledge. Someone had filled a jug with summer flowers.

'Ellen, Marjorie, I would like you to meet an old friend of mine. Master John Willock has recently come from Scotland. John, this is my good-sister, Ellen, and Miss Marjorie Bowes.'

Master Willock bowed.

'Mistress Knox. Miss Bowes.'

'You're from my own parts, I think, Master Willock,' said Ellen. 'The west.'

'Ayrshire.'

'You must have been sorry to leave.'

'I had no choice in the matter. I do not make such a stramash of it as my friend here, but I found I was no longer welcome in my own country.'

'He knows better how to smooth the ruffled feelings of his enemies,' said Knox.

'I prefer not to make them into my enemies in the first place,' retorted the other. 'But they chose to think of themselves as such. And here I am. I am on my way south to London.'

'What takes you there?'

Marjorie, taking off her cloak and laying it along with Ellen's on the pallet in the corner of the room, understood they were making conversation to set everyone at ease. It was not an everyday situation and there was tension in the room.

'I go to take up a post as chaplain to my Lord Suffolk in London.'

'I hope you will find it congenial.'

Master Willock turned to John and Marjorie who were now standing hand in hand listening quietly to this exchange.

'Are you sure?' he asked.

'I'm sure,' said Marjorie.

'I have never been so siccar of aught in my life,' said John.

'You understand,' Willock said, frowning slightly. 'I cannot marry you. It cannot be done without the consent of your father, and you do not have that. I can only witness your handfasting, along with Mistress Knox here. You understand about handfasting? It is a binding oath, not to be abused or set aside.'

Marjorie nodded.

'But although it is binding, it is not yet marriage. For that there has to be another formal ceremony followed by consummation.'

Marjorie drew in her breath. She looked at John. He shook his head. 'We dare not...'

'It is enough,' said Marjorie to Master Willock.

They stood, the two men and the two women and looked gravely at one another.

'Now?' he asked her.

She nodded.

Knox and Marjorie held hands. It was Knox's place to begin.

'I, John Knox, take thee, Marjorie Bowes, to my wedded wife, till death part us, and thereto I plight thee my troth.'

'I, Marjorie Bowes, take thee, John Knox, to my wedded husband, till death part us, and thereto I plight thee my troth.'

John put his hand into his pocket. He showed them what lay in the palm of his hand. It was a gold coin, cut in two.

'Had you not come today I would have spoiled good siller for nothing.'

He put one piece of the coin in the palm of her hand, closing her fingers over it.

'I will keep the other, and you will keep yours, and one day we will be united.'

They stood together in the ensuing silence, looking at each other, and Marjorie could feel his cool hand in hers and she knew in her heart deep down that she loved this man dearly and meant every word of what she had just said.

'We are married in the eyes of God. No one can take you away from me now,' he added softly, she squeezed his hand and smiled her delight.

He turned to the others. 'And if you are ever asked, then you can swear that you witnessed this.'

Master Willock lifted out from a cupboard a plate of cold tongue and salad leaves and a bowl of strawberries, and there were cups of wine in which they drank toasts to the bride and the groom and then toasted Ellen, who had supplied the food, and who suddenly, perhaps with the emotion of the moment, began to display an uncharacteristic giggling girlishness.

When they had finished eating, Master Willock offered his arm to Ellen Knox and offered to escort her down to the yard. He closed the door behind them, leaving John and Marjorie alone together.

They kissed, and she clung to him.

'Soon,' said John. 'Soon.'

*

'Perhaps it should have been more special,' said Ellen as the two women made their way back to the house by the harbour.

'It was special, Ellen. It was all I wanted.'

97

Chapter 19

The sweating sickness swept from London throughout the country.

The soldiers and workmen of Norham Castle were confined to barracks. Captain Bowes increased the provision of ale and ordered the men to drink milk laced with sorrel and sage. They all waited and watched anxiously as the days passed. They eased their shoulders carefully, watching out for the pain in the back that was the first symptom, and the chill that followed which meant you were a dead man in three hours.

In the end they lost no one. The north escaped lightly. When eventually messengers were allowed to travel once more, they learned that many thousands had died in the south and most particularly in London, where even the King's closest circle could not defy the terrible death. When the Duke of Northumberland's daughter was taken, many said it was a punishment. There were even those who dared to say that all was the wrath of God, revenging Himself on a people who had turned their backs on the true religion. Some of the people who said this too loudly were hauled before the magistrates and severely punished.

The restlessness cannot be attributed solely to the sweat, wrote Sir Robert to his brother. *People whisper that under Somerset (who has become the good Duke in many eyes) there were no burnings, there was toleration of dissent. My Lord Northumberland deems it best that all such dissent be stamped out. It is in the interests of good government.*

Captain Bowes showed his wife the letter.

'Look at this,' he said. 'Since Robert was made a member of the King's Privy Council he considers anything the Duke of Northumberland does as good government.'

'What about the King?' asked Elizabeth. There had been rumours that the King was unwell.

'What about him? He doesn't mention the King.'

He bent and held the letter in the flames, and they watched it burn. In nervous times, anything in writing is dangerous.

*

Then there came an opportunity to be away from Norham for a time. Marjorie's sister Philippa had been married for two years and was expecting her first child. She wanted her mother there. Alnwick, where Philippa lived, was close to Newcastle.

'Please, Richard,' Elizabeth sounded calm, but Marjorie was aware of the subdued excitement that her mother was feeling. 'I would like to go. I'm worried about Philippa. She is not robust, you know.'

'What can you do that her own women cannot?'

Both women were aware that Captain Bowes knew they corresponded regularly with John Knox. All letters in and out of the castle passed through his hands. Elizabeth had never ceased writing to Knox. She sighed over these letters, sitting hunched at the table, her quill scratching at page after page, and Marjorie could almost hear his sigh when he read them. He always answered, equally long letters with reassurances and apt quotes from the scriptures. How much of the treasured quiet days he set aside for studying and praying were devoted to writing these missives she could not begin to estimate.

Marjorie made sure she had no need of any of that. She added to her mother's letters a small scrap containing no more than the reassurance that she was well. His letters to Elizabeth always concluded with his respects to Marjorie and to Captain Bowes. It was not a courtship the balladeers would ever sing of, she thought, but it suited.

Captain Bowes agreed, reluctantly, that they could both go. It was September and the danger of infection from the sweat had passed.

Philippa's husband owned a large estate near Alnwick. From some parts of his land the castle could be seen, distant on the skyline. The house had been built new for his bride, though the bride had been chosen only after the house was nearly complete, such were Jonathan's priorities.

The windows in the family quarters were glazed and there were large fireplaces in every room, and no shortage of fuel, for they were within easy reach of the coalfields. At first Marjorie found it stifling after the chill of Norham, but she became used to it. She had never been close to her sister Philippa, who had been invalidish as a child. With delicate features and soft pale skin she was considered one of the prettier ones in a family where none of them had much beauty. She had been a little pink and white doll sitting on the sidelines crying during the more boisterous of the nursery games.

After a few days Marjorie was sorry she had allowed herself to be brought along. She was excluded from most of the intimate confidences Philippa shared with her mother in the private parlour. The room which her brother-in-law designated as the library was almost empty. The steward was to order books from London, he told Marjorie, but in the meantime there were regrettably few.

Jonathan had been one of the men brought to Aske with a view to marrying her, but he had asked for Philippa instead. If Philippa, welcoming their arrival, had surreptitiously watched Marjorie for some sign of jealousy she was wasting her time.

Marjorie was happy to accompany Jonathan as he did his rounds of his estates. He was undemanding company, and Marjorie was content to jog along beside him. He pointed out to her the changes he would make; a planting here, the felling of a wood here, fencing there, clearing off those old cottages. Enclosures? Oh yes, enclosures, but he would do it slowly. He would not deprive his villagers all at once of too much common land.

He was large and blonde, a man of flamboyant gestures and loud talk. He had intentions of going into Parliament, he told her, but meantime he had his new house, his new wife, and soon he would have a new son. Marriage into the Bowes family had done Jonathan no harm.

'See there,' he said, pointing with his whip. 'I'm going to divert that watercourse to there,' and he twisted in his saddle and pointed towards the south. 'I'm increasing the sheep stock, for the wool prices are good this year, and will get better. They're exporting more than ever from Newcastle.'

Marjorie let him warble on for a while and then asked, 'Do you ever hear of the preacher at Newcastle? Knox is his name.'

'Not liked,' said her brother-in-law. 'Should have had the sense to keep his head down, you know, keep to the rules, no one would mind. People round here don't like change. See those oaks on that hill. Fine timber there. Good offers from shipbuilders. The King's wanting to build up the fleet.'

'Do people complain about Master Knox?'

'I'm a magistrate and I'm supposed to keep the peace, but surely, Marjorie, I can't be expected to knock heads together in church, now can I? I don't know who has the right of it.'

'There are fights?'

'He doesn't do things the way he's supposed to. Too outspoken. Too many opinions. Doesn't do any good.'

Her mother had already told Philippa that Knox was a friend of the family. And since Philippa in her delicate condition could be refused nothing, he was invited and came. Knox, who had grown up on a farm, could talk easily with Jonathan. Marjorie heard with some amusement a long discussion about diseases in cattle, after which Jonathan admitted that perhaps the preacher wasn't so bad. Knox gave Philippa his serious attention, sitting beside her with his head bent, nodding at her every inanity, and she was charmed.

He could only occasionally snatch a moment to have a word with Marjorie.

'It's good of you to take the time to write to my mother,' she said quietly to him, as they stood in the window embrasure looking out at the setting sun.

'It helps me. Her doubts are often my own. She forces me to confront them.'

He was invited again. And again. Soon he was as frequent and welcome a visitor as he had ever been at Norham.

And so it was at Alnwick in the house of her sister that Marjorie saw her mother once again in the arms of a man. But she was no longer six years old, and the man was John Knox.

Chapter 20

He looked up and saw her and flushed red, and Elizabeth started back and looked up into his face before turning and seeing Marjorie.

Marjorie ran. She ran through the gallery and down the stairs and out into the garden. She ran till she reached Jonathan's young orchard. She paused, and sank down below the hedge. All was quiet save for the slight rustling of the wind in the leaves now browning ready for winter. She knelt in the earth and crushed her fists in her eyes. She could hear herself wailing, a soft open mouthed wail, the wail of one bereft.

And then he was kneeling beside her, with his arms around her and cradling her head against his chest. She struggled to free herself but he would not let her go. He stroked her hair and murmured soothing noises, the noises a mother breathes to a baby. She was still then, but her heart felt like a leaden weight. She stilled herself, so that he would stop.

'It doesn't matter,' she said, and he released his hold. She eased herself from his arms, and stood up.

'Marjorie,' he said.

'It doesn't matter,' she said again. She turned away. He grabbed her hand and held it, gripping till she winced with pain. He continued to kneel at her feet.

'I love you,' he said.

'So what was all that about?' she asked.

'It's not what you think.'

She was silent. He let go of her and got to his feet then, clumsily. The agility of youth had been lost.

'Your mother wanted comforting.'

103

Suddenly she was shouting. 'As I did just now? As other women do? Who else? My sister? My maid? The gardener's wife?'

'No. No, Marjorie. Listen to me.'

'I listened to you at Norham. Fool that I was.'

She turned then and ran. At the door she shook the leaf mould and dirt from her skirt. She walked through the hall and upstairs, ignoring the servants. There were always people about in this house. Composure in public was essential. She walked upstairs, the perfect picture of the sister of the lady of the manor, the clever one, the bookish one, the one with the broken heart.

Her mother was with Philippa in her parlour, sitting sewing at a baby vest as if nothing had happened.

'Where have you been, Marjorie?' asked her sister peevishly. 'Why can nobody settle today?'

'I'll play for you, shall I?' said Marjorie, and she sat down at the spinet and began to thump away at a vigorous galliard.

'Where is Master Knox?' asked Philippa.

'Gone,' she said.

'It's too bad of him. He did not say goodbye.'

Marjorie hit a wrong note and went over the phrase several times. From the corner of her eye she could see her mother, bending over her sewing, but the needle wasn't moving.

Then Jonathan came in and they all had to be merry. She avoided her mother all the rest of that day.

Elizabeth came to Marjorie's door that night and tapped gently.

'Marjorie,' she whispered. 'Let me in.'

Marjorie lay silently, the bedclothes covering most of her face. She heard the door open and sensed her mother bending over her. 'Marjorie?'

Marjorie kept her eyes closed. Her mother knew she was awake. Who could sleep after such a day? She forced herself

104

to lie still and silent, digging her nails into her palms to stop herself from screaming. After a few moments Elizabeth went away. Marjorie lay all night like one dead.

She could not avoid her mother forever.

'Marjorie, it is not as you think.'

'What do I think?'

'I was distressed. Master Knox was being kind. It was not . . . . not a true embrace. There was nothing in it would worry your father.'

'My father?' Marjorie stared at her in amazement. 'My father has nothing to do with it,' she said. 'It is I you have offended. We were to be wed, John Knox and I, and you have spoiled that.'

As soon as she said it she was sorry. But it would have to come out some time, and why not now? When it was over.

'You foolish girl. What romancing is this?'

'No romancing, mother. We were handfasted before witnesses.'

Elizabeth went white. 'It is impossible.'

'It is very possible. Or was. Till now. Perhaps he has spoken to you in the same language he used to me. Perhaps he is false to both of us.'

Her mother walked slowly over to her chair by the fire and sat down. She picked up her embroidery silks, and with great concentration chose a green one, while Marjorie stood in silence and watched her.

'You would shame our family, Marjorie.'

'You are not one to talk about shame.'

'You will marry according to your father's wishes. If you are soiled then no one will want you.'

Marjorie cried out at that.

'John is honourable.'

She knelt down beside the chair, trying to look into her mother's face. 'What have you done?' she cried.

Her mother's face was twisted in grief. She had her needle in her hand and for a queer moment Marjorie thought she was going to stab her with it and drew back.

'Mother, I have four sisters still unmarried. Father can choose husbands for them as much as he wants.'

'It is not . . .' Elizabeth was struggling with her tears. 'Don't tell your father. He mustn't know.'

'It is too late anyway,' she said.

'What do you mean? You are not . . .? Marjorie, are you having a child?'

'Little chance of that,' she said. 'Not now.' She was shaking.

'I could not bear that,' said her mother.

Marjorie rose to her feet.

Elizabeth went on. 'Don't you understand? If your father knew of this, he would forbid you. We could not speak to John again, or hear him preach, or correspond. We would never see him again. It would be the end.'

'It's all right,' said Marjorie. 'We won't talk of it again. It's over anyway. For me. You can keep your spiritual adviser.'

For the rest of their stay at Alnwick they did not speak save when courtesy demanded it and other people were present. Marjorie received one letter from Knox, which she dropped in the fire unread.

Philippa's time was close. Her slight body ballooned with rolls of fat and she lay on her couch, peevish and restless. All Saints Day came and went. It was difficult for them. They each in their own way spent the day remembering with sorrow those who had gone, trying to ignore the sounds of revelry that came from the servants' quarters. Jonathan, anxious for his wife, moped about the house, but did not have the heart to tell his household that since there were no saints any more, then All Hallows Eve was banned as superstition.

106

'Why does not Master Knox come?' asked Philippa. 'I want to talk to him.'

'Well my dear, I think perhaps it is better that he does not come. You see, he has done something very foolish,' said her husband.

'What?' asked Philippa, and Marjorie saw her mother raise her head and stare at Jonathan. She herself was indifferent.

'I have had a letter from your uncle Robert Bowes.'

'What about him?'

'Master Knox has preached a sermon insulting to the Lord Protector. Your uncle says it bordered on sedition. I had heard something of this, but thought it was exaggerated.'

Marjorie smiled, in spite of herself. 'The stories are probably not exaggerated,' she said.

'He told the congregation that the arrest of my Lord Somerset was a Roman Catholic conspiracy to set one champion of Protestantism against another and destroy the new learning. He threatens that the downfall of Somerset will also bring down the Lord Protector. He even questions the Lord Protector's honesty.'

He looked at them almost plaintively.

'I always thought there was something fanatical in the man. Sir Robert knows about our friendship with him. I have now written to Knox to forbid him the house. Your uncle's orders.'

Philippa became agitated. 'Jonathan, I want to see Master Knox.'

Her too, thought Marjorie. He charms them all. 'I am sure my uncle's advice is good,' she said.

Philippa glared at her and struggled to sit upright on her couch, crying that it was unfair, that her uncle had no right to interfere in such matters. She sobbed for a bit, then subsided in hiccups while her mother and her maid fluttered

107

round her, for fear her agitation would start the baby before its time.

Marjorie stayed in her corner of the room, watching, and her thoughts were bitter.

Soon after that Philippa gave birth to a large fair son, and they had a message from Captain Bowes, ordering them back to Norham.

Chapter 21

Marjorie stood in the curve of the stairwell and listened to her parents quarrelling.

After the comforts of Alnwick, Norham Castle was more cramped and cold than ever, and with winter setting in, damp and claustrophobic. The women sat in their parlour, grimly passing the time, her mother with her embroidery, Marjorie usually crouching by the window attempting to read in the grey winter light, and Sarie stitching at their linen, bemused by the chill in the atmosphere, and dreaming of her lover.

There had been little festivity at Christmas, when the noise of the men celebrating in the bailey had set off a headache in Elizabeth and she had retreated to bed, leaving Marjorie and her father and the steward in the holly decorated parlour toasting the King in a half hearted fashion.

Her mother moped. Her father became more and more short-tempered. Never one to spend much time in the family's quarters, he now was hardly ever there. Every day when weather permitted he was drilling the men, who grumbled and swore. There were some desertions, men who chose to take their chance over the border with the Scots rather than submit to the discipline of the garrison. Especially worrying for the Captain were the rumours that spread, even though at every turn he tried to contradict them, of more unrest in the south.

The debasement of the coinage, rumours of war, and insidious suggestions that the King was in poor health, all contributed to the unease and uncertainty. Now the tensions within the family were breaking out.

'I am sick of it,' she heard her father say. 'The pair of you moping all day, snapping at each other. You'd be better to return to Aske for all the use you are to me here.'

'I don't want to go back to Aske.'

'Then try and be a proper wife to me.'

And then her mother's low voice. 'Find a husband for Marjorie.'

Her father's pacing stopped. He was always on the move, pacing, twitching, never at rest, a man of such tremendous energy he could never be still.

'What? Is that the problem? Should she be wed?'

'The visit to Alnwick unsettled her. The new baby.'

'Ah.' This was something a man could understand.

'Send her away.'

'Back to Alnwick?'

'No,' Elizabeth's voice was harsh. 'No. Why not to London? Your brother Robert could find her a suitable husband. He has often said as much.'

And so it was arranged. No one asked Marjorie what she wanted. It was true she wanted to get away from Norham, and she didn't much care where she went. Perhaps she could have gone back to Aske, but when she thought of her younger siblings there, in the care of her aunt, she could not bear the thought of living in a household of women and little girls.

It was arranged that her sister Isabella, who was thirteen years old, would come to take her place as companion to her mother.

As soon as the weather turned milder, and the roads became passable, as soon as Isabella arrived from Aske, round eyed and scared to be away from home for the first time, Marjorie set off from Norham with Sarie and an escort of soldiers, on the long road south.

110

Chapter 22

She hated London.

She hated the oppressive feel of the house, surrounded on all sides by other dwellings with only a courtyard between the front door and the street, and a small garden at the back to walk in. Her uncle's wife – call me aunt, my dear - talked continually of the large house Sir Robert was building out beyond Gray's Inn where he had his chambers. He had sold part of his land here in Aldgate to fund the costs, and there was a new raw brick wall across the end of the garden and beyond that a new house was being raised, one that would overlook the garden. Nowhere was private.

She walked in the garden every day, and longed desperately for the sight of hills and green fields, until the head of a workman popping up over the wall drove her indoors again. She crumbled lavender and thyme, now no more than withered dry stalks, in her hands and imagined the scent of them. Anything to kill the pervasive smell of smoke. Even at Norham with hundreds of men crammed together, the winds blowing across the high moorland kept the air clear. Here, there seemed to be no wind, and the air was full of ash and everything was smutted with soot.

The Fleet River was foul and stinking and even the noisy crowded Thames, which they said was the greatest river in the world, was sluggish and murky compared with the sparkling waters of the rivers of the north.

And everywhere, indoors or out, there was always the noise, constant hammering on building sites, constant rumbling and creak of wagons and shouts of men and women and the yelling of children, never resting, always on the move, travelling round and round and in and out of the city, buying and selling.

In the night when she lay awake she heard the cry of the watchman as he sounded the hours, and the occasional dull thudding of horses' hooves as they passed nearby, and that roused fears, for what reason and by what authority could any man be out in the dead of night, long after the curfew was rung and the city gates were closed?

Lady Alice went out into the streets every day to do the marketing for the household. She called it that though in fact the steward and housekeeper managed the provisioning of the house between them. But the wife of an important man must see and be seen. They paraded in style, a man in front of them to push a way through the jostling crowd, a man following to carry the baskets.

'Your future will be here, Niece. You must become accustomed,' she said.

So Marjorie went with her, stupid from lack of sleep, trying to keep up with her aunt's brisk pace, concentrating on where she was putting her feet for fear of standing in ordure or slipping on rotting vegetables or fish tails. The lewd remarks thrown at her by men lounging outside the taverns made her blush. Lady Alice did not seem to notice. Perhaps in time the continual noise made people deaf.

There was a holdup in the street. She was becoming used to this, the regular pause to make way for a crush of people, or a horseman edging through the narrow streets, or a noblewoman in a closed litter arriving in the city and making her way towards the big houses along the river. Now she could hear Lady Alice murmuring a question, and the servant's reply.

'See, Niece. That's how we deal with cutpurses in London.'

The crowd were roaring their appreciation as a woman, her filthy shift trailing on the ground, naked breasts grimed with dirt and runnled with sweat, stumbled towards them on bare feet. Behind her two men with short nine-tailed whips were lashing out at her. Blood from the woman's back dripped onto the cobbles. As the trio passed Marjorie could hear her sobs and the animal grunts of the men. She was no more than a girl. They passed, and the crowds closed up.

'What's she done?'

'Stolen something, I expect.' Her aunt seemed indifferent, but seeing Marjorie's face, perhaps some sensitivity roused itself, for she whispered. 'I know it looks cruel, but it's necessary. Don't you see? If they're not punished, then everybody would be thieving.'

Once at Aske a cleaning maid was caught with a piece of lace from a visiting lady. Elizabeth Bowes talked with the girl. She has never had anything beautiful in her life and had been overcome with the wish to touch it. After she had handled it, it had been soiled with the dust from her fingers and she had hidden it, too frightened to put it back.

She was moved to the kitchen where she could not come into contact with guests, but Elizabeth gave the girl a little piece of lace of her own, an old piece to be sure, but still pretty. The girl cherished it. When Marjorie went into the kitchens she would see the girl wearing it draped round her shoulders. The other servants jeered at first, but soon grew tired of mockery. In time the lace became torn with too much handling and grubby from the grease and dirt of the kitchen, but the girl still wore it.

That girl had been simple minded, and tolerated by mistress and servants alike. Had anyone troubled to find out whether the woman they had just seen whipped shamefully through the streets had all her wits about her? Marjorie shuddered. After treatment like that it would not be surprising if the poor child lost her wits.

Lady Alice took her duties to her husband's niece seriously. Family mattered. The clothes which Marjorie had brought with her were not, apparently, good enough for London. Her aunt lifted up the kirtles and bodices as they were unpacked from their box, and tossed them onto the bed with a sigh of despair.

'My dear girl, you cannot possibly be seen in company in clothes like these. Did you use them in the north for berry-picking?'

She shook her head over a set of sleeves of grey linen. 'Grey,' she muttered. 'People will think you have not the means to wash them. And look at this clumsy patch. Did one of your father's soldiers do your mending? I'll order some more clothes made for you. Your uncle is in the King's service, and destined for high office. He must not be ashamed of us.'

She shook out a gown of blue velvet. 'Oh yes, I remember choosing this cloth for you, one for your mother too..' She tutted. 'Would you look at the detail on it, the style. Well, that was all very well for Norham Castle but it won't do here.'

Her uncle had brought that blue velvet north with him on one of his visits, as a gift. The tailor in Berwick had made it up from a book of patterns of the latest designs from London and Paris. Not late enough, obviously.

Marjorie thought Lady Alice tried too hard. She was a countrywoman eager to become a Londoner: too many ribbons on her gown, too many pearls on her hood.

But Lady Alice had no children of her own to dress, and she enjoyed herself discussing Marjorie's needs with the seamstresses. Marjorie's patience with the talking and the fittings, which her aunt did not recognise for the indifference it was, endeared her to Lady Alice. She professed herself well satisfied with her new relative. And Sarie remarked how well she looked in the new gowns.

As her nights became more rested, Marjorie began to fit in with the rhythms of the household. Her uncle was rising in the King's service. Once an adviser to the Duke of Somerset, when that great man fell he moved smoothly into the service of the Duke of Northumberland, the Lord Protector.

The family rarely dined alone. There were always other people: young men from her uncle's law chambers, merchants from the city, other privy councillors. They talked and talked, discussing, arguing, laughing, disputing, reminiscing. On these occasions the women sat demurely, apparently uninterested, but absorbing much to discuss among themselves later.

Marjorie thought at first the conversation of Lady Alice and her friends as they visited one another in the afternoon was all about fashion and babies. But gradually as they became accustomed to her presence and were assured she was harmless, just another relative to be found a husband, the women's talk turned to their husbands and the court. Always the court and the business of government. Who was on the way up, who was destined to fall; more and more, whispered remarks about the King, and illness, and shaking of heads. The women would sigh and pull themselves up, and eye Marjorie as a possible profitable wife for a younger son with his way to make in the world.

Her uncle seemed different here at home. He was softer and sleeker, and watching him by the side of his silk-clad, perfumed wife Marjorie had difficulty remembering how he had looked, dressed in leather, travel-stained, alighting from his horse at Norham. Here there was no need for the alert aggressive swagger of the ex-soldier, the King's man keeping the peace of the border. Here was the quietly confident privy councillor, sensitive to the shifting moods of his fellows, open to every opportunity.

*

Spring gave way to summer.

Marjorie was sitting outside making the most of the mild sunshine able to penetrate the haze when she sensed that she was being watched, and turned. There was a man standing

115

by the door, a stranger to her. He had made a slight noise to attract her attention. As she grew to know him she saw him do this, make people aware of his presence by a gentle cough or movement as much as to say, I am here, but pay me no attention, I am not eavesdropping and I do not wish to interrupt.

He bowed slightly. Marjorie smiled and he approached. He was older than the young lawyers who came to the house, but not as old as her uncle or the other men of the court. Like them he was dressed in black, with gleaming white linen at neck and wrists. Unlike them he lacked the stoop of a man carrying affairs of state on his shoulders.

She rose. 'Sir, I will tell my aunt you are here.'

'No need. The servant knows. No ceremony, please. I am an old friend of this household. We have not met. I have been away on business. My name is William Cecil. You must be the niece.'

Lady Alice had talked of him. Like so many of them he had been Somerset's man and now he was Northumberland's man. When Somerset fell, Cecil spent three months in the tower, but he was known to be useful, and had been recently appointed one of the King's Secretaries of State.

'Yes, Sir. I am Marjorie Bowes.'

He nodded. 'I know your father. I did my stint with the army. He was one of the officers. A fine soldier, much respected by the men.'

They sat down.

'How do you like London?'

'It's too big. Too noisy. Though it seems quieter today.'

'Ah.' He looked over her head towards the west. 'That is because everyone has gone to Smithfield to see the entertainment.'

'Entertainment?'

'They are executing two heretics,' he said.

She felt a cold thump in the pit of her stomach.

116

'Catholics,' he said gently. 'Those who would deny the King is head of the Church.'

'Perhaps they believe that for the King to call himself head of the Church is the heresy.'

'They do believe that. And they will die for their belief.'

'I thought that such punishments were in the past.'

'No, as long as men disagree about religion there will always be death for some. *Cuius regio, eius religio.* You know the Latin, Miss Marjorie?'

'Sir, the religion of the ruler is the religion of the state.'

'It is a sensible doctrine, do you not think? The worst thing that can happen to a nation is to have two religions, each vying for supremacy. Two religions cannot live side by side. Events of the last few years have demonstrated that.'

'Master Cecil, would you die for a religious belief?'

'No,' he said. 'Those who would die for their religious beliefs make very uncomfortable friends. It is kinder, do you not think, Miss Marjorie, to keep one's thoughts on such matters to oneself?'

She understood. It was not a subject for civilised conversation.

He offered her his arm. 'Shall we take a turn round the garden?'

A clever man, her aunt had said. He's learned to be cautious. He did one foolish thing in his life and will be more careful in future. What foolish thing, Marjorie had asked. Married young, for love, without his father's consent. The wife died. He remarried more wisely, and he has learned sense.

Lady Alice saw them from the house and came to hurry them in, and soon there were more people arriving and the servants were waiting with basins of water for the guests to wash their hands. Marjorie offered Master Cecil the drying cloth.

At the table they were seated together.

117

'You are family and I am a family friend. We can be comfortable together,' he said. 'What would you like to talk about? Some safe subject.'

'Is the King's health as poor as they say?'

'That's not a safe subject. He has a small cough which keeps him to his room.'

'It has been remarked that no one has seen him in public for some months.'

'The cold air is not good for him. When the weather is warmer he will be seen by his people. Come Miss Marjorie, some other matter.'

They talked about books. One of the compensations of living in London was that there was ready access to books. Her uncle had a large library. William Cecil confessed to being an addict of the printers at Paul's Cross.

'They lie in wait for me, Miss Marjorie. I can never pass by without they have some choice morsel they claim to have laid aside especially for me.'

After the meal was over William Cecil remained behind.

'Come through to my library, William,' said Sir Robert. 'We have plans to make.'

And those plans, Lady Alice told Marjorie when they were alone, concerned a proposed visit north. The Duke of Northumberland was going north to inspect the Bishopric of Durham. It was too large: he wanted it broken up. Bishop Tunstall was now an honoured prisoner in the Tower of London, less for his religious beliefs than for the power that he had in the north. He was in no position to object. The duke would make a tour of the north to include an inspection of the border. Sir Robert Bowes, as Depute Warden of the East Marches, and Master Cecil, would be in the party.

'If you want to send messages to anyone, you must say.'

Marjorie bent her head over her sewing.

'My respects to my mother and father,' she said. 'Who else would there be?'

118

Lady Alice was watching her. 'I will send a message to your mother,' she said. 'I will tell her that we have in our acquaintance many families we would be proud to be connected with. I can reassure her we will soon find a husband for you.'

In a momentary flash of loneliness Marjorie considered confiding in her aunt. Telling her she was betrothed to John Knox and could not marry another. Was she still betrothed? She couldn't be sure any more. How binding was it, when one of the parties had betrayed that promise, and when there was a likelihood they would never meet again? She could imagine the sharp response Lady Alice would make. Nonsense girl, you cannot possibly imagine yourself bound to such an unsuitable man as that.

Chapter 23

A man stood in the hall, considering her uncle's coat of arms, the colours still gleamingly new, that hung on the wall. He turned at the sound of her footsteps.

'John,' she said.

'Marjorie.'

They spoke together.

'Your beard has grown long.'

'You look different.'

'It's the clothes,' she said. 'The London fashions.'

'You have become a princess.'

Round them the servants moved briskly. The torpor of the last few weeks in the absence of the master was gone. Now all was vigour and activity. Her uncle appeared, with a servant scurrying after him helping him on with his cloak, and his secretary clutching his bag of papers.

'There you are,' he said to Knox. 'Come, come.'

He hardly noticed Marjorie. The door closed behind them. Marjorie sank down onto the stair. A passing servant glanced over at her. 'Are you all right, Miss?'

The hall emptied. Marjorie rose and returned to her own room, whatever errand she had been on forgotten.

Her uncle sent for her that evening.

'The Duke heard Master Knox preaching in Newcastle. The Lord Protector recognises when someone has a talent which can be usefully used in the service of the King. That is why we have brought Knox back with us. The intention is to appoint him as one of the King's chaplains. A temporary appointment. Then he will return to Newcastle.'

Marjorie stood with her hands clasped in front of her and her gaze on the floor.

'We need not acknowledge the previous acquaintanceship. I do not like the man. If anyone asks you,

you will say as little as possible. Have I made myself understood?'

'Yes, Sir.'

'I will not ask him to dine. But we may be asked to dine in houses where he has been invited. You will avoid speaking to him.'

'Yes, Sir.' She glanced up. He was looking at her suspiciously. 'I am sure you know best, Uncle,' she said.

In her room she found Sarie sitting by the small fire, stitching a torn shift while she waited for Marjorie to come to bed. She dropped her work into its basket.

'You look feverish,' she said. 'Do you want anything?'

'No, I'm fine.'

'This London air isn't good. Did you know Master Knox has come to London?'

'Yes.' Marjorie started to undress. 'We are not to know him.'

'Is it true he's to preach to the King?'

'Is there anything the servants' hall doesn't know?'

'Not much.'

Marjorie sat patiently while Sarie brushed her hair, a ritual that Sarie enjoyed more than she did.

'Miss Marjorie?'

'It's all right, Sarie. You are quite right. This London air is not good for us.'

'I just wonder what's going to happen, that's all.'

'Nothing will happen. We are unlikely to have much to do with him.'

She dismissed Sarie and climbed into bed. The fire died, and outside the noises of the London night quietened. She found herself unable to summon up the anger she had felt against John Knox that last time she had seen him, that terrible day at Alnwick. There had been no mistaking the joy in his face as he turned in the hall and saw her standing there. Or the leap of happiness in her own heart.

She had to find out where he was staying. Whatever her uncle said, she would meet John. In this busy household there would be a chance. If she took Sarie they might not insist on a manservant, and even if they did Sarie could maybe keep the man occupied while she talked to John. The underworld of the servants would know where he was living. Sarie could find out.

She was thankful for the freedom which women in London had. More than one foreign visitor to her uncle's house had remarked on it. Women in Dresden, or Antwerp, or Copenhagen, would not have the freedom to go out in the streets accompanied only by a maidservant.

Planning, she fell asleep.

Chapter 24

It was the household's habit to attend regularly at St. Paul's Cross to hear the public sermon. All except Sir Robert himself, who deemed it expedient to attend every Sunday at the King's Chapel in Westminster. The King was not always there, but everyone else who mattered was. Whether he was enjoying the sermons of John Knox, who regularly took his turn, he did not say.

Attendance at Paul's was always large. Today the crowd seemed quieter than usual. They clustered in groups, heads close together, talking, but at the same time watchful, as if they expected something to happen. Several times Marjorie heard a murmured reference to the King.

The servant found Lady Alice and Marjorie a place in the shelter of a great buttress where they were free from the crush of the crowd but could still see and hear. The windows of the houses round about were crowded with people, some sitting quietly waiting for the sermon to begin, others hanging out of the window and calling to their friends below. A little boy at one window had a catapult and was firing pellets at random at the crowd below. As Marjorie watched, his mother appeared behind him and struck him over the ear and hauled him back out of sight, his mouth a round O with a yell.

She listened to the talk around her.

'A dog walking calm as you like through the streets carrying a dead child in its mouth, and none dared touch it, for it was an omen.'

'Daftie. The child was a rabbit, and who would be frightened of a dog?'

'It was an omen. The King is going to die. He's the dead child, see.'

'Oh aye, and who's the dog? The Pope?'

There was laughter at that, but it was nervous laughter and the speakers were looking round them to see if they had been overheard by authority.

The preacher climbed into the pulpit and began his sermon. He warned the crowds that they must attend to God's word, else God would bring the kingdom to its knees. Had not the Duke of Somerset become cold to God's word before his death, preferring to spend his time worshipping stones and mortar and building ever greater and greater houses for himself? 'Aye,' said the crowd. They all knew the Duke's great palace on the bank of the Thames, now sitting empty.

'And did he not suffer God's judgment on him?'

And so the sermon went on, the preacher alternately wooing and castigating the crowd. When he had finished he descended from the pulpit and fought his way back into the cathedral, many following him, arguing. The rest of them settled down with their bread and cheese to debate the sermon, and no doubt to pass amongst themselves more rumours and omens, the bloodier the better. There would be another sermon in the afternoon.

As soon as the throng of people cleared a bit Lady Alice led the way towards home. Marjorie felt a touch on her arm and whipped round, ready to shout if it was a cutpurse, but it was only a little girl. She thrust something into Marjorie's hand. Before she could speak the child was lost in the crowd. She tucked the tiny wad of paper into her glove and hastened after her aunt.

The note was unsigned, but she knew the writing. He would be walking in Paul's churchyard between the hours of eleven and twelve on Monday, and on Tuesday, and on Wednesday, and on all the days of the week until she came to him.

The next morning she sent Sarie to her aunt to say she had a headache and pleading permission to stay in her room. Lady Alice bustled up and felt her forehead and questioned her about the symptoms. Marjorie felt guilty. Lady Alice was worried that there was genuine illness in the house. It was not so long since the last time the murderous summer sweat had swept through London.

'Have you a backache?'

'It's only a heaviness in the head, Aunt. I think perhaps it was reading too much with only a candle for light that caused it.'

'If it was up to me I would forbid you to read books at all. It is unnatural in a woman and causes more harm than good. Perhaps after this you will listen to me. Shall I fetch the doctor?'

'No, no Aunt. I shall be well if I may just keep to my room today and rest quietly. I do not want any food.'

'We were to dine with Lady Allen. Had you forgotten?'

She said meekly 'I had forgotten. I am most sorry to miss that.'

'I'll make your excuses.'

She had reckoned on Lady Alice going to Lady Allen's without her. She would stay there for most of the day, for they were old friends with a wide circle of acquaintants to gossip about. They would enjoy it more without an unmarried girl hanging about. Their talk could range more freely, and more deeply into matters which were not considered suitable for her ears. They were more blunt in their talk than Marjorie was accustomed to hearing in the north, but even so it had not escaped her notice that when the conversation began to verge on the personal or the medical the women would glance irritably at her and lower their voices or change the subject. Well, today they would have all the freedom they wished.

She was left in peace after that. She lay listening to the sounds of the household. Her uncle had already left in the early morning to go to Westminster for a privy council meeting. She heard Lady Alice leave, with her usual fussing.

She changed her mind about taking Sarie with her. It would not be fair. Her aunt might ask questions of Sarie and Marjorie could not expect Sarie to lie on her behalf. She therefore sent the girl to the housekeeper's room, to help with the repair of the household linen. Sarie patted the bedclothes straight and looked at her sideways, opened her mouth as if to speak, then nodded, and went meekly away. The housekeeper might not see Sarie, for Sarie had a new love, one of the footmen.

In the hall one of the dogs lifted its head and looked at Marjorie, murmured a sound in its throat and lowered its head back onto its paws. She slipped past them and opened the door. The front courtyard was deserted at this time of day, save for the sentry who lounged under the canopy by the gate. One of the kitchen skivvies was with him and they were talking in low voices. They broke off and glanced up as Marjorie passed. The maid curtseyed and then the two returned to their talk. It was the sentry's duty to stop people entering. Family leaving were no concern of his. The skivvy would not remark on it, for she should not have been there.

Paul's Churchyard was quiet on a Monday, with only some scavengers picking over the detritus left by the crowds of the day before, and a few visitors to London, noticeable in their country dress, picking over the offerings of the stalls round about. Marjorie knew where John would be. She made her way to the side where the printers had their shops.

There he was. She stopped to watch him as he leafed through a volume, exchanging cheerful comments with the printer, who was leaning forward, pointing to the woodcuts. She heard them laugh. He looked up and saw her. She drew back. He completed his purchase of the book, glanced round, and walked towards her. They greeted one another gravely, as two acquaintances meeting by chance. They walked north, towards Cripplegate, and out under the great city walls into the green space of Moorfields. Soon they had left the washerwomen's drying fields behind them and were

126

walking among trees and streams, talking, talking, talking. Marjorie breathed in the scent of the dogroses.

'It's like coming alive again,' she said.

By mutual consent they turned down a path that led to a hollow among the trees that hung over the stream. He spread his cloak on the ground and they sat. He took her in his arms and kissed her.

'We are handfasted but we never slept together to make us man and wife,' she said.

He stroked her hair. 'Not now,' he said. 'Don't tempt me.'

'Why not now?'

'For I would have you mine in the eyes of the world and of God. No subterfuge. Nothing hidden.'

'We can tell them we are betrothed.'

'And they would steal you away to some hidden tower and I would have lost you forever. I could not bear it.'

'Patience is not one of your virtues.'

'Then I must cultivate it. I have waited this long. I can wait a short time more. I am in favour at court. Wait until the time is right and I will speak to your uncle.'

He kissed her, hard and passionate. He stood up and pulled her to her feet.

'You must return, before you are missed.'

As they walked back he told her, 'My return north may be delayed. I have been given other work to do, apart from preaching. There is to be a new Book of Common Prayer and all the churchmen are asked their opinions. You know my opinion of the old one. A mixter-maxter of a book. Let us hope they can get it right this time.'

Chapter 25

Marjorie had become familiar with the first Prayer Book and Order of Service for the Church of England, the one that had rendered the Latin mass into English, the one they said had been written by King Edward himself.

John Knox always refused to use it. It omits the litany of the saints, quite rightly, but changes little else, he said. Now, he told her, Archbishop Cranmer and his committee of churchmen were preparing the revision. Out went most of the forms of the old mass. The wording of the baptism and marriage sacraments was modernised. The burial service no longer included prayers for the dead. There was no mention of the Virgin Mary.

It was the communion service that turned out to be the one causing the most trouble. The bread and wine became the body and blood of Christ, the Church had said for centuries. Not so, said the modern churchmen. They are only a symbol. In the new Prayer Book the congregation were to kneel to receive the bread and the wine from the hand of the priest. When it was his turn as a royal chaplain to preach in the King's Chapel John Knox lambasted this.

Sir Robert Bowes returned from Westminster that Sunday shaking with anger.

'The man is dangerous,' he said. 'What right has he, a common country priest, a renegade priest in exile from his own country, what right, I say, has he to come and criticise a fine piece of work by our English archbishop?'

Knox called it idolatry. Kneeling implied worship of the bread and the wine itself, when worship should be to God alone. Sitting was good enough for Jesus. It should be good enough for the faithful. Sitting together to share food was a sign of friendship, of joy.

'Why, John?' asked Marjorie. She paused in her walk to watch the sails of the windmills turning in nearby Finsbury Fields. 'Just because you cannot kneel because of the rheumatism in your knees, why cannot others do as they wish?'

'It is not fitting to make jokes about the sacrament,' he said huffily. 'Nor about my poor knees.' She had her work cut out to tease him back into a good humour. Archbishop Cranmer reminded the Privy Council that of course Jesus sat at the Last Supper, but if we all followed the custom of the time we would be lying on cushions like Turks and Tartars.

'Do Turks and Tartars lie on cushions?' Lady Alice asked her husband.

'How would I know? All I know is the King has ordered that the printing of the Prayer Book be stopped while the matter is considered. This is costing money. The printing was nearly done.'

The royal chaplains met and a compromise was reached. The printed pages were examined and it was found there was room for a note, a rubric, which would say that kneeling did not necessarily mean worship of the bread, since the bread and wine were only symbols. It was too late to print this rubric in red like all the others so it would be printed in black. It was a weak compromise, and John Knox had made enemies among the churchmen.

'They think I am meddling in matters that are the preserve of the bishops,' he told Marjorie. 'I was not trying to lay down rules. I just thought men should be free to follow their consciences without being dictated to.'

His old congregation in Berwick, who had not been accustomed while he was there to using the first Book of Common Prayer, were confused even more by the new one. Knox received bewildered letters from them, all asking the same thing. Are we to give up the sharing of communion as you taught us, as Jesus taught, and do it the way the Prayer Book says?

He showed Marjorie the letter he was writing in reply. 'The best I can tell them is that they must obey the secular authorities.'

'That is a weak argument.'

'I have no other.'

'Are the authorities to be obeyed no matter what? No matter if they themselves are wicked and unreligious?'

'So long as they leave men to obey God in their own consciences,' he said.

She let it be. She could see that John was uneasy in his own mind. He, who had always had his own way in Berwick, had been out-argued by the churchmen. He felt he had failed.

*

Sir Robert was appointed Master of the Rolls, a position which gave him authority over all the law courts, and his sense of his own importance grew accordingly. He was seldom at home. Lady Alice ordered more gowns for herself and for Marjorie. Hours were spent with seamstresses.

Marjorie became aware that Lady Alice was watching her more closely. She found herself more in demand to accompany her aunt on her visits. She had less and less time to herself. It was inevitable. It was to be expected that word would soon reach her uncle that she was meeting John secretly. After the first meeting she took Sarie with her, for propriety's sake, but Sarie had the sense to distance herself from them so that their conversation could not be overheard. Whenever they could they left the city by one of the easterly gates, where fewer of her uncle's acquaintances could be found, but still they must have been seen.

The household entertained more often. Now fewer of the guests were lawyers and merchants, and more were minor ambassadors and the younger sons of the aristocracy.

Sir Robert might be too busy to remember his promise to Marjorie's parents to find her a husband, but his wife was not. She had resumed her efforts with a new urgency. Some of the unmarried men and widowers who were invited were of an age to require more a nurse for their final years than a wife, but some were young men who knew this was a family worth marrying into, for its wealth and for the potential of power. The men exercised their best efforts at flattery towards Marjorie. She was not fooled. She was not handsome, and she knew she lacked the slick flirtatious charm of southern women. But still, had she never met and loved John Knox, she might have succumbed.

She took refuge whenever she could in the company of William Cecil, who regarded these manoeuvrings with amusement.

'I wish they would leave me in peace,' she said to him one evening as they sat quietly in a corner watching others of the company dancing noisily. This did not happen often in this household, but it was Sir Robert's birthday and only close friends were present. 'I have no wish to marry.'

'But you must. It is a comfortable state.'

'Is that the best you can say of it, that it is comfortable?'

'If we have that, we should content ourselves. Any of the gentlemen brought here for your inspection would make an excellent husband. If you would take time to get to know them you would find something to admire in all of them.'

Marjorie looked up to see her aunt, momentarily standing aside from the dance to catch her breath gazing at her, slightly frowning.

Later she scolded Marjorie. 'You are too forward with Master Cecil.'

'I am sorry, Aunt.'

'His wife is in the country.'

'I know that. But what has it to do with me? Oh Aunt, you cannot think I would set my cap at Master Cecil!'

She began laughing. Her aunt went on stitching at her embroidery. It was not a very pretty piece. Lady Alice had eye for colour, and a measure of impatience which made

131

the stitches uneven and the linen wrinkled. It was only the most inclement weather that kept her indoors stitching when she would rather be out visiting.

'You do little to encourage any of the suitors we have brought to the house. Why is that?'

'I have no wish to marry.'

'I have some sympathy for you, Niece. I understand. You think you will not marry because you cannot have the man you have set your heart on. I know what it is like to be young and to be infatuated with a man who is most unsuitable.'

'Aunt?'

'There are some friendships which are all very well in country places, but it is one that your uncle particularly dislikes.'

'I do not know what you mean.'

'Don't be so foolish, Niece. You should think of the reputation of the family.'

'You speak of Master Knox. He is a good man. There is no dishonour in his friendship.'

'Disabuse yourself of any idea that there can be more between you than simple friendship. And it must end when your marriage is arranged.'

'There is no marriage arranged.'

'Not yet. But soon, I hope. In the meantime, take care. I must tell you, that against my better judgment your uncle wishes to invite Master Knox to this house. That is why I must warn you. You must not be too forward.'

What was coming? There must be a catch somewhere. Her uncle never did anything without some profit to himself.

'It appears,' said Lady Alice, 'That Master Knox has found such favour with the King that there is a likelihood he is to be made a bishop.'

Chapter 26

Scurrilous pamphlets flooded the streets, pamphlets which attacked the King's advisers. They were as quickly seized and burnt by the authorities. Every printer denied they came from his workshop. Many of the pamphlets had the imprint of stationers abroad, in Antwerp or Geneva and other places, but the speed with which one seized pamphlet was replaced by another in the same tone suggested their source was more local.

'John, did you write this?'

He took it from her and examined it. 'No, dearie. I had nothing to do with it.' He started to read it.

'Leave it, John,' she said. 'Do you mean some of them might be yours?'

'Mmmh?'

'You had to look at that one to make sure it wasn't yours?'

'Nay, but it's good, lass, listen to this - '

She snatched it back from him and threw it on the fire.

'John, it's imprisonment if you write this stuff. It's punishment just to be reading it.'

'That's my brave Marjorie. You brought it to me. Did you walk through the streets with it in your hand, or did you hide it in your pocket?'

'I would be all right. I would say I was taking it to my uncle to show him. So that he could find the culprit.'

'You just made sure the culprit isn't me.'

'Might it have been?'

'Marjorie,' he said seriously. 'They cannot imprison the whole population of London. The whole country. We do not know how far afield these works are distributed.'

'Not everyone can read.'

'Enough people can.'

'And they can imprison people as an example. And hang them too.'

'There will always be others. Make as many examples as they like, hang as many as they like, others will always be found to continue the cause. And die for it if necessary.'

'What cause?'

'Any cause,' he said impatiently. 'When men feel it in their gut.'

They were in John's lodging. Sarie was sitting in the stairwell outside and they could hear her occasional shriek of laughter at the joshing of the landlady's son, who was thrilled to have a fine lady's maid to flirt with.

John's desk under the window was covered with papers and books. He had been writing when she came in. She decided not to pursue the matter further. If she did not know, then she could not answer questions that might be asked.

'You are to be invited to dine at my uncle's.'

'The invitation has already come. I am in two minds whether to accept. Am I to be exhibited like a prize won in a fairground?'

'You cannot refuse. We need my uncle's good will.'

'Very well. But to answer your question and set your mind at rest, no, I have not been publishing any pamphlets attacking the government. I owe my freedom to this King. I am grateful that I have been given sanctuary in England. I would not abuse that.'

*

He put on his best tunic and came to dine and was declared a charming man by Lady Alice, though she watched the flagon of wine as it circulated. She had heard that Scotsmen were prone to excessive ill-behaviour when drunk. But John Knox when in sober company, drank but little.

'I can understand why the Duke favours him,' said William Cecil.

134

'Do you like him, Master Cecil?' asked Marjorie, watching John at the end of the table talking to Lady Alice and making her smile.

'Very much. I have come to know him well these last few weeks. He is a straightforward man in a twisted world.'

'I am puzzled, Master Cecil, why there is talk of making him a bishop.'

'Why not? There's a vacancy. The King enjoys his preaching. You should be glad. The Bishopric of Rochester will allow Master Knox to spread his wings. It will provide him with a good income. I think he has not been used to such.'

'John doesn't much care about money.'

'No.' This was said thoughtfully. Cecil was watching Knox. 'Even among our modern churchmen that is rare. Even those that care little for material benefits want power. That is a more dangerous craving, do you not think, Miss Marjorie?'

'John doesn't want power either.'

'Perhaps not. But I fear that he is not a man destined to have a peaceful life.'

*

She had not meant to eavesdrop.

The air was damp with the November chill, and she was the only person lingering in the garden. She had been gasping for breath inside the overheated house. The kitchen people had left an ale cask by the side of the house to be collected later. She wiped the edge of it with her handkerchief and leaned against it and closed her eyes and imagined a house in Rochester.

Where was Rochester? In Kent they said. South, south of London. Did bishops have to live in their diocese? The only bishop she'd ever met was old Bishop Tunstall, still out of favour in the Tower of London. He had lived in his diocese but it had been enormous, covering almost the whole of the north of England. Poor man. Several palaces to chose from one day, confined in the Tower the next.

It was a new thing for priests to be married. She would be a bishop's wife. There had been none such before, or none acknowledged, though there were rumours that Archbishop Cranmer had a wife hidden away. She would not be hidden away. Would she have to run a large household? Her mother's training would be useful then. She missed her mother.

'I don't like the man.' She heard her uncle's voice.

She had not realised she was so close under the window of his library. She did not want to overhear confidential conversations. She held her breath and stayed still.

'He has a large following and many friends,' said William Cecil.

'Oh, the women like him.'

'The King likes him.'

'He's a troublemaker. I don't understand what it is Northumberland sees in him.'

'Why, precisely that,' Cecil gave his dry laugh. 'The Duke thinks that Knox will keep Cranmer alert. A whetstone is the word the Duke uses. Not a man given to flowery speech, my lord Duke, but he has this image in his mind, I believe, of sparks flying when Bishop Knox and Archbishop Cranmer try to work together.'

'How will that serve the Duke?'

'The churchmen are acquiring too much power.'

'So he would set them to fight amongst themselves?'

'Witness the trouble over the new Prayer Book. There is more work to be done on the Articles of Faith for the Church, and if Knox has the power to argue over the detail of it, why it will keep them busy till kingdom come.'

'Knox would do that without being made a bishop.'

'There are other reasons. Item two, there are anabaptists lurking in Kent, and Knox would smell them out. Item three, the Duke does not want him back in the north. If

136

employment is not found for him here then he must return to Newcastle when his appointment as royal chaplain ends.'

'He was less of a nuisance in the north. In fact, I would have thought the Duke would prefer him there to rout out Catholics.'

'Not so. If not kept on a tight rein Knox will ignore the new Prayer Book completely, and that appeals to the Scotsmen who flock over the border to hear him preaching. We do not want them settling in England, certainly not as far south as Newcastle. The border is reasonably peaceful just now but who can say when trouble might erupt again. Their queen is but a child, and where there is a child anything may happen.'

She heard the door of the library open and close and there was silence above her head. She sat on for some time, until she realised she was shivering. The house and garden were silent, and no one had seen her. She stretched her cold limbs and made her way slowly back into the house and up to her room. She crouched by the fire, glad now of the heat, and rubbed feeling back into her hands and thought about what she had heard.

*

'I have already refused.'

'Refused?'

'I visited the great Duke in his lair this morning and told him I did not wish to be a bishop.'

She pulled her cloak tighter round herself. The day was raw. 'They say no one refuses the Duke.'

'He was not overjoyed.'

'Why did you refuse?'

'I'll not be one of the Duke's pawns. I have no taste for nitpicking with Cranmer and the other bishops. The Duke accused me of ingratitude. William Cecil was there, heartily amused by the whole business.'

137

They were walking in Paul's Yard, John occasionally stopping to pick up a book from one of the stalls. She told him what she had overheard in the garden. He was not surprised. It confirmed he had made the right decision.

'I have no place here,' he said. 'The court is rotten at the very heart of it. There is treachery everywhere, no man stays loyal for long. No one can be believed. All seek advancement. They are like rats on a dungheap, scrambling over each other for whatever offal they can feed on.'

She saw Sarie and her cabinetmaker journeyman, her latest admirer, lingering beside a stall selling ribbons. No one was paying them any attention.

'Marjorie,' said John. 'I'll be leaving soon for Newcastle. I have to preach the Christmas sermon there.'

He looked carefully around and put down the book he was holding. He walked a few steps to a quieter corner. She followed.

'But that is not what I must say to you, Marjorie. Listen to me. No one speaks about it, but the King is very ill. He's a good lad, Marjorie. Clever. He has a great deal of learning but he is ignorant of the world. I used to teach boys of his age. They are usually boisterous, and rude, revelling in hunting and running. Wrestling. Competing at the butts. I doubt if the King has had much of those pleasures.'

'Were you sweaty and rude as a boy?'

'No, I preferred my books. But it was never my destiny to be a leader of men. The government of a kingdom will never rest on my shoulders.'

'He could still be a good King.'

'He will not live long enough. He has death in his face. Sssh. Say nothing to anyone. It is not to be spoken of. At court they are all manoeuvring round an event which none will acknowledge.'

'What will happen?'

'There is no other heir save his sister Mary. Mary is a papist. She will reverse all her brother's reforms. There will be danger. We will all be safer in the north, I think, when that time comes. Write to your father and ask if you can return to Norham.'

'I will only go back to Norham if you are there.'

'I will be, lassie. Cling to our handfasting. We will be married. We can take advantage of the King's favour. Your father couldn't refuse. But lass, when I leave here, my duties done, never, never will I return to London. It is a cesspit of iniquity.'

He glowered at some women who were soliciting customers round the doors of the cathedral. He gripped her arm.

'It is no place for us. Marjorie, come north and let us be wed, and live in peace.'

His duties at court soon finished, and without seeing her again, he left for Newcastle.

Soon after Christmas, he was arrested on a charge of treason.

Chapter 27

'It was his Christmas Day sermon in Newcastle,' William Cecil told Marjorie.

They were speaking in low voices, standing by the fire in the hall while they waited for Lady Alice to finish preparing herself for the visit to Gray's Inn. William Cecil was to escort both women there for the annual masque being performed by the apprentices at her uncle's chambers.

'The mass again?'

'Worse. A rant against treachery, disloyalty, and greed generally, not what most people would regard as suitable subjects perhaps for a Yuletide sermon. He named names. If anyone in Newcastle was in doubt about the iniquity of the King's court, Master Knox has spelt it out for them.'

'Did he name my uncle?'

'No, even Knox knows better than to cast calumny on one of the north's own. Besides, Marjorie, I do not think your uncle could be spoken about in the terms that John used.'

'Who did he name, then?'

'The Duke of course. Names him as the worst of traitors. He accused the Duke, along with the Privy Council en masse, the courtiers, all the King's advisers, of merely awaiting the death of the King in order to betray the Protestants and turn back to Rome.'

'He said that?'

'Loudly and clearly. And none misunderstood.'

'What will happen?'

'His licence to preach has been suspended.'

'And then?'

'That is all I know. Imprisonment, possibly.'

She felt her legs give way under her and she sat down on the stairs, only to have to make way a minute later for Lady Alice, overwhelming in green silk, still being fussed round by her maid. Master Cecil was being kind. Marjorie knew the penalty for treason. It was death.

Later, sitting among the lawyers and their guests, watching the apprentice lawyers cavorting in front of them, she went over and over the conversation in her mind. Beside her Master Cecil was explaining to her aunt who the characters in their flamboyant costumes were and assuring her that this was tame compared with what used to be performed.

'We have grown polite under a most sober King.'

He had seated himself between the two women, with Marjorie in the corner, with his back half turned to her, shielding her from the others. She was grateful for his thoughtfulness. The shrieking from the floor and the laughter round her reached a crescendo until she felt she could scream. She began to tremble. William Cecil, sensing this, turned back to her. He pressed his hand on hers.

'Courage,' he whispered. 'It won't be long now and you can go home.'

'I have no home. I don't belong here.'

'Sssh. Time to despair when all is lost. There is a long way to go yet.'

'What are you saying to Marjorie, William?' cried Lady Alice on the other side.

'I was explaining that there is still more to come of the charade, my lady.'

It was four days later, four days of agonising waiting, smiling and moving calmly about the house with an air of tranquillity as if she had not a care in the world, four long days later, that she received a letter from John. It had come by a roundabout way through several messengers, the last of whom, a man in the service of Master Locke, a London merchant, told her they had all taken precautions for Master Knox did not want to get anyone into trouble.

'He says it is better,' the messenger reported. 'That he is believed to be without friends.'

The letter was his farewell. It had been written while he waited for the men to come and arrest him. He would not run away. He had run away when his great mentor George Wishart had been taken and subsequently burnt at the stake, but he would never run away again. Not he. He was aware of what he was doing, and was ready to die if need be for the cause of Jesus Christ and the truth of the gospel, as George Wishart had died. There was much more of this. He expected never to see Marjorie again. He could write no more.

'Stupid, stupid, stupid,' she cried aloud.

'Miss Marjorie?' A startled Sarie put her head round the door. Marjorie burst into tears. Sarie came and put her arms round Marjorie, nearly suffocating her.

'If I'd been there, I could have stopped him,' she wailed.

'No you couldn't,' said Sarie.

*

'If anyone asks you, you have only the mildest acquaintance with him. Do you understand, girl? He was merely the garrison preacher at Berwick when you were there.'

They were in her aunt's parlour. It was nearly midnight. The guests had all left. The servants had finished their work and gone to their quarters. Around them the house was silent.

'Sir, everyone knows we have had him here to dine.'

'I will answer for that. It was a matter of courtesy to one of the King's preachers. No more. It was not a personal matter. There was no friendship. Is that understood?'

'Yes, Sir. Please, Uncle, may I return to Norham?'

'No. You will stay here.'

'You are not to leave the house, Marjorie,' said her aunt. 'If you go out, it must be with me.'

She did not dare ask if John was in prison. She wrote to her mother to ask if she knew. Her mother replied eventually, an anguished missive, carelessly scrawled and blotchy with her tears. John was still in Newcastle. Although under arrest, he was too ill to be moved from his bed. He had pain in his head and stomach and was in low spirits. Captain Bowes had forbidden his wife to visit him.

January was cold and raw and the wind whistled down the river Thames and round street corners. Snow fell and turned to slush and mud which was trailed into the house. Everyone shivered and sneezed and took their temper out on friends and servants alike. Slowly the weeks passed.

*

It was the first day of March.

The whole house was in a flurry. Today King Edward would open the new session of Parliament at Whitehall. Sir Robert's robes of state had been pulled out of the wardrobe press a week ago and hung to air in the top gallery. The maids had been picking over them carefully for moth and other damage, and cleaning the gold thread where it had become tarnished.

Now Marjorie stood with her aunt at the window watching as the men gathered in the courtyard, spilling out into the street, gawped at by passing urchins hoping for a penny.

'He never before had to have armed men with him. Not in London,' said Lady Alice.

Some of the men below checked their pistols and hid them carefully inside their cloaks. All of them wore swords.

'Will they all be armed, in the parliament building?'

'Very likely. The lords will have large numbers of their people with them.'

Sir Robert appeared in the courtyard and mounted his horse. The gates were swung open, and he led the way out, his men following in rough formation. It was very quiet save for the tramp of their feet. The gates closed behind them.

He was late back that night. She heard him return as she lay wakeful in bed. In the distance she could hear shouting and pistol shots. The men who came to London with their masters, both Lords and Commons, were ignoring the curfew and causing trouble in the city.

Sir Robert came into his wife's parlour the next morning while she was going over the household account books with the steward. Lately, mindful of her duties to Marjorie, which she remembered in a fitful way sometimes, she had been taking the opportunity of instructing her in the running of a large London household. Marjorie, listening half-heartedly, did not bother to remind her that her mother had taught her the management of the household at Aske, far larger than anything Lady Alice had ever had to deal with.

On Sir Robert's entrance, his wife signalled to the steward that he should leave, they would return to the figures later. Sir Robert sat down heavily in the chair by the fire. There was silence in the room apart from the crackling of the wood in the fireplace.

'The Parliament has been postponed. The King is not well enough to attend.'

'But he was there yesterday?'

'Yes, he was there. But it was quickly done. Rushed.'

And then would come the plotting, always the plotting, thought Marjorie. All the men round the King would be scurrying to protect their backs.

'The King did his duties well. But it was a pointless exercise, calling the Parliament. If the Duke has his way it would not have happened. He has filled the Commons with his placemen. The Privy Council's powers are to be reduced. Master Cecil has been given instructions to work out the new procedures and regulations for the King to despatch all the business himself.'

'But if he is ill he cannot do everything.'

144

'No.' said Sir Robert. 'When the Privy Council loses its power to advise the King, and the King is ill, who can say what tyranny we might be subject to?'

The tyranny of the Duke. It was unsaid.

'What talk is there in the town?' he asked.

'Talk? About what?'

'About anything. About the King.'

'We do not gossip, Robert.' said his wife primly. 'Have you not many times said to us that we must be careful and reserved for there are matters heard in this household that are secret?'

He made an impatient gesture with his hand. 'Madam,' he said. 'I ask again what gossip there is in the town. This is not time for tomfoolery.'

'They say the King is dying.'

'Ah.'

Marjorie spoke up. 'And there are omens and prophecies. Stars have been falling from the sky, and a sheep has given birth to a wolfcub.'

She started to explain that of course she did not believe in these silly things, but he grunted and she shut up.

'There is a prophecy that the Thames will run with blood,' Lady Alice shuddered as she spoke.

'Dear God, where do these things start?'

'There are some who say Edward is already dead. But of course that cannot be true if he opened the Parliament yesterday.'

'Obviously not.'

'But he is never seen, Uncle. Some people say that he will just disappear, like the little princes.'

Lady Alice nervously stroked the cover of the account book.

'People wonder,' Marjorie continued. 'They wonder if the King were to die, who would be the next King. Do you know who would be the next King, Uncle?'

He did not answer her. He turned away and bent over the fire, warming his hands. They were grown knobbly, the joints swelling, and caused him a lot of pain in cold weather. He was getting old, living in this unhealthy, damp city. There was little left of the vigorous soldier he had been. He had grown fat and stiff, and had to sit for hours with others arguing about what advice to give the King, knowing it was futile, and all the time wondering what the future held. His tired eyes, sunk in darkened flesh, suggested he did not sleep well at night. Marjorie, who had once been frightened of him, now felt pity.

She opened her mouth to say more, but caught Lady Alice's warning frown and was silenced.

'After Easter the King will move to the palace at Greenwich,' said Sir Robert. 'His health is very much improved and he will enjoy the fresh air there. He is expected to make a full recovery by the summer, and all will be well again.'

'Oh, I am so glad. That clever boy,' said her aunt.

Sir Robert sighed and looked from one to the other of them.

'That is what you are to tell people.'

'Oh, I see,' said Lady Alice, understanding.

'But is it true, Uncle?'

He rose and left the room without a word, his tread heavy, tired.

'We will do as he says, Marjorie. Tomorrow. Yes, tomorrow we will go visiting as many people as we can.'

'Aunt, who will be King when the King dies?'

'Only God knows that. They breed nothing but girls, these Tudors. Mary and Elizabeth, and then their cousins the Grey girls. And look at Scotland. They have a little girl for a queen and much good it does them.'

Sir Robert went every day to Westminster Hall where the Privy Council met, and returned home late each night. The household hardly saw him, and on the occasions when he was at home he was bad-tempered, and the sensible servants stayed out of his way. Occasionally he would return early with Master Cecil and was closeted in his study for hours. When Marjorie went downstairs to the hall she would find Master Cecil's men lounging there, casting dice with the footmen.

Master Cecil's men were armed all the time. It was said that no nobles and no members of the Privy Council, no one connected with the King, now travelled without armed guard. Many of them now travelled only at night, secretly. People were waiting. But for what?

They were now in the season of Lent. The churches were crowded, and so many people surged towards Paul's Cross for each sermon that some were trampled underfoot. Some of the sermons caused an uproar. One preacher lambasted the loose morals of the court. Another prophesied plagues that would carry off all the sinners. And now the most daring of the preachers talked of the death of the King, though that was treason.

The authorities were harsh with those they caught spreading rumour. Cutting off the ears was a common punishment. Marjorie and her aunt saw a poor garrulous soul nailed to the pillory in Houndsditch by his ear. He crouched on his knees, his neck twisted, obviously in agony. Marjorie heard later that eventually the flesh of his ear had torn, and he had run away, leaving part of his ear still nailed to the wood, where it eventually rotted. But he was lucky to be alive. Such punishments failed to stop the rumours, but Sir Robert's household were all careful what they said in public, and even in private, for who knew who might be listening?

Then one day Master Cecil brought more personal news to Marjorie. By order of the Duke the charges against John Knox were to be dropped.

'Did you speak for him?'

147

'No, no. I do not have that kind of influence. I am only the clerk to the Council. Knox has been writing himself to the Duke. I saw the letter. I am afraid our friend had to grovel a fair bit, but with success. All is forgiven.'

'But why? Men have had their tongues cut out for less.' She was bewildered.

He hesitated. 'I do not know. I do not know what goes on in the mind of the great Duke. But Knox is to return to London.'

'Just like that? As if nothing has happened?'

No more, she thought. No more of London. No more of this cat and mouse. In favour. Out of favour. The King's chaplain. An arrested traitor. A favoured preacher again.

'It would be better if he stayed in the north. Out of harm's way.'

'John Knox will never be out of harm's way. He is not that kind of man.' Cecil looked at her shrewdly. 'You of all people should know that.'

Chapter 28

'Two days ago I was summoned to see my lord Duke. His message said he had a position for me. I had to wait in his antechamber with all the other supplicants for his attention for nearly three hours. So much for his assurances that I was valuable and could have access to him at any time. No doubt he says that to everybody.'

They were in Knox's room. He was back in his old lodging. Marjorie had gone there as soon as he'd sent word that he was back in London. Sarie was downstairs gossiping with the landlady in her kitchen.

'When I saw him eventually, he was distracted by lackeys running to him with notes and papers to sign. There is no peace round that man. He will have no peace in his heart. He is an unhappy man, Marjorie. I could see it in his face. He is striving and striving and for what? For worldly power and gain. I feel sorry for him.'

'What did he want with you?'

'These courtly men talk round and round and round a subject and cannot speak straight out and say what they mean, and for that matter, how can we ever be sure they mean what they say? A man should speak plain and the world would be a better place for it.'

She waited patiently.

'Marjorie, I do not know where God is calling me. God is offering me too many choices.'

'Is it the Duke who is offering you the choices?'

'Is the Duke God's messenger or the devil's?'

'John, forget God and the devil for the moment. Tell me what the Duke wants you for.'

'What great ploy does he have in hand that he can forgive John Knox? Ungrateful was the word he used. This

149

ungrateful preacher, bring him to London and offer him a position. Good question, Marjorie.'

'What position?'

'He has offered me a church here in London. All Hallows. You know it, I think. In Bread Street? The corner of Watling Street. You must pass it regularly.'

'I know it.'

'He has offered me the living.'

'What did you say?'

'Thanked him. Said I would consider the matter. I was very gracious. I am learning the elegant ways of the court.'

'Why do you hesitate?'

'I wanted to speak to you first.'

'Do you want it, John?'

'This would be a respectable position. Your family might permit us to marry. You would be the wife of the vicar of All Hallows church in London, in favour with the King. Not perhaps as grand a position as the wife of a bishop, but good enough.'

'It is what you wanted, a church, a congregation.'

'Yes.'

He was pulling at the casement window, trying to open it. It was filled with waxed paper. This house was too poor to afford even the cheapest glass. As he tugged, part of the wooden frame came away in his hand. He looked at it ruefully.

'What do you think, Marjorie?'

'I think you should find more comfortable lodgings.'

He sighed. 'Aye, no doubt. I have been offered such. Mistress Locke has offered me accommodation in her house.'

'Mistress Locke?'

'You know her.'

'I know of her. The merchant's wife?'

'Important in the city. Good faithful Protestants, both. But a man who is one day accused of treason and the next invited to preach the Lenten sermon before the King is not a comfortable friend to have.'

'Preach at Lent?'

'Yes, that too. Did I not say?'

'Are you going to accept the Duke's offer?'

'Do you want me to?'

He stood there, still with the spar of rotten wood from the window in his hand, looking at it in a puzzled way as if he had forgotten how it got there. Marjorie heard the shouts of the traders in nearby Leadenhall market and smelt the sweet smell of the rotting vegetables that would be tossed aside there after the day's trading, to be scavenged by the poor and starving.

'If you wanted it you would have accepted him right away.'

'I do not trust these people. He will have some mischief in mind and thinks to use me.'

'But supposing his plans are sensible and his purpose is just?'

'I still do not trust him. I question his sincerity. I think he cares nothing for the Church and everything for himself. I'm sorry, Marjorie.'

What could she say? Her father and uncle would argue this was a chance for John to find his way back into favour with the Church and the Privy Council. They would say he was being foolish to hesitate, as he had been foolish before. He had offended the Duke once, would he do so again? But he would have to be more careful in his sermons, less outspoken, more conciliatory.

'John, we will always be honest with one another, will we not?'

'Always.'

'I do not want to live in London but if that is what you want then of course I will do it.'

He dropped the spar of wood onto his desk and pulled her to him.

151

'You do not like London? What, shake your head so emphatically? Why, Londoners consider there is no place like it on Earth.'

'There probably is not.'

He laughed. 'I dislike the place also. But I thought you would want to stay. Here you can have the latest gowns and caps. You could spend my stipend on coloured ribbons. Would that not tempt you?'

'You know me well enough not to tease me like that.'

'I could thole being respectable and compliant if it would allow us to marry.'

'Then we must wait a bit longer.' It cost her an effort to say this, but it was for the best. Marriage would never compensate him for the restrictions he would have to endure if he agreed to the Duke's offer and became subservient to the Bishop of London.

They heard the bells of the nearby church tolling the hours. It was three o'clock. She stirred. 'I must go, John. You will be careful.'

'I'll avoid cutpurses and knifemen.'

'I don't mean that. I mean, with the Privy Council and in the King's Chapel, you will be careful what you say.'

'I have to say what I think, Marjorie.'

'That is what I fear. Don't get yourself into more trouble, not now.'

'Come, you need to get back before you are missed.'

The rain was now falling steadily. They passed round the river side of St. Paul's where the stallholders were packing up for the day, for though it was not yet dusk, there were few customers about in this weather. People were hurrying home, well cloaked against the drizzle. In doorways people were sheltering, and here and there two or three were gathered, murmuring in low voices, which ceased as they approached. As they passed a tavern loud voices were raised in argument.

152

'All is uneasiness,' said Knox. 'It's different from when I was last here. Mind your step there.'

'Yes. Will it be dangerous?'

'The mob will be dangerous if roused.'

They came to her uncle's house. Sarie slipped in at the postern gate and left them alone. John pulled Marjorie into the shelter of the wall. They stood close together. He touched his forefinger to his lips and then touched hers.

'Marjorie,' he whispered. 'Thou art mine.'

He stroked his finger along her jawline and let her go. She knocked on the gate and was let in. Knox melted away into the gathering dusk.

*

Who does he think he is?' roared Sir Robert. 'This man dares to refuse the Privy Council. To refuse the Bishop of London who is prepared to take him back into his diocese.'

'Perhaps that is the trouble,' said Master Cecil. 'Perhaps he would not be willing to use the new Prayer Book and fears the Bishop will force him to.'

'No one forces Master Knox to do anything,' Marjorie murmured to her aunt as they sat in the corner by the window, quietly sewing and hoping not to draw too much attention to themselves. Marjorie did not want the men to withdraw to her uncle's library where she would not hear their conversations. It was cold though they were into March, and she did not intend to lurk outside again in order to eavesdrop.

'He is holding out for more.'

'Do you think so?' asked William Cecil.

'What else?'

'If that were true it would make my task easier. The Duke will not take no for an answer,' said Master Cecil. 'He has set me the task of trying to persuade him.'

'I don't know why the Duke is so patient.'

153

'Knox has a great deal of charm, in his rough Scottish way.'

'I would wish him back in Scotland.'

'To be sure, but since we have him among us we must make the best of him we can. Or in the best way the Duke can. The Duke does not understand why a man would turn down such a splendid route to advancement. The trouble is, my dear Bowes, and this is something I find difficult to explain to the Duke, I suspect that John Knox is a man who will not be bought.'

Chapter 29

'A friend of your family is presently housed in the Tower.'

Marjorie felt her legs go weak, but took a firm grip of herself.

'Bishop Tunstall, formerly of Durham,' said Sir Robert. 'Who did you think I meant?' His voice was surprisingly kind.

'Sir, these are uneasy times.'

'When you were at Norham, the Bishop visited there. You recall the occasion?'

'Yes, Sir. He was doing a northern circuit of his diocese. He stayed at the castle for some weeks.'

'You saw much of him?'

'We were bidden to dine sometimes.'

'Was that just the family?'

'There were always other guests. My father seldom. His duties kept him busy.'

'Your father's loyalty has never been in doubt.'

'Sir...'

He hastily drew a chair forward for her to sit down. She drooped her head and swallowed the bile that had risen up in her throat.

'Sir,' she said. 'My mother's loyalty is not in doubt either.'

'No, no. I never said it was.'

'Does someone say so?'

He didn't answer her. He had returned to sit on the other side of his table. His fingers, heavy with rings, were clasped rigidly. The room smelt of paper and candlewax. 'These priests,' he said, almost to himself. 'Always the priests.'

'Sir, my mother is true to the King's religion, as am I.'

'As are all our family, I hope. Would you like to visit him?'

'The Bishop? In the Tower?'

'Yes, yes, that is who we speak of.'

'Do you wish me to?'

'It would be a kindness to an old man. He will die soon.'

'Sir, why do you not visit him yourself?'

'It would not be seemly. He is now considered an enemy of the state. You may take him sweetmeats. I will tell my wife to have some prepared. Your basket will be searched when you go in and again when you come out. They search all for seditious literature. Of course, nothing he is writing must be smuggled out. You must not, under any circumstances, discuss any matter of religion with him.'

'We would not have any matter of religion in common, Sir.'

'No. And no talk concerning the King, or the Parliament.'

'So what are we to talk of, Sir?'

'His health. Is he comfortable? That sort of thing. You will not discuss your visit with anyone, before or afterwards. If anyone learns of it, it is a private visit to someone who was once a friend of your family. Is that understood?'

'Yes, Sir.' She felt total bewilderment.

He rose to his feet. 'You may go tomorrow. I've already instructed one of my men to act as guard.'

Bishop Tunstall was housed in a room high up in the east tower. It overlooked the green. The rays of the late morning sun slanted across to the Chapel of Saint Peter ad Vincula, but made only a small moving patch of light on the wall of the room. There was a brazier in one corner, not yet lit. The room smelled damp and faintly of urine, the nest of an old man. In one corner there were two trestles supporting a small board spread with papers and books.

He rose from the desk when he saw her. Tears came into his eyes. He held both her hands between his, and became choked up and could hardly speak. She hastened to fill the moment.

'My mother is well, as is my father, Sir. I am living in London now with my uncle. My mother is still at Norham with my father.'

'Norham was my northern seat, you know. I often went there when I still had work to do.' He lifted a paper from his desk. 'I still have work to do. I write, you see. Look, I never had time before. Now I have time.'

'Are you comfortable, Sir?'

'I have more than the desert fathers had. Of course, the desert is warm, and England is cold. Cold to the truth.'

'We must not talk of religion, Sir,' she said, nervously glancing towards the door, which stood open. There was a warder sitting outside.

'Are you yet married, Marjorie? There was talk of it. You were to marry a cousin.'

'He has married someone else.'

'And your mother, she is well?'

'Very well. Life at Norham is pleasant in the spring.'

'I am writing a treatise on the true meaning of the blood and body of Christ.'

There was a hiss from the open door.

'They allow me to write what I wish because they think the matter is pointless and of no account. Perhaps they are right. When I die, my papers here will be dropped onto the bonfire and consumed. Do you think it better my papers be burnt rather than my body?'

She was silent, lost and unable to follow the old man's thoughts.

'It makes no odds, in the end. I am done with the body. They may do what they like with it.'

'Sir, I have brought you some sweetmeats from my aunt's kitchen.'

She rummaged in the basket and brought out some gingerbread and candied fruit. There was a little pot of honey.

'Thank you my dear,' he said. 'Will you share it with me?' He had hardly any teeth. She shook her head.

'I will eat it later then.'

She began to babble. She told him of the marriages of her sisters and the careers of her brothers, all soldiers like their father, and how the port of Berwick was busy with ships from the Low Countries, and how noisy London was and how much she missed the quietness of the north. He nodded as she talked, but she became conscious that he was only half listening, and this visit probably meant little to him. She was interrupting his peace. Now and again his hand would twitch towards his papers.

She had nothing more to say. She rose to leave. He struggled to his feet too, though she tried to stop him. He made as if to sign the cross over her. She froze, for she could not have refused him, though such was now anathema to her, but how could she shrink from such an old, tired man? It made no odds anyway. The sign of the cross was but a movement of the hands, and if she did not think it meant anything, then it meant nothing. What it meant to him was his own affair.

He paused and glanced at the doorway. They were out of sight of the warder there, but still the Bishop retained sufficient caution from his years of compliance with new learning he did not believe in. He dropped his hands. He leaned forward and whispered to her.

'I am not allowed, but it is in my heart, dear Marjorie. Consider it done.'

She nodded, and edged her way from the room. Outside the warder searched her basket again.

'To make sure you're not smuggling out any of his writings.'

'He seems comfortable.'

'He's comfortable enough. He's like to die soon anyway. A man his age. Will you come again?'

'Perhaps.'

'He doesn't see many people. I reckon they've forgotten about him.'

The manservant her uncle had sent with her was waiting at the door of the tower. There seemed to be a lot of people about. They were led past the orchard to the passageway that took them through the gate in the inner wall. They crossed the moat towards the second gatehouse. There was a shout at their back and they were roughly ordered to stand aside. Her escort pulled her into an embrasure in the wall of the gatehouse. As they waited, light carts came out of the inner court of the Tower, their contents hidden under tarpaulins. These were followed by heavy bullock carts, laden with small cannon and barrels of gunpowder. They rumbled across the bridge of the moat and turned onto the road that led down Tower Hill.

'Where are they going?' she asked.

'Best not to ask that,' said the servant. But he was watching closely. She was silent, realising he was counting the carts. Was he also noting the contents? The carts were followed by a contingent of soldiers. The procession passed and disappeared out, leaving behind only a cloud of dust and silence, as the few men left closed the heavy gates and dispersed to their business.

The guard let them out at the postern and they walked home. Later that evening as she passed through the hall she saw the servant who had been with her in the Tower come out of her uncle's room. He saw her and nodded and went off in the direction of the kitchen. Sir Robert called her into his room.

'Tell me about your visit.'

Carefully she recounted her visit. 'We did not talk of anything religious, or political. Indeed, we talked of very little. He was having difficulty concentrating, I think.'

'You are a good girl, Marjorie.'

'It surprises me that anyone could be interested in the conversation of a girl and an old man.'

159

'In difficult times, all conversations are of interest. You must be careful. Did you see anyone you know?'

'No, Sir.'

'Anyone you have seen before in this house?'

'No, Sir.'

She was dismissed. That night, Master Cecil came to the house and was closeted for hours with her uncle.

She was not asked to visit Bishop Tunstall again. She never knew why she had been sent in the first place. She wondered whether the cake she took him had been poisoned, but the Bishop continued to live.

Chapter 30

On the 2nd of April John Knox preached the Lenten sermon in Westminster Abbey before the King.

Lady Alice and Marjorie crowded into the benches set aside for the wives and daughters of Privy Councillors, women who covertly examined each other's clothes and waved to catch the eye of people they knew.

The dimness of the abbey on this cold spring day was hardly lifted by the banks of candles. Not votive candles now. It was forbidden to pray to the Virgin Mary or to the saints for the soul of your dead in Purgatory since there was no Purgatory, and to whom would you be lighting a candle if not to a saint? But the candles were still necessary and Marjorie wondered who paid for them now that the poor people no longer put their penny in the box to buy one.

In the front were the members of the Privy Council full of themselves in their robes of state. Behind them came the Lord Mayor and the aldermen, along with the deans of the various guilds, less important here outside the city but still resplendent in their furs and gold chains of office. Round about crowded the lords, those not in the King's circle of advisers, and the members of the Commons, finding space where they could. Dismissed as of less importance than the lords, still many of them were large landowners, able to summon up armies of followers at will.

Behind the women sat the merchants and their wives, glittering with jewels, and behind them stood a double, a triple row of servants and discreetly armed guards, to protect the gentry from the moiling crowds of common people who were now surging in through the doors, to stand at the back.

The trumpeters announced the arrival of the King and everyone stood, but strain as she might Marjorie could not see him. The King was hidden from all, seated in the King's balcony overlooking the altar. Only the person in the pulpit could see him. Not even then, her aunt whispered to her, if the King chose to have the curtains closed. He could hear but not be seen.

They settled themselves.

John Knox entered the pulpit. He spoke without notes. Marjorie had seen him write rough outlines of his sermons, working them up, but he did not need notes when he was preaching. His voice was large, and filled the space. He still had his Scottish accent, but he spoke in English. He announced his text. *He that eateth bread with me hath lifted up his heel against me.*

Not a sound could be heard in that vast abbey.

Many godly princes, he said, had officers and chief councillors most ungodly, who traded with enemies of the true religion, and who were traitors to their princes. There was a ripple of sound, a mere sigh, throughout the abbey. This was going to be good. All knew that young King Edward was, above all, godly. None needed it spelled out to them whom Knox meant. As he was talking he turned most often to the balcony where the young King was sitting. I'm talking to you, he seemed to say. Take care.

He lashed out at the King's advisers, calling them traitorous councillors. As he spoke he leaned forward and glared at the men seated in front of him. He quoted those stories in the bible where young and innocent kings had been deceived by evil councillors. He had them all. He became personal. He compared the Lord Treasurer, sitting in the front row, to Shebna of the bible, a crafty fox who could show a fair countenance to the King. The Lord Treasurer shifted slightly in his seat. Perhaps he was wondering whether to get up and walk out.

Knox likened my Lord of Northumberland to Achitophel, whose counsel was like the oracle of God. Achitophel was a clever man, but one who betrayed David the King.

162

Dear God, thought Marjorie, this man if mine is a fool. Does he think the Duke will forgive him this? He has gone too far this time. It was one thing to say this in far-off Newcastle, quite another to say it in the heart of the court itself. She wondered if he was deliberately angling to have himself exiled from London.

He brought his examples up to the greatest of all. He talked of Judas who sat down to eat with Jesus and then betrayed him with a kiss. By this time most of the privy councillors were stony-faced, sitting with folded arms, gazing at nothing. Her uncle was among them. Marjorie could see Master Cecil at the end of a row, leaning back, his eyes closed. None dared leave. They could not, as long as the King was there.

'David and Hezekia, princes of great and godly gifts and experience were abused by crafty councillors and dissembling hypocrites. What wonder then, that a young and innocent King be deceived by crafty, covetous, wicked and ungodly councillors?'

There was some mild cheering behind them, among the common people, and a flurry of noise and banging doors as some were ejected from the building.

The sermon finished triumphantly and Knox leapt down from the pulpit and strode out of their sight. The trumpets sounded and the King left, still unseen by the congregation. And then there was a roar of sound as the tension broke and everyone began to talk at once.

Northumberland had been out of the church in a flash behind the King. The privy councillors crowded forward to leave the church by the side entrance, accompanied by jeers and shouts from the crowd inside and outside. There had been many outside the abbey who hadn't heard the sermon but who had it relayed in bits and pieces to them by those nearest the door, and how much had been accurately rendered was anybody's guess, but the gist of it would be clear to the people.

163

The women guests would normally have been escorted out quickly, protected by their servants, but one of the guards came forward with a message that they were to wait until the rabble had been cleared from round the abbey. It would not be safe to go out now. For the most part they were silent, cautious as their menfolk would be. One young wife, too young to know better, began to chatter about the sermon. What had he meant, who had he been talking about? But she was quickly shushed by older and wiser women. Some elderly women, and others young and clumsily pregnant, began fidgeting and chuntering and some slipped away into dark corners behind the pillars.

No doubt the more sensible ones were wondering if any of this mattered, how it would affect their husbands and fathers. But there had been other fierce sermons here at Westminster Abbey and in the open pulpit at Paul's Cross and nothing much came of any of them, except a few hours of unrest among the commons and ill-temper among the men of power.

And presumably, thought Marjorie, John was not telling the King anything he did not know already. Or anyone else for that matter.

Gradually the crowds outside were cleared away. The women determinedly started some idle small talk about children as they were allowed out into the sunshine to wait in the queue at the abbey's jetty for their barges.

Sir Robert did not come home till very late.

John Knox was summoned to the Privy Council a few days later.

No one, said her weary uncle, telling them about it in the privacy of his wife's parlour, dared challenge him on the sermon. How could they even give a hint that they thought it might apply to them?

'He had us at a disadvantage,' he sighed. 'How could anyone point to my lord Northumberland and ask why he was likened to Achiphotel? So all we could do was ask

164

Knox why he objected to kneeling, and to the wafer. Why did he insist on using ordinary bread? All the old complaints. We asked him again why he had refused the charge of All Hallows. He declined to give a reason. Your friend sails close to the wind, Marjorie, and if he is not careful his barque will be overturned one of these days.'

'Is he being sent back to Newcastle?'

'He is not. They don't want him. He is to be sent into Buckinghamshire as a travelling preacher where it is hoped he can do little damage.'

Chapter 31

It was not often now they had guests for dinner. It was unseemly in Lent, said Lady Alice. It would appear ostentatious, eating when the rest of the world went without. Marjorie knew this was nonsense. She did not believe that in a city like London where wealth was flaunted there could be such sensitivity. Sarie picked up from gossip amongst the servants that entertaining had not stopped for Lent in previous years. The present restraint, in the opinion of the servants, was nothing to do with Lent and everything to do with people not wanting to be seen to be conspiring.

'Conspiring against whom?'

But Sarie couldn't say. Against anybody, Marjorie supposed. Just because you were rich and powerful didn't mean you were safe. People still remembered how the Duke of Somerset, aye, even the King's uncle, had been accused. His unfinished mansion house on the bank of the Thames stood silently, a monument to grandiose ideas and the death of a traitor. Though nobody, Sarie whispered, really believed the good duke had been a traitor. There were still many who mourned him.

Besides, people didn't want to go out at night. The market people coming in to London made sure they were gone well before the curfew. The traders brought talk of armies on the move in the countryside round about. Or at least crowds of men travelling silently at night, armed. Some people said they were the ghosts of old armies, but Sarie didn't believe this herself. She knew they must be living men. But she herself would not go out at night, for there might really be ghosts and the moon was coloured red the last time it was full, wasn't it, and what did that mean but trouble?

Today therefore it was just a small family supper. Sir Robert displayed an unusual cheerfulness.

'The King is in Greenwich,' he said, as he carved the fowl. 'His health is very much improved. It is as we said all along. He is on the mend.'

'Oh Robert, that is wonderful news indeed.'

'Rest and fresh air, that is what people need when they are ill, not these physicians clustering round like flies round a ....'

Carcase? Was that the word he was going to use?

'Rotten fish,' he concluded.

'What is the nature of the King's illness, Uncle?' Marjorie asked.

'Just a slight rheum. Nothing to worry about. It was allowed to get a grip and lingered when it should have been thrown off earlier. His doctors were incompetent. He's recovering fast.'

He looked round at the servants who were dishing up the food to make sure they had all heard. One of them smirked at his fellows.

Sir Robert sat down and began to eat. 'He is so well that he will show himself to his people. You may see him. Would you like that Marjorie? Something to tell your brothers and sisters when you go home.'

'Am I to go home?'

'Yes.'

'Not yet, Robert, surely,' said her aunt. 'I am so enjoying having her here with us.'

Marjorie picked at the pale meat on her plate. So John was expected to stay in the south. That would be why there was talk of a return home for her. Take her as far away from him as possible. Don't let them see that it matters.

'The Privy Council is summoned to Greenwich on Tuesday. You may come with me. While I am in the palace you may have a day's outing in the country.'

167

Word had obviously been well spread and on Tuesday as Sir Robert's barge made its way downstream the river was crowded with similar craft, with wherries and other small boats dodging in and out of the larger river traffic of laden barges, and the occasional fast sweep of a nobleman's barge as it raced past. The oarsmen had an easy task. The current was with them. The path along the river bank was thick with people making their way on foot.

They arrived at Greenwich in the late forenoon. The riverbank was crowded with people going ashore. The oarsmen pulled into the jetty of the Palace, and the guards there, recognising the barge of Sir Robert Bowes of the Privy Council, pulled it in. They stepped ashore. The boatman handed up the baskets filled with food, and then steered the boat away to make way for others. Lady Alice and Marjorie followed Sir Robert over the boarded walk to the gardens of the palace, and here he saw them settled in a sheltered corner on some raised ground under the trees, a manservant hovering.

'See,' he pointed to the first floor windows of the palace. 'The third window along from the left. That is the audience chamber. Behind it, you cannot see it, the room where the Privy Council meet when the King is here. If he is pleased to appear, you will see him there.'

He left them then, striding towards the palace, his secretary running to keep up. His wife looked after him proudly. In her opinion he was a fine figure, in his velvet and silk. She believed everyone was looking at them admiringly.

A family of boisterous young people approached and settled near them, chattering. They had walked from London, leaving as soon as it was first light. Marjorie watched as others splashed ashore over by the marsh, for the guards at the jetty would not let the passengers of the wherries ashore there. The guards looked sour and unsmiling. They straightened up as the gilded barge

168

belonging to my Lord the Duke of Northumberland arrived. He alighted and strode towards the palace, looking neither to right nor left, surrounded by armed guards and followed by secretaries. He looked proud. Marjorie remembered what John Knox had said about him. A tired, worried man.

The day was warm and spirits were high. Children ran about shrieking. There was a cry of 'cutpurse!' and a ruffling of the crowd, and someone was brought to the ground as men fell on him and began punching. Guards appeared from nowhere and dragged him away. Even as this was happening, Marjorie saw a slattern in the crowd slip a purse from the britches pocket of a man who was too drunk to notice what was happening. She was about to cry out when her aunt seized her arm and shushed her. Don't become involved. Don't draw attention.

'It serves him right,' she said primly. Marjorie had observed before how Lady Alice had a horror of drunkenness. Anyway, the thief had disappeared into the crowd and Marjorie could not have identified her, for she was no different from many of the other poorly dressed white-faced women. Here and there were groups of richer people, standing out in their brighter colours and cleaner linen, protected by a servant or two. Everyone, it seemed, had come to see the King.

'It's a waste of time,' said a man near them. 'We won't see him. The King is already dead.'

'Nay,' he was shouted down. They had been told he was here, and had not the Privy Council assembled for normal government business? And the King was in charge of them.

Time passed. The morning gave way to afternoon. The food-sellers were doing a roaring trade, and those who had brought their own food had long finished it. People were lying on the ground enjoying the sunshine, some of them now the worse for drink. The children who had earlier been splashing in the shallow waters of the river were becoming fractious. People started to drift away.

And then everything fell silent, gradually, starting with the people nearest the palace, and spreading to the outer edges of the crowd, the chattering dying away as it will in a flock of grazing geese when a swift sudden shadow passes over the sun. The curtain of the window had been drawn back. A figure stood there, and people were craning to see. But it was only a servant in the Tudor colours of green and white. He opened the window.

'The King,' someone shouted. 'Let's see the King.' The crowd took up the chant. The King, the King.

And suddenly there he was, a slight figure, lifting an arm in greeting, behind him the shadowy forms of other men, larger, darker. The crowd erupted with cheering and then the cheering died away. It began again, raggedly and uncertain, but that too soon ceased.

They saw, and understood the truth. They sensed the thin and wasted body which the fine clothes could not conceal. The sleeve fell away from the raised arm to reveal white skin stretched over prominent wrist bones and a skeletal hand. His face was tiny, his cheeks sunken. He looked to left and right, acknowledging the crowds. As he moved, the furred gown round his shoulders barely shifted as if it were too big and hardly touched the body underneath. No one watching could have any doubt that the King had been very ill indeed.

He stood there for only a few minutes, and then he was gone out of their sight. The servant closed the window and pulled the curtain across it. The silence ended and the crowd began murmuring again. They were subdued, some shocked by what they had seen, but not many surprised. That much Marjorie gathered from the talk she could overhear. No one, it seemed, had believed in the good health of the King, no matter how often the bulletins from Westminster proclaimed it, no matter how much the councillors appeared cheerful and positive, or how much the churchmen claimed he was God's special favourite. They were right, the doomsayers were right.

170

There was nothing to be said. Any pretence that the King would recover was mere bravado. Stories of his returning health were lies. They knew it, all of London now knew it.

'Poor boy.'

'What will happen, Aunt?'

'God knows. We can only pray.'

Chapter 32

The King was dead. No one could cry *God save the King* for there was no other.

The city was silent, the markets and taverns closed, no one was working. Crowds gathered at St. Paul's. It was not true the King was dead, said some. It was not true, it was a trick of the French, or the Spanish. Why else were the guards at the Tower being reinforced? Why else were there warships sailing up and down at the mouth of the river? There would be war. Hadn't building work in the city ceased for weeks past while the carpenters worked on new battleships?

Be careful, said some. You know what happened to men who said the King was deadly ill. It was the pillory for them, and worse. So watch what you say. But those who had been to Greenwich and had seen the King at his window told what they had seen, and said there was no doubt. They had been looking at a dead man.

At each of the water conduits and on most corners, and everywhere where the streets were wide enough, stood groups of soldiers, armed. While they were out one day, Marjorie and her aunt saw one such group jostled by the crowd. They drew their swords and the crowd fell back. At any other time a soldier threatening a Londoner would have been overwhelmed, but people were subdued, uncertain.

'What are your instructions?' Lady Alice asked imperiously of the man in charge. Marjorie realised how unreal the situation had become, that Lady Alice should thus draw attention to herself in an incident in the street. But anxiety was making Lady Alice almost aggressive.

'We've been sent to keep the peace, my lady. In case there is rioting.'

A people less likely to riot could hardly be imagined. Lady Alice was known as the wife of a privy councillor and people gathered round her.

'Beg pardon, Ma'am,' said one, courteously enough but keeping his cap on. 'Can you tell us what is happening? Who is to be King now?'

'I don't know any more than you do.'

But that was the question they were all asking. Who? Princess Mary, people said, the old King's daughter. But this led to more uneasiness. England had only once had a woman as sovereign, and that was a long time ago. And hadn't that led to civil war? But who else was there? The last civil war, the cousins' war, when the crown was disputed between the houses of Lancaster and York was within the memory of the oldest there.

New rumours began. The Lord Mayor and the Aldermen of the City had been to Whitehall and made to swear an oath of loyalty. But to whom? None of them would speak of it, and they were all closed up in the Guildhall. A crowd gathered there, waiting for a proclamation. None came.

Now there was a new rumour. Lord Robert Dudley, the brother of the Protector, had been seen leaving London with his retinue, heading north-east. Gossip from his stables told that he had gone to fetch the Princess Mary back to London.

Sir Robert Bowes sent word that he would not be home that night. The next day Lady Alice said they could not go out wandering the streets and gawking and waiting for news like any common servant. Besides it was dangerous.

'Shall we send the servants instead, Aunt?' asked Marjorie.

They found that many of the servants had already slipped out of the house, on one excuse or another. And then they heard the sound of running steps in the streets round about. Even before the servant arrived to tell them what was happening Lady Alice had sent for her cloak and gloves.

'They say the new queen is sailing in her barge to the Tower!'

'Queen Mary? Here already?'

They pulled on their hoods and hurried out of the house. They made their way as briskly as they could, overtaken by people running towards the Tower. They approached as near as possible to the water's edge, wriggling through the crowds, in a way Marjorie would not have thought possible for one of her aunt's build. People made way for them, and they had a good view of the river. And there, sure enough, came the royal barge, glittering golden in the sunshine and flying the royal pennant. It pulled up at the water gate and the escort in the Duke of Northumberland's livery disembarked and stood to attention.

A tall man dressed in white and gold helped the slight figure of a small woman out of the barge onto the jetty. She was dressed in green velvet embroidered with gold. The French hood set well back on her head revealed red hair. Someone in the crowd raised a ragged cheer but had little encouragement and the sound died away. She was whisked out of sight into the Tower.

'But that's not the Princess Mary,' said Lady Alice in bewilderment.

But the men waiting at the water gate had knelt to her.

'Who is she?' the question surged round the crowd.

The Princess Mary had been at court as recently as last Christmas. She had processed through the streets to Whitehall Palace and many in the crowd had seen her then. This was not the Princess Mary.

'She's the King's cousin, the oldest of the Grey girls. She's Northumberland's new daughter-in-law. That was her husband with her,' said Lady Alice quietly to Marjorie.

'Is she going to support the new Queen? As lady-in-waiting?'

'She's not dressed,' said Lady Alice grimly. 'As a lady in waiting. Come, Marjorie, let's go home. There's nothing more to see here.'

But as they walked back home they heard the sound of guns from the Tower. Everyone stopped and held their breaths. Another thunder of guns and then all the bells of the city began to ring. And apart from that, still the restless silence, of a people waiting, not sure what was happening. A herald came out of the Lord Mayor's office and tacked a notice to the door of the Guildhall. The crowd surged forward to read it. There would be a proclamation at seven this evening.

In the continued absence of Sir Robert at Westminster, that evening Lady Alice and Marjorie went to the Guildhall. They joined the crowd and waited. At seven o'clock exactly, two trumpeters sounded and then a herald came out and read a proclamation.

The King was dead. Long live Queen Jane.

There was a sound from the crowd. A low growling, almost like an animal in pain, and then the silence again. The herald hastily retreated inside. The crowd continued to stand there, stunned and disbelieving.

One man began shouting. 'That is not the Queen. The true queen is Mary. Why do you accept this imposter?' He leapt up onto a bollard and shouted at the crowd. 'Don't accept this. Stand up to them! Stand up to the usurpers!' Two soldiers came forward and dragged him down and he was hustled away.

Her aunt became frightened then, and they went home. Sir Robert came soon after. He found them in the garden, for it was a warm evening, and dropped wearily onto a bench beside them. When he heard they had been out on the streets he said, 'I would not have allowed it, had I been here.'

'What will happen now?'

'God knows. It was the King's wish, you see, that his cousin be queen. He made a testament, a "devise for the succession" he called it. All the privy councillors had to sign it, and we were sworn to secrecy.'

'Even from me, Robert?'

'Even from God, I think. For it has overturned the old King's will. But it was what Edward wanted.'

'And what my lord Northumberland wanted,' said Lady Alice sharply. 'So now we know why he was in such a hurry to marry his son to Jane Grey. We thought it was because she was pregnant.'

'Hush, my dear.'

'Did everyone sign?'

'Almost everyone. Those who refused were invited to spend some time on their estates in the country. Archbishop Cranmer refused initially. But he's been promised the new religion will be protected and strengthened and all the old canon law abolished. He'll be more powerful than the Pope. He signed.'

They sat on in the growing darkness. Marjorie leaned back against the wall of the house, feeling the daytime warmth stored there. A servant came out of the house and signalled to Sir Robert, who half rose. But the servant was followed by Master Cecil who joined them, throwing aside his cloak. He was carrying a pistol in his belt. He settled down with a sigh. Lady Alice nodded to the servant, who brought out some welcome ale, cold from the buttery.

Cecil raised his glass. 'I am free,' he said. 'The King's death has freed me at last from that miserable court. I will have no more of it.'

He pulled a pamphlet from his pocket.

'This is already being distributed,' he said. 'It celebrates the sacrifice of Potter.'

'Who is Potter?'

'He made a scene today. Harangued the crowd.'

'He did. We were there.'

176

'He has had his ears cut off. He was lucky not to have his tongue cut out as well. This pamphlet urges Londoners to rise on behalf of the Princess Mary.'

'And will they?'

'No one knows where she is. When Robert Dudley reached Hunsden she had already gone. It may be she is planning to flee abroad.'

'Do you think she will?'

'She's still old Harry's daughter. She may have inherited something of his nature. Both her parents were stubborn people. If so, she will not flee.'

'Will there be civil war?' asked Lady Alice.

'God knows.'

'So what do you do now?'

'Keep the peace as best we can,' said Sir Robert.

'Personally,' said Cecil. 'I am going to join my wife in the country. Perhaps the Princess Elizabeth will find a place for me in her household. I have served her before. We will live quietly, and moulder happily with our books and memories.'

They sat on, unwilling to go in, and darkness fell on the city, and people waited.

For many days there was a subdued air in London. People began to go about their business normally. The taverns opened again. The carts still came in from the countryside in the morning filled with produce, but they brought with them rumours that some towns had disbelieved the news of King Edward's death, and when they had been convinced of that, had disbelieved the news of the proclamation of Queen Jane. Many believed they now had a Queen Mary.

Sir Robert returned each day from Westminster weary and sad. He and the council were doing their best to hold things together, but they still had to keep guards on the streets in London. Edward's body was being embalmed and would be brought upriver from Greenwich to lie in state in Westminster for the people to see, but not yet.

There came another night when he did not return home. He came in the evening of the following day.

'My dear,' he said. 'For the first time in my life I think that Master Cecil is right. It is better to live quietly in the country.'

'What has happened, Robert?'

'We have spent the last two days considering a letter received from the Princess Mary. She claims she has not been officially notified of the death of her brother. Nonsense of course. She ignores the fact we sent Robert Dudley to tell her, but she had fled before his coming. She now claims the crown of England by right of the will of her father. She offers to pardon all of us in the Privy Council for what we have done in proclaiming Jane Grey as Queen.'

He paused while the servant pulled off his boots and then went on.

'She will pardon us all so as to avoid the bloodshed which would ensue were there to be a civil war. Her words.'

There was a shocked silence. Marjorie could see the servants beginning to gather at the door to the kitchens, listening.

'But,' Marjorie said. 'Surely she is the true Queen? She is the sister of the king who has died and the daughter of the king that went before. Why should she not be queen?'

'That is what people will be asking. I could hear them as I came through the streets. They could call Jane Grey Queen, they can call her the Virgin Mary for all they want, but the Council cannot make her anything other than little Jane Grey. That is what people say. And that is the truth of it.'

'What will the Council do?'

'Play for time. We have sent a reply to say that we are astonished to receive her letter. She knows as everyone does that she has no claim, having been declared a bastard – we put that more politely of course – and that the Lady Jane has been proclaimed our sovereign queen. If she persists in her claim she will cause great grief and suffering to the subjects.'

'That was sent?'

'Yes. And the Council wanted to prepare a proclamation denouncing Mary's claim. But William Cecil refused to draft it. Point-blank refused in the face of Northumberland to pick up the quill. Sat there with his arms folded. I must say that caused more than a little astonishment.' He laughed. 'William Cecil has made up his mind.'

'It was brave of him.'

'It was courage verging on folly. In the end Northumberland wrote it himself, in a fury. But that was not his difficulties. It was agreed that my Lord Suffolk, Jane's her, should be sent to Norfolk to apprehend Mary and ng her back. So we adjourn for some food and rest, and n later we are told that little Jane, I beg her pardon, that Queen Jane had pleaded with her father not to go, and his wife was advising him that in his state of health it would be dangerous, so he is refusing to stir from his house. Evidently the danger of going to arrest Mary is greater than the danger of defying the great Duke.'

'So what is to happen?'

'My lord Northumberland is going himself. The Council agreed that his military training made him the best man for the job. Nay, we were more than eager to persuade him. He is preparing to go tomorrow, leaving, as he said, the Queen in the care of the Council, trusting implicitly in our fidelity to her.'

'Do the Council have any fidelity to her?'

'Many took the view that since we are all in it together we have to stick together. What is in their hearts I cannot say, but I think I will emulate the Duke of Suffolk, and suffer from an indisposition that keeps me at home.'

The next morning the drums of the Duke's muster sounded throughout London. Silent crowds lined the streets, mostly women and children and old, old men. The young men had the sense to stay well out of sight. The great Duke and his men marched away, laden with the cannon they had taken from the tower, six hundred men from the yeomen of the guard and many who had been soldiers under him before. He was considered a great leader in the field, and men who had fought under him would follow him anywhere. It looked a formidable fighting force.

They left behind them a silence as people thought about what was happening but gradually the city roused itself and went about its business.

The wives of the privy councillors found excuses and time to call on one another. If their husbands sent them to assess the mood of their fellows, they did not say. They learned that the Lord Mayor was organising a collection in the city for the customary present to the new sovereign, but the money was slow in coming, and besides, which sovereign was it to be given to? They learned that the goldsmiths at their assembly had advised all their members to try and remain aloof from any quarrel. They learned that once the Duke had left London the Lord Mayor had quietly ordered a watch to be kept at all the gates to prevent any more arms entering or leaving the city.

And then more rumours circulated that Edward was not dead after all. No one except those closest to him had seen a body, they said, and who was to say whether the body which would be laid in state was his? It was sealed within a coffin. Who was to say there was even a body there? Then there were the rumours that the Duke of Northumberland had had Edward poisoned so as to put his own son on the throne.

All this news Sarie brought excitedly to Marjorie. Lady Alice expressed the very mildest of reproofs that a maid should not be wandering about the streets gossiping.

The carters bringing food in to the city brought with them stories that towns outside London were proclaiming for Queen Mary. In some places the Duke's messengers were being harassed and run out of town for attempting to proclaim Queen Jane. People were flocking to Mary's cause.

Sir Robert had been forced to give up any pretence of an indisposition. The Privy Council were now meeting in the Tower, and his family had not seen him for some days. William Cecil came to dine again, and told them that the councillors were quarrelling amongst themselves. There were factions in the council who were breaking away and obviously wished to support Mary.

'I think I will go abroad,' he said. 'The shires are not far enough for safety.'

'What, William, flee?'

'Northumberland's last card,' said Cecil, 'Is the argument that the Princess Mary is a devout Catholic and if she were queen we would all be bowing the knee to Rome again. I could not do that.'

'Would you not stay and fight and die for your beliefs, Master Cecil?' asked Marjorie.

He looked at her seriously and considered.

'We talked about this before,' he said. 'No, I would not die for my beliefs, but I would live very uncomfortably.'

And so for a brief moment he made them laugh, but it was hard to tell how serious he was about going abroad.

The next day the navy mutinied. The ships ordered to arrest Mary should she attempt to flee abroad refused to leave port. The captains and crew proclaimed for Mary and refused to follow orders from anyone else. Perhaps it was then that everyone knew Northumberland and his son and Queen Jane had lost.

Marjorie heard a wail from her aunt's room and hurried to her. Lady Alice had a note in her hand. 'He's a prisoner! My husband has been arrested.'

Marjorie seized the note from her and read it. 'No, Aunt. Please, Aunt. It is not as bad as that. Please do listen. He's not been arrested. It's all of the Privy Council. They're all still in the Tower.'

She read it again. Queen Jane's father, Lord Suffolk, was refusing to allow the Council to leave the Tower. The gates had been locked and Queen Jane had the keys.

'Don't worry, Aunt. Queen Jane cannot hold the Tower. She does not have an army. She'll have to give up the keys and let them go.'

And all this time Marjorie had no word from John Knox, who was somewhere in the country.

Chapter 33

I am back in London.

That was all the note said, but it was enough.

Without asking her aunt's permission, Marjorie slipped out of the house with Sarie. Lady Alice was too distracted with anxiety about her husband to notice. The streets were still quiet. Here and there groups of women were gathered, waiting to see what would happen. They fell silent as the two girls passed.

'I'm scared, Miss,' said Sarie.

'Don't be.'

'I wish we could go home. Back to our own country.'

Suddenly Marjorie felt an overwhelming longing to be back in the north, away from these dirty stinking streets with dark houses and ugly mean people pressing on all sides, and all the anger and fear. She felt such a desire for the high moors and the sighing wind, with nothing above her but God's sky, that she had to stop, weak at the knees.

John's landlady let them in and Marjorie ran up the stairs. It was no time for coyness or pretence. She went into his arms. They kissed and murmured incoherently and she cried a bit, and kissed away the moistness in his eyes too.

'What's to happen, John?'

Before he could answer they heard a commotion in the street. Sarie came bounding up the stairs. 'Miss, miss, the Lord Mayor. They say he's going to make a speech.'

'It's of no interest,' said John, still holding Marjorie in his arms.

She shook herself free of him. 'No, John, we'll have to see. If it is about the Princess Mary, we should know about it.'

The three of them joined the crowd surging towards the Guildhall. The Lord Mayor appeared on his balcony, with

183

several aldermen beside him, and some of the nobility. The Lord Mayor raised his arms to call for silence and the crowd became still, expectant. John had one arm round Marjorie to protect her from the press of the crowd and his other arm round Sarie. They clung close to him.

The Lord Mayor signalled to his herald, who raised his trumpet to his lips and blew three loud slow blasts. In a voice that echoed round and round from the surrounding buildings the Lord Mayor of London proclaimed the Princess Mary to be Queen of England.

There was a huge roar and much tossing of caps in the air. The Earl of Pembroke threw gold coins into the crowd and there was a great scrabbling for them, and one woman had her arm broken and had to be carried away, screaming and laughing alternately, but still biting hard on a coin in her mouth. As some pressed forward, the people at the front began to squeeze their way back through the crowd. People were running through the streets crying 'Long live Queen Mary.' Many people stood quietly, for had they not been ordered to cry 'Long live Queen Jane' no more than ten days ago, and been punished for refusing?

'Two Queens?'

'Do two Queens equal one King?'

John and the two women were pulled by the crowds to St. Paul's. It seemed to be the natural place for the Londoners to gather. To their astonishment they saw the Bishop of London leading a procession of the nobility, a shuffling, ragged kind of procession, into the cathedral.

'He hasn't wasted any time,' said John.

People crowded in behind, and those that couldn't get into the cathedral settled in the precincts and the graveyard. From the open doors came the voice of the Bishop.

'Surely not,' groaned John.

The Bishop was saying a full mass. He said a full mass such as had not been heard for years and the crowd knelt and crossed themselves and murmured the responses as if

184

they had never known how to do otherwise. John and Marjorie stood at a distance, and heard the chanting Latin echoing through all the streets round about.

'It has been all for nothing,' said John. He stood there, dazed. 'All for nothing.'

'Come away,' said Marjorie. He looked down at her, and there was anguish in his eyes. 'Come,' she said gently.

They walked away, Sarie clinging close to Marjorie's heels. At the New Gate the guard recognised John and let them out. In the fields, all was quiet and the air was scented with the roses growing thickly on the bankings.

'She has swept all before her. This is a sad day for England.'

'It was to be expected,' she answered. 'She has it by right of blood.'

'You English are a sentimental nation, Marjorie.'

'No, we're not,' muttered Sarie.

'It's well known you cheerfully break hearts, Miss. But no matter if Mary was the devil's wife herself, she would be made queen because she is old Harry's daughter. They'll be sorry.'

All day the celebrations continued. The weather was warm and as the long July day ended and darkness came, fires were lit all along both banks of the river and everywhere there was the smell of roasting meat. The air was full of the sound of fiddles and drums, and people danced, cups of wine and ale spilling.

The bells of the city were still pealing. They had been ringing all day but now the sound was discordant, as if the bellringers were drunk, or collapsing from exhaustion. The printers' shops were brightly lit as they worked all night turning out leaflets with the words of the Lord Mayor's proclamation, and these were eagerly seized and passed, still damp, from hand to hand.

John and Marjorie returned reluctantly to the city and walked slowly along, watching. Sarie had disappeared,

185

absorbed somewhere into the general celebrations. Marjorie ceased to care whether her aunt would wonder where she was. For all she knew her uncle was in the Tower under arrest for supporting Queen Jane. More likely the Council were making preparations to welcome the new Queen and swear loyalty to her, and Lady Alice would be already worrying about her gown for the coronation.

'What will become of the child Queen Jane?' she wondered, but John had his mind on other things. They paused to watch some shrieking drunken people splashing in the shallow waters of the Thames. All along both banks of the river to where it curved out of sight there were bonfires, and the sounds of laughing and singing, and an occasional cry of anger as a drunken quarrel arose. The river was filled with boats that found the way practically impassable there were so many of them. As they watched, a wherry was tipped over by some nobleman's barge pushing its way upstream. The wherryman waded ashore, shaking his fist and shouting curses at the barge.

'Come,' said John. 'It's time you went home.' They turned up into the city.

'I don't want to go home just yet,' she said. 'Can we go to your room?'

All was quiet at the pend entrance to his lodgings. He called to his landlady. There was no answer. 'Gone to join in the fun.'

They climbed the stair. The whole building was deserted. In his room John struck his flint and lit a candle. Together they leaned out of the window and listened to the distant sounds of revelry. The room was warm, for it faced south and the sun had been hot all day.

'John,' she said as he opened the cupboard to look for ale and cups. 'Do you still have the half gold piece which you cut up for our handfasting day?'

'Yes of course. Shall I show you? Do you think in all my travels I failed to keep it safe?'

186

He opened the small travelling kist that went everywhere with him. Burrowing deep he pulled out a leather pouch and tipped into his hand the half gold piece. He laid it on the desk. She dug into her pocket and pulled out her own half coin. Without looking at him she laid it on the desk, sliding it forward so that the two broken edges met and fitted into one another.

'Lassie, what are you saying?'

'I'm saying we've waited long enough.'

He put his hand under her chin and turned her face up to look into his.

'The world has gone mad,' she said. 'No one knows what tomorrow will bring.'

'On our betrothal day John Willock asked us both if we were sure,' said John. 'I ask it again now.'

'And I asked you the same question then.'

'And my answer now is the same as my answer then. Never more sure.'

She reached up and stroked his cheek. 'We've waited long enough,' she repeated.

Afterwards he saw her safely back to her uncle's house. It too was almost deserted and no one remarked on her late return. She crept up to bed and lay there, exultant. There had been no mistake. They would do very well together.

*

The next day was quieter. Many people were sleeping off their drunkenness. Gradually and slowly as the days passed the city resumed its business, while waiting tensely to see what would happen next. A few days later came the return of the Duke of Northumberland, under arrest with his friends. They rode through the streets, prisoners, on their way to the Tower where his son and daughter-in-law were held. Stones were thrown. The Duke himself was splattered with mud and rode along with his face grim and expressionless.

Gilbert Potter who had been mutilated by having his ears cut off for crying against Queen Jane, was raised shoulder high and carried along beside the Duke, shouting insults at him, while the crowd roared with laughter. But the laughter had to stop sometime, for people had to go on living their lives, and there were new uncertainties.

Sir Robert came home badly shaken by his sojourn in the Tower. Feeling helpless was a new experience for him. The Privy Council had grovelled and been pardoned for their support of Queen Jane, but most of them were dismissed nonetheless. He resigned his position as Master of the Rolls, whether under pressure or not Marjorie did not know.

It was only a few days later, in early August, that Mary made her state entry into London. Sir Robert and his wife and niece were guests of a family with a window overlooking the entry route so they saw her in all her proud glory.

The Princess had, it was said, three thousand of her followers with her. They were welcomed at the gates of the city by the Lord Mayor and all the city dignitaries. She wore a deep purple gown which shone with jewels and pearls, and her horse was caparisoned in shimmering gold. The pretty young Princess Elizabeth was beside her, dressed all in white, and they were followed by hundreds of ladies and gentlemen all in red and green velvet. The crowds went wild. There had not been such a sight or such an occasion for more than twenty years.

Mary processed through streets decorated with banners and streamers, halted regularly by tableaux where young girls made pretty speeches. It was astonishing, thought Marjorie, that London could produce all this in such a short time, as if it was something they did every week, instead of once or twice in every reign. At the Tower of London the Princess forgave many who knelt to beg her pardon.

188

There was official banqueting all over the city that night and for days afterwards. The great conduit in Cheapside was filled with wine by the city fathers, and free meat was given out. There was considerable drunkenness but little fighting. The mood was joyful and the reason for that was clear to anyone who cared to listen to the talk of the citizens. The illness and death of the King had created uncertainty, uneasiness. Now there was a strong hand once more, a Tudor. Now, it didn't seem to matter that she was a woman, for she was clearly her father's daughter, and for Londoners King Henry had been a popular king. Moreover the Queen had been at the head of an army, and while it had not actually fought a battle, it had been ready. In that respect at least she was all a monarch should be.

Three weeks later the Duke of Northumberland was executed by beheading in the Tower. In his speech on the scaffold he claimed to die a good Catholic.

'It was all for nothing then,' said John Knox. 'If even the man who leads the country does not believe in what he is doing, we all stand on shifting sands. One day there is firm ground where you may be sure of your footing, the next day it becomes a treacherous sandbar and you find yourself sucked under the waves.'

'What else could the Duke say? He leaves a family at the mercy of the Queen.'

'Did it sit so lightly? The new truth? That it can be denied without a fight?'

'Would you risk the lives of the people you love for your beliefs?' Marjorie asked him.

'Many die for their faiths.'

'It was not for his faith that he died. He died because he over-reached himself in his lust for power. Were his family to die too?'

Some of the preachers spoke out. They warned that there would once more be popery in the land. Fights broke out in churches between supporters of the old and supporters of the new. John Knox's voice was one of the loudest. He had stones thrown at him.

Bands of apprentices roamed the city, unhindered, in search of Protestant preachers. Young men who could have barely any memory of the old religion, were embracing it with fervour, thinking they were rebelling, because it was contrary to what they had been taught. John, now a familiar figure in the city, was an early and easy target. Marjorie found him one day in his lodgings ruefully trying to wash egg stains from his shirt.

'And worse, I think,' he said, sniffing it and plunging it once more into the basin of water.

'Let me,' she said and took it from him. He gave it up willingly, and paced up and down the small room as Marjorie rubbed and scrubbed at the linen.

He was feverish almost with anxiety and anger.

'They'll be sorry,' he said. 'They don't realise. Whatever the Queen says, however much she may proclaim freedom of religion, she is in thrall to the old Church and the Bishop of Rome. They will be vicious in their revenge.'

The attacks, unchallenged by authority, showed signs of becoming more violent when one preacher was discovered battered to death in the street. Knox moved into the house of the London merchant John Locke for his own safety. Marjorie had never met John Locke or his wife Anne, but they had become good friends to John Knox. They were convinced by the new learning, and were staunch Protestants. There were many such in London, among the ambitious shrewd merchants of the City, merchants who were beginning to open up trade to the New World, where the writ of Rome ran faintest. John spoke often of them. They were kind to him and he was absorbed into their circle. But despite the prosperity they brought to London the merchants' situation was becoming difficult.

It was not long before the new Privy Council passed a law restoring the full mass. The Bishop of London was delighted, and those bishops who had only reluctantly conformed under King Edward now returned readily to the old ways. The priest once more turned his back on the congregation and spoke Latin to God. Bishop Tunstall was released from the Tower.

Protestant preachers who claimed the Pope, the Antichrist, was once more among them lost their licence to preach. The Queen banned the use of the words 'heretic' and 'papist'. Anyone saying or, worse, publishing those words would be punished.

One day a dagger was thrown at the preacher at Paul's Cross. After that, the Bishop of London, surrounded by soldiers, preached there. He ordered that all would return to the old ways and the old faith. The Scriptures would be in Hebrew and Latin as before, and the English bible, that Great Bible of old King Henry, a copy of which stood in every church, was to be destroyed. He doubted if it was accurate anyway. Persons found with any English translation would be punished.

Marjorie was in the crowd listening to the sermon with her aunt, and she saw the grim faces of the booksellers and stationers who made their living in the shadow of St. Paul's. Perhaps they were mentally calculating the numbers of English bibles they had in their storerooms.

*

'I want to see Sir Robert.'

The voice that could fill a great abbey echoed through the house.

'No. It's his orders,' said the steward, a burly man who had been one of Sir Robert's soldiers in those distant days of the border wars. Beside him John looked slight and fragile.

'I'll stay here till I can speak to him.'

'You can say nothing he wants to hear.' The man stood there, arms folded, implacable.

191

John looked up and saw Marjorie hastening down the stairs. 'Marjorie, can you make your uncle see me?'

'Miss, he's given orders that Master Knox is not to be admitted,' said the steward, but his expression softened. The servants had a weakness for a romantic story, and Sarie had spread the word amongst them that John and Marjorie were a couple who loved each other but were thwarted by family opposition.

'Wait,' she said, and ran back upstairs. She found her uncle in his library.

'Please, Uncle, will you not see Master Knox?'

He scowled at her.

'I will not,' he said. 'He's one of Northumberland's men.'

She gasped. 'Northumberland's men? Oh, but he's not, Uncle. You know that. He disobeyed and disobeyed my lord Northumberland and called him names and displeased him. How can you say he's Northumberland's man?'

'Did not Northumberland employ him to preach against the Catholics? Did he not do that in obedience to the Duke? Everywhere he went he cried out against popery. He calls the Bishop of Rome the Antichrist, does he not? What else but in obedience to the Duke, to rouse up feeling against her that is now Queen?'

'It is his own beliefs.'

'And those beliefs will be the death of him.'

'Will you not see him?'

'No.'

She went slowly downstairs. 'John, it's no use. He won't see you. He's frightened, John.'

He looked round. For a moment she wondered whether he was going to force his way past the steward, but the moment passed, for Knox was not a violent man. His weapons were words, not muscle, and they were of no use here.

She noticed how shaggy his eyebrows were, and his beard was uncombed. He had grown somewhat wild in his

192

looks. Her uncle was not the only one disorientated and at a loss. Her heart ached for him.

'Go, John,' she said quietly. 'There will be a better time.'

'Don't you see? The Queen will soon forbid priests to marry. We will lose our chance.'

She could only shake her head helplessly.

'Marjorie, come away with me.'

'What?'

'Come. Come with me. Pack your shawl, whatever you need. Leave here.'

'Leave everything?'

'We soon may have to.'

'John...' She was breathless. To be away from here, and all this distress and uncertainty, to be settled with John somewhere.

'Where would we go?'

'Anywhere. We'll leave England.'

They crouched there in the corner of the hall out of earshot of the servants. She felt his urgency and need, and her own. But then her aunt came running down the stairs and was upon them. She took Marjorie's forearm in a tight grip.

'Go,' she said to Knox. 'You are not wanted here.'

He looked into Marjorie's eyes, a last pleading look, and straightened up.

'Yes,' whispered Marjorie. 'Yes. But go now.'

He walked out, and the big door was slammed behind him.

Chapter 34

'I no longer want to be responsible for you,' Marjorie's uncle told her.

'I'll be travelling north shortly.' He paused, and there was something like relief in his expression. 'Queen Mary has given me a commission to assess the defences along the border, as I have done in the past.'

He was being offered the road back into favour, using his expertise and knowledge of the border, responsibilities he had now exercised under two previous sovereigns. But had it come too late? His step was heavy and his movements weary. Marjorie wondered whether he still had the stamina to travel the distances on horseback. She forced herself to concentrate on what he was saying.

'You'll travel north with me. I'll return you to your father.'

It was late October when they were finally ready to leave. They left behind a much subdued London. There had been a brief amnesty for Protestants, and most took the easy way out and reverted to the old religion. Many foreigners who had come to England seeking refuge from persecution in France and Spain, now gathered up their possessions once more and left. When the amnesty expired, no one had any illusion that the Queen would continue to be easy on Protestants.

She was going to marry the Spanish King. Everyone knew what else came from Spain. The Inquisition. They had all heard the terrible stories. Nurses frightened their young charges into good behaviour with threats of it. Those who had particular reason to fear it waited with a sense of horror for it to come to England.

Marjorie paced her room, her mind in agony. What would John do? Renounce his religion he would not. She had no doubt about that. But he was too well known, and had too many followers to be ignored.

'He is as good as dead,' was her aunt's opinion.

Marjorie was confined to the house, but Sarie, who had found herself a beau among the apprentices in Master Locke's business, brought word that John was in Kent, preaching. His friends were fearful of his arrest at any moment.

Quickly Marjorie wrote a note and gave it to Sarie to pass to Anne Locke in the hope that it would reach John. *Leave England,* the note said. *Go while there is still time.* She received a reply from him within the week.

I will try and come for you. I willingly jeopardy my life for the deliverance of my own dear flesh and blood. I will come for you. Wait for me, my beloved. The note was unsigned.

Sir Robert Bowes' entourage made its way northwards in slow stages. Winter was setting in and the going was wet and unpleasant. They travelled mostly in silence, for her uncle had forbidden his men to speak to the women, and the men-at-arms who rode beside Marjorie were changed frequently in case there was a temptation to familiarity. She wrapped herself in her furs and closed off her mind to the present discomfort, dreaming of happier days in the past. Numb with the physical misery, she gave no thought to the future.

Their lodgings on the road were usually the houses of the nobility or of gentlemen, for the authority of the Queen opened all doors to them. Occasionally there was no great house and they made their beds as best they could in a wayside inn. Wherever they stayed, Marjorie and Sarie would be shown to a chamber and locked in, their food brought to them, prevented from communication with anyone. She was no better than a prisoner.

Sarie wept as they talked in the quiet of their bedroom prison, while Marjorie rubbed soothing ointment into the girl's toes and bandaged them up. She suffered dreadfully from chilblains and the tips of her fingers were cracked and bleeding. She hated the cold and was hating this journey. Marjorie felt badly about bringing her, but when she said this the girl wept more. They clung to one another, closer than sisters.

But no security is ever truly secure. Sarie was riding pillion behind a different servant each day, with orders from Sir Robert that they must not speak. But there were a limited number of men, and by turns she found herself on the same horse as one who had made a particular favourite of her back in London. This of course was unknown to Sir Robert and his wife, for there were so many servants in that house, as befitted the household of a privy councillor, that particular friendships passed unnoticed.

So Sir Robert had unwittingly brought along one who had been considering Sarie for a wife, had she had a mind to settle. And inevitably from time to time on the road they found themselves on the same mount. When the horses were strung out over a rough road and a bleak wind was blowing loudly enough to smother all sound, he was able to tell Sarie bits of news in snatches of whispered conversation.

Thus they learned that John's licence to preach had been revoked and the authorities were looking for him. He was believed to be travelling north secretly, by night. He had turned up in various places, preaching to eager audiences. So far no one had betrayed him. By the time the authorities heard about it he had moved on.

Sarie told her that one of the men had heard about the arrest of a messenger, believed to be John Knox's man, trying to get letters through to Marjorie. If this was true, her uncle said nothing to her about it.

At last they came to Alnwick, to Jonathan and Philippa.

Philippa greeted her sister with squeals of delight, and rushed her to the nursery. Her son was now an active imperious toddler, and she was with child again. Her husband set himself to charm Sir Robert. Oblivious to the nuances of the ebb and flow of power among the Queen's servants he thought still to use family connections to progress his ambitions. Sir Robert listened silently.

They stayed there two nights, for everyone was weary and needed a rest. Since they were family, her uncle could hardly demand that Marjorie be kept under lock and key, so for once she was able to relax.

Philippa chattered inconsequentially to Marjorie while the men were in the room. What were the fashions in London? What caps were being worn? What shape of sleeves? Was Queen Mary pretty? The Princess Elizabeth must be well grown. Was she pretty? Prettier than her sister? But that night, when her uncle had retired to his chamber, they were at last alone with Jonathan. He began on the subject of Knox.

'It is as well the friendship between you came to nothing.'

'Yes, Brother.'

'It would have meant great trouble for our family.'

'He was here, you know,' said Philippa.

'Here?'

'We gave him shelter for one night.'

'More than that we could not,' her husband took up the story. 'He is a danger to everyone who protects him. I had a long talk with him, Marjorie. I reminded him that you are safe as long as you are with your family. Our name is protection enough. He is a heretic and a traitor. You would suffer along with him.'

'He told us,' blurted out Philippa. 'He told us you wanted to marry.'

'For your own good you have to give up this crazy notion,' said Jonathan.

'It's not crazy. We would be safe abroad.'

'Would he exile you from your family, from those who can protect you? What kind of life could he offer you, a vagabond life, wandering from town to town? What kind of

197

living could he make, now that he has lost his position at court?'

Marjorie said nothing, but sat staring at her hands. She felt tears pricking at her eyelids, tears of weariness and anger and despair. She willed herself not to cry. She could imagine the effect of such words on John. She could imagine the agony of mind he would be in, wanting her and at the same time acknowledging that he was putting her in danger. How dare these people make decisions for her! How dare they interfere!

'Where is he now?'

'He told us that his brother's ship is leaving shortly for the continent. He intends to be on it. It may have gone by now. He left a letter for you.'

Her sister lifted out some of her sewing threads from her box and found the letter.

'Wasn't that a clever place to hide it,' she said. 'What man would think of looking for it there?' Jonathan gave a snort. No one would be searching his house. But if his wife chose to indulge in womanly intrigue, he would not stop her.

Greetings. This friend is about to take ship for Antwerp. Greetings, too, to your gracious mother. He wishes you well in the future. That was all.

Jonathan said, 'That's that then.'

As soon as the door closed behind him Philippa said, 'That's the one Jonathan saw.'

'There's another?'

Philippa dug deeper into her sewing basket and lifted out an unfinished baby gown. Folded inside it was another paper, which she handed to Marjorie. It was much longer than the other.

He poured out his heart in love for her, frantic that he might never see her again. *I have been a fugitive in my own country and a fugitive in England, but the happiest time I ever had was in England with you and the country is dearer to me than my*

198

*own because you are there.   But if I stay here will be only death
ahead and what is more it will place you in gravest DANGER.
You are safe in the protection of your family but married to me you
would be in danger too so I will leave England for good.   I am a
faint-hearted and feeble soldier, and in truth it is not from fear of
death that I flee. Have mercy on me, O Lord, for I am weak.   Since
it is uncertain we shall ever meet again in this corporeal world I
write as though I should take from you my last goodnight on earth.
Farewell my dearest love.*

Marjorie knelt and held both letters in the flames until
they caught. She dropped them into the heart of the fire and
watched them burn.

Chapter 35

She was shocked at her father's appearance.

Richard Bowes, who had always been lean, was almost skeletal. His scalp, which he had always kept shaved, was now bald and encrusted with pustules. His face was sunken, cheeks hollow in a grey skin.

'He is not well,' said her mother. 'He says he is, but he has pains in his chest.'

Marjorie cried then, her face buried in her mother's shoulder. She could not say for whom she cried. She wept for her father and mother and herself and John. She wept for loss. Her world had fallen apart. She was put to bed and slept for nearly twenty four hours, waking in the dusk of the next day to find her mother sitting by her bed, her hands on her lap and her eyes closed.

Her sister Isabella, who had been living at Norham this last while as companion to their mother, put her head round the door when she heard their voices. She was nearly sixteen now and well grown. She looked with awe at Marjorie and barely spoke, shy of the big sister who had lived such a sophisticated life in far-off London.

'I was not at court.' In vain Marjorie tried to persuade the timid girl that she was still the same Marjorie. But she was not the same girl who had left Aske all those years ago. London had hardened her.

Sir Robert ordered the defences at Norham to be strengthened and the rest of that winter passed in a constant flurry of noise and hammering, with carts of stones trundling past, stones to raise the battlements even further, and build extra walls. Queen Mary had married her Spaniard King, and there was talk of war with France. And war with France meant war with Scotland.

The fog sat heavy over the land and everyone coughed and choked on the stone dust, for the high cleansing winds that Marjorie had dreamed of were stilled. The Bishop's quarters were closed up and given over to mice and bats. The great keep lay silent and empty, no longer welcoming guests, for none had reason to come here.

A new priest, one thankful to cast off the new ways and revert to the old, had been appointed to the Berwick garrison. He came once a week to Norham to hold a mass in the garrison chapel, and the family were obliged to attend.

The altar was back in place and draped with an embroidered cloth. It was threadbare and was probably the one that had been in use in the days of King Henry. For who would sew another? Her mother would not and there was no one else in the castle to do it. The biggest change was that the walls were half covered with paintings. Marjorie peered at them. They were images of the Virgin Mary and the Christ Child. They were in muddy colours and fairly crude in places, but there was some skill in the rendering of hills and trees in the background.

'It's Cuthbert, miss,' said a voice behind her and she turned to see the blacksmith, dressed in his Sunday tunic for the mass.

'My brother Cuthbert. It was him was given the job of whitewashing out the old pictures, and he remembered what they looked like so he's painting them back in.'

'Do you like them?'

'Oh yes, Miss. It's like coming home, isn't it? To see everything like it was before.'

Her mother sat through each mass with clenched fists. When they had to kneel at the elevation of the host she excused herself on the grounds of painful knees, and no one could argue.

'John taught us that it is an abomination,' she reminded Marjorie. 'What a comfort he has been to me. Such a dear, dear man.'

201

She went into the kist in her bedroom and pulled out a bundle of letters.

'See Marjorie. See how often he has written to me. He is a loving friend.'

'I did not know he was writing to you.'

'All the time he has been in London. Every week.' She handed them to Marjorie. 'You can read them. They will be a comfort to you too.'

Marjorie refused to take them. 'I do not want to read your private correspondence. You should not have kept them. Don't you understand? John is outlawed. If you were found with these there would be trouble.'

'I cannot part with them. I would defend them to the death.'

'Oh mother. No one is going to ask for your death.'

Not yours, she thought. Not yours.

She did not care. She did not care whether she knelt to pray or not. She did not care if the words she intoned without giving them much thought were in Latin or English. Men were dying in defence of one or the other, but that was the foolishness of men. They were only words. But she did not say any of these things. Her mother, forced to attend the mass, was once more in torment for her immortal soul and the best service Marjorie could render her was to keep her thoughts to herself and her tongue repeating the smooth words her mother needed to hear.

For didn't John Knox himself write regularly to his congregation at Berwick, urging them to hold fast to the truth? Obey your consciences, but obey the law. God will understand if under pressure you have the appearance of conforming. There were many in Berwick who could say that it was all very well for him, safe in Geneva, to urge them to obey their consciences, but he was not the one who risked jail. Older heads said what could he do? There was no future in being a martyr.

The now forbidden English bible had disappeared, burned on pyres in town squares, but many were hidden away in doocots and thatch to await better times, or to be eaten by rats.

John Knox was in Geneva, he was in Dieppe. He was back in Geneva. He was called to minister to the hundreds of Protestants who had fled England and settled in Frankfurt. There were quarrels. The old argument, apparently, over using Archbishop Cranmer's prayer book or not. Some said yes, he said no.

He was back in Geneva. He was there, he said in one of his letters, to consult with Master Calvin on questions that were troubling him. Whatever Master Calvin said to him, he remained troubled. His letters to Marjorie – which came safely now, delivered to the hand of his brother's captain in Dieppe, and brought to the castle with the delivery of fish – were full of his sadness and love, but between the lines she could see the struggle he was going through. He was alone in a strange land, without purpose, without money, without any hope for the future.

People were good to him, he wrote. He had left England in a hurry and did not claim the last instalment of his stipend as a royal chaplain. *The Queen owes me £40 but I thought if I claimed it she would offer me lodging in the Tower, so better I be homeless and poor, what do you think my Marjorie?*

He was being well looked after among English friends. *And you would not know your man, Marjorie, grown fat on pies because he dare not offend the good wives of the town.*

Letters. Her life was whiled away with letters. Letters do not keep a woman warm in bed. Letters do not make babies. And she knew, because she had seen it here in Berwick and again in London, women liked John, and he liked the company of women. One day he would meet someone, someone perhaps who reminded him of Marjorie, and soon after that there would be a letter that told her John Knox was married.

But still she waited.

*

Word came from friends in London that King Edward's Protestant bishops had all been arraigned and tried by an ecclesiastical court and found guilty. The Queen was asking Parliament what should be done with them. What were they to say? They had lost the argument over her marriage. They wanted her to marry an Englishmen and she had married a Spaniard. Were they going to give her more advice she did not want?

She wanted the bishops to burn, and burn they did, Archbishop Cranmer among them, before a silent crowd beside Balliol College in Oxford.

Marjorie knew that by the time they heard that at Norham, Knox would also have heard it at Geneva. She knew he would feel only sorrow. He and Cranmer had had their quarrels, but it had all been procedural, not profound; their foe had been the same - Rome.

Word came too that the Lady Jane Grey, the child used as a pawn in the power politics of her family, had died, beheaded on Tower green. Marjorie remembered the small, thin girl she had seen at the Water Gate and grieved for her, and wondered at the vindictiveness of Queen Mary.

There was also cause for sadness closer to home. Soon after his return home to London Sir Robert Bowes had taken to his bed. The winter travelling and hard work, and the excessive efforts to ingratiate himself into favour with the Queen had been too much for him. The news of his death came to them, and plunged them into mourning.

It changed many things.

'We are leaving Norham.'

Her weary father seemed to have much of the life drained out of him as he told them this. Marjorie was so taken up in her own misery that she had not paid much attention to him.

204

He had grown old in the service of his sovereigns but had won little glory or fame. The battles in which he had fought, and in one case been taken prisoner and ransomed, were remembered as minor skirmishes of not much consequence. He had done his duty and now that duty was being taken from him.

'Where are we to go, Sir?' Marjorie asked.

'Back to Aske.'

There was a breath indrawn beside her, and she turned to see her sister Isabella in tears. 'I will be so happy to go home,' the girl sobbed.

Her father looked at her grimly and left the room.

*

'I have sent a message to him,' said Elizabeth.

'What message? To whom?'

She smiled. 'To John. Now that your uncle is dead there cannot be any objection to your marriage. Your father never disliked him the way Robert did.'

'What have you done, Mother?'

'I have asked John to come back.'

Marjorie screamed at her then. 'Mother, John cannot come here. If he sets foot on English soil he will be arrested. It is dangerous for him. And for any who help him. Would you have his brother and his friends in trouble? Mother, you should not have done that.'

'He will come.'

'He won't. He's not that stupid.'

Chapter 36

They were packing to leave Norham.

The work fell to Isabella and Marjorie, for her mother, pacing round the room, from the window embrasure to the fireplace, to the dresser where she stood and fingered the plate ranged there, then round and round again, seemed to have no interest. Marjorie, folding clothes and linen and packing them with sweet herbs, watched her and worried.

Outside the light shimmered in the steady rain and the distant hills were shrouded in mist, which darkened and lightened and drifted and parted, giving a glimpse now and then of the moorland. Beyond the moors lay the sea and beyond the sea, John was working. As soon as her mother told her she had written to him, Marjorie sent another message. *Do not come. It is too dangerous.*

'I will not destroy his letters,' said her mother. 'If they should fall into the hands of my enemies I will die a martyr.'

'Mother, you have no enemies. And the Queen does not burn women.'

This was perhaps not true. Disturbing reports had come from the south that there were indeed some women who had gone to the stake for refusing to recant their beliefs. But no woman of quality had died. Perhaps such as there were had been shut up in isolated manor houses in the country, hidden by their frightened menfolk.

Her father only lingered briefly with them for meals, for he had much to do to prepare the castle for handing over to his successor. The men of the garrison were also packing up, for they were men under his commission. The new captain, whoever he was, would bring his own men.

Sarie, working beside Marjorie and Isabella, her eyes red with tears, would not be going south with them. To her own surprise, she learned her sweetheart at Norham had stayed loyal to her, so she had decided to settle to her fate as a wife and mother. Her soldier would soon be a soldier no longer and would return to his father's farm, taking Sarie with him as his bride.

Messengers travelled constantly between the castle and London, Berwick, York and Newcastle. But from John there was nothing. Marjorie began to watch the road in case he appeared. She was frantic that he might come in defiance of the authorities, against all common sense. If he did there was only so much protection might be afforded him by his friends in Berwick, for every day the messengers brought rumours that the Queen was behaving more and more harshly towards avowed Protestants, and the fires of Smithfield were burning night and day.

One of the windows of their living quarters above the gatehouse overlooked the village of Norham. This small cluster of dwellings was settled by people who serviced the castle and valued the protection it offered in this land where murderous reivers in pursuit of this vendetta or that were always a danger.

Marjorie, prowling round checking that every one of her books was packed away, looked out and caught a glimpse of a figure standing in the doorway of the nearest cottage. She caught her breath and her heart gave a lurch, but when she looked again the figure had gone. She put on her cloak and hurried out.

'Who was here?' she asked. 'Was someone here?'

But the people looked at her vaguely and there was much headshaking and denying. There had been no one there, no stranger, no visitors. No, no one they knew from the past. Courteous but indifferent, they turned away. Except for one child, snotty-nosed and mucky, who followed her shyly almost to the gate of the castle. He opened his clenched fist and showed her some sticky dates and then pulled from somewhere in his clothing a note.

Could Marjorie come and see Mistress Ellen Knox and make her farewells? Marjorie sought out her mother.

'May I go? She has been kind to us.'

Elizabeth was indifferent. 'Go, go. Say my farewells for me, too.'

At the harbour Marjorie dismissed her escort to the inn to rest the horses and enjoy some ale.

She had grown close to Ellen Knox in the last few months. Ellen was still in awe of the Captain's lady, but treated Marjorie as a sister, occasionally indulging in an air of unspoken intrigue, for like many sensible practical women, she had a sentimental streak, and sometimes treated Marjorie as a lovelorn maiden, though Marjorie laughed at her for this. It was Ellen who enclosed the letters to John with the documents which were going overseas on her husband's ships, and made sure his messages to Elizabeth and Marjorie were delivered. That some of those ships also brought prohibited Protestant literature to Berwick for onwards distribution throughout England, Marjorie was certain, but it was never spoken of. None of it reached Norham Castle.

Today when she saw Marjorie at her door Ellen reached in and pulled her cloak from its nail inside the door and hurried her back outside and along the quay.

'I need some fresh air,' she said. 'Let us walk. Tell me, have you ever been on board a ship?'

'No, never.'

'Do you see my husband's vessel? There, the *Heron*.'

The ship was riding low in the water. Among all the bustle of the harbour it had little activity round it. One man stood leaning on the rail, idly talking to another sitting below him on the quayside, mending a torn sail.

'She has come from Dieppe. She has only put in to take on more water. She's on her way to Leith in Scotland, carrying claret. They're particularly fond of claret in Edinburgh.'

'Sandy!' Ellen hailed the seaman leaning on the rail and stepped lightly up the gangplank. Marjorie followed her awkwardly.

'Mistress,' said the sailor, lending them a hand to step onto the deck, before going back to his rail and contemplation of the jetty and his fellow seaman below.

Ellen led her briskly down some stairs and through narrow passageways. She clearly knew her way about. She had only once sailed on her husband's ship, Marjorie knew, and never wanted to do so again. She was terribly sick. But she was frequently on and off the ships in harbour carrying messages and helping check stores of food for the voyage. To make sure the tradesmen are not cheating them, she told Marjorie once. Though to be sure the people round here were very honest.

Now she tapped gently on the door of the captain's cabin. The door was flung open. John Knox stood there.

Ellen eased herself back behind Marjorie.

'There you are,' she heard Ellen murmur. 'I'll wait up on top if I'm needed.'

John's hair was more grey, his beard longer. But he looked well. Exhilarated. He hugged her so close she felt the breath being squeezed from her body. She gasped and released herself.

'I told you, didn't I?' He was almost boyish in his excitement. 'I told you I'd come back for you.'

'You took your time. Why didn't you warn me?'

'There was no time.'

'Was it you at Norham Village?' She was half-crying, half-laughing.

'I was going to march in and claim my Marjorie, but my nerve failed me. I feared the soldier at the gate would run me through and tip me in the moat.'

'John, it was foolish of you. It's dangerous.'

'It's my last chance. When your mother wrote me that you were moving south I knew I would never have another.

And Marjorie it's all coming together. I'm told I will be welcomed back in Scotland. The past is to be forgotten. So I'm going there.'

'And you just happened to call in on your road past?'

He slid his arms round her again. 'Lass, do you think anything except you would bring me back? I would have refused Scotland no matter how much they pleaded, except it let me come for you.'

He eased her cap off and stroked his hands over her hair.

'Marjorie. Will you come with me? Come to Scotland? Or have your feelings changed?'

'My feelings have not changed.'

'I canna promise you the life you're used to. You'll not be the chatelaine of a fine estate like your sisters. There'll be precious little siller. But Edinburgh's a grand city, Marjorie. Would you be content to bide there wi a plain man?'

'I will, I will,' she was shouting.

'That's my Marjorie,' he said. 'This ship sails on the evening tide. Get yourself home, gather up what you need and come back.'

He put his hands on her shoulders and steered her towards the door. 'Hurry. There's no time to be lost.'

Dazed, she found her way back onto deck where she found Ellen leaning beside the sailor on the rail, where they were conversing in soft voices about mermaids. She turned as Marjorie approached and without a word led her ashore.

As they walked back towards her house Ellen said quietly, 'Well, no need to ask whether you were pleased to see him. You are glowing.'

'I must get home. Oh Ellen, how am I to manage this?'

She was all conspiracy. 'Are you able to leave the castle after dark?'

'No. It's locked up tight and guarded well.'

'Then you'll have to leave earlier. Is it possible for you to go home, say I am ill and ask permission to return to sit with me?'

210

'Oh Ellen, is it really happening?'

'Aye, lassie. It looks like it. I'll be well pleased to see John settled at last.'

Chapter 37

Back at the castle Marjorie dismissed her guard and took her horse to the stables. She told the boy to rub him down and let him rest, but to get him ready for her to ride again in about an hour's time.

She found her mother in her parlour, a pile of plate in front of her. Sarie had set her to counting the pieces and wrapping them in rags ready to pack. But she was sitting listlessly, hands idle.

'Mother,' she said. 'John Knox is come. He is on his way to Scotland. I'm going with him.'

She started up, sending the pile of plates crashing and skittering across the floor. 'He is here? Here in the castle?'

'In Berwick. He's travelling on his brother's ship.' Marjorie looked out into the passage to see whether anyone had heard the clatter and come running to see, but there was no one. Everyone was too busy with their own duties to pay attention.

'He daren't set foot on land. You know that. Mother, I must go.'

In her own room she pulled the kist from under the bed. It had already been packed but she knew she could not take everything that was in it. There would be no mules and baggage trains where she was going. Isabella came in and stood and watched.

'Where are you going, Marjorie?'

'Scotland.'

'They're heathens there.'

'I don't think so.'

She pulled out her other wearing dress, and her spare caps. Her pretty embroidered kirtles and velvet gowns she tossed over to Isabella.

'Here,' she said. 'Take these to Aske with you. They will fit you or some of the other girls.' She rolled everything else up into a ball and tied her winter cloak round it.

Her mother stood in the doorway watching.

'You're running away?'

'Yes.'

'What am I to tell your father?'

'Where is he?'

'In the gunners' storeroom.'

'I'll tell him myself.'

She could not lie to her father. He might not accept John into the family. It would be too dangerous for them all. But neither would he stop her now. He could disown her, especially when she was away in another country. And besides, she no longer cared. Her heart and her head were both so full of joy she cared nothing for anyone else.

'You'll leave me all alone?'

'What?'

'I said . . . '

'Mother, you have plenty of other daughters.'

Her bundle was light. To a casual eye it would look as if she was taking some old rags for alms.

'Mother?'

Reluctantly Elizabeth stood aside. Marjorie pushed past her and hurried outside.

The gunners' room was on the far side of the inner bailey. As she approached she could hear the chief gunner's voice listing the munitions. Her father was standing by as a clerk noted the details called out by the chief gunner, while the gunner's boys were carrying the cannon balls being counted from one end of the store to the other. The open boxes stood by, spilling straw. It was her father's duty to account for every item of armaments in the castle and leave it well stocked. Normally it was unthinkable that she, or anyone, would interrupt her father. But the urgency had made her

213

determined. He looked up and saw her in the doorway. He nodded to his clerk and came out.

'What's to do?' he asked. 'Is your mother ill?'

He spoke absently. His mind was clearly on his duties.

'Father,' she spoke softly, so as not to be overheard, though she knew that the gunners' duties made them all deaf. 'I must leave Norham. John Knox has sent for me. I will go away with him.'

He glanced at the bundle she was carrying.

'So suddenly?'

At the gatehouse he spoke briefly to the guard and turned up the stair. Marjorie followed him. Instead of going into any of the rooms, he continued up to the battlements. They stood side by side on the narrow walk. He looked out over the river towards the hill, beyond which was Scotland. She stood by his side, waiting for him to speak, flicking glances at his stony profile. She was nervous. She would have to go to the privy before she left. She hoped he wouldn't start shouting.

But anger had never been his way with his family.

'Don't do this mad thing.'

'I must, Father. I will go with him.'

'I am sorry for it,' he said. 'You did not think to ask my consent, like a civilized Christian?'

'John cannot come into England,' she said.

'There's no more to be said then.'

He turned to go down. 'Do you need an escort to wherever you are to meet him?'

'No, Father.' He could still do his duty by the Queen and order the arrest of John. She was not going to travel with soldiers charged with that duty.

'I can ride there. I will leave the horse to be returned to you.'

He snorted. 'You have it planned. Keep the horse if you wish. One horse more or less. One daughter more or less. I would not have had him arrested. You need not think that

214

badly of me. Go to your man if you must. Write to your mother. She will miss you.'

She could not see his face. 'I will miss you,' he said.

She clutched at his arm. 'Father, I'm sorry.'

'It's too late for tears. Go and be a good wife to your preacher. Be happy.'

He turned and went down the stairs. She wiped her eyes and followed him. Her mother was waiting for them on the landing below.

'The girl is determined,' she said in a low voice.

'Yes.'

'Richard. I am going too.'

Marjorie sank back against the wall. Oh no, she thought, please not.

'Go where, Elizabeth?'

'I'm going with Marjorie and John. My place is with them.'

'Your place is with your husband.'

'I cannot.'

He took her arm at that, and hustled her into the parlour and closed the door hard behind them. Marjorie waited, straining to hear, with a sudden flash of a memory of doing this once before, in a different place, but the details eluded her. The door was heavy and there was no sound from within. Isabella came and crouched down beside her, white-faced and scared.

Marjorie rose and with a hiss at Isabella not to follow, she hastened out into the bailey and to the stables where the boy had her horse ready. She packed her bundle into the panniers. She had to get away. But a man from the kitchen came into the stables and told the boy to saddle another horse for the lady mistress.

Marjorie had to stop at the gate. Her mother was standing there. She came close and whispered, so that the guards, who by this time were watching them from the corners of their eyes, would not hear. It must have been all round the castle by this time that something scandalous was happening.

'Wait, Marjorie. I am coming with you. Give me time to collect some belongings together. I have sent word to the stables to saddle another horse.'

What could she do? She thought of the ship making ready to sail on the evening tide.

'Hurry, mother,' she said. 'There is not much time.'

Marjorie turned once as they rode across the drawbridge, to see Isabella standing, forlorn.

And so they left Norham Castle and the protection of their family, two women with no more than the bundles they could carry with them, and a horse as a dowry.

She never heard from her mother what words had passed between her and her husband. Elizabeth wept all the way to Berwick.

Chapter 38

They were married in Edinburgh. The celebration afterwards was crowded and lively. Marjorie looked up from her plate to see a grave young man watching her.

'Jamie,' cried John and he rose quickly from the table. He took the young man by the hand. 'Come meet my wife.' He chuckled. 'Does that not sound good, Marjorie?'

'Marjorie, this is Lord James Stewart. I am right glad to see him again.'

Lord James was a short, sturdy young man, with very black hair and beard. He was not many years older than Marjorie. His clothes too were black and among the gaily dressed wedding party he looked funereal. But the black was well cut, and of a very fine wool.

'Mistress Knox.' He bowed.

She laughed. She had only had a small goblet of wine but she was intoxicated with joy. 'It sounds strange. After all these years of waiting.'

He raised his glass in a toast. 'I hope you will be happy in Scotland.'

He was drawn away then, to talk to other people. 'Who is he?' she asked John. It seemed to her she had been asking this all day.

'Half brother to the bairn that is Queen. Bastard son of the late King.'

'You know him?'

'He was at St. Andrews. And I met him again in London. He once visited the court of King Edward.'

Later Lord James told her that yes he had been in St. Andrews at the time of the siege of the castle. 'But not of course on the side of Beaton's murderers. I was Prior of St. Andrews. A meaningless title, you understand. I was only a boy. But with a boy's curiosity I went there against my guardian's wishes to see what was happening.'

He smiled. 'I went expecting to do glorious deeds to defend my family. Instead I found a bunch of ruffians and a dominie turned reluctant preacher. John did not need to be taken prisoner. There were months of truce, and there was freedom of movement between the castle and the town. He could easily have left when the French fleet came. He chose to stay. Ruffians or no, he was their pastor. He would care for them.'

In the following weeks Marjorie, though she was in a glow of happiness, had much to do to prevent her mother slipping back into melancholy. Elizabeth clung to John as if she were his wife and not Marjorie. She fretted. She wanted him to sit with her and talk. He had no sooner succeeded in alleviating one anxiety than she would find another, gliding from one to the other as easily as a child on icy ground.

He had never, since he saw them walking along the quayside while he paced on the deck of the ship, given by as much as a hint by word or deed that he would have preferred if Elizabeth Bowes was not there. Privately Marjorie told him that it was no wish of hers. Her mother had made her own choice, and defied her husband.

John merely rubbed his hand down his beard and shrugged and said, 'Aye, aye, well well.' And there was no more discussion of it.

The only time Marjorie had him to herself was in bed.

They were lodged with an Edinburgh burgess. Master Syme and his wife had a fine house off the Canongate with a view of the Crags above the Palace of Holyrood. It was a big house by Edinburgh standards, but small compared with the manor at Aske. It was more comfortable than Norham.

Still her mother grumbled. She grumbled that the Scotswomen had little manners. There was a roughness to them. A Scotswoman, they found, did not consider one who carried a title any different from one who laundered clothes

218

for a living, and spoke as plainly to one as to the other. Marjorie was in agony in case Mistress Syme, who was unfailingly kind to them, would be hurt. Marjorie sensed in her a mild impatience with one she considered a soft and pampered Englishwoman. Aware that she should be careful not to be too sensitive she was yet alert in case Mistress Syme, who did have a sharp tongue, inadvertently invited retaliation from the easily offended Elizabeth.

Marjorie told John they should seek accommodation of their own.

'My mother would be happier if she had the management of a household, even a small one. She is too idle. She knows no one and she makes no attempt to find friends.'

'Are you happy?' he asked.

'I am content. But our own home would give us more privacy. You would have peace for your writing.'

He accepted this, and within a week he found them lodgings of their own.

In fact, the translations and tracts he wished to write had to wait. There was a constant stream of visitors to the house. The arrival in Edinburgh of John Knox had caused a sensation. Whenever Marjorie looked out of her window she would see people hanging around the house, hoping to catch him. As soon as he went out, they engaged him in conversation, walking with him to his destination, discussing, arguing, talking all the time.

When she went out with her mother strangers asked them how they did, and settled into conversation as if they had always known them. They were not used to this.

'Marjorie, why do people behave like this. What right have they to address us in the street. We do not know them.'

'It is their way, Mother. They are being friendly.' The only times she saw hesitancy and reserve were when there was a Frenchman within hearing.

John in a domestic setting was different from Master Knox in the pulpit. In Berwick and London she had not

219

often seen him in general company. In Berwick it had been in church, or privately at the castle, and occasionally at the house of his brother. Now she saw a different John, one relaxed and comfortable in his own home, among friends with whom he could share a joke, tease and charm the women while talking about matters other than their immortal soul. And happy as a married man, frequently even in the midst of talking to another, reaching out to take her hand and smile at her, his wife.

And then one evening she heard shouts of laughter in the hallway and hurried down to find John embracing a man who had just arrived.

'Master Willock,' she was equally delighted to see him.

'Mistress Knox. Delighted I am to call you that. I knew when I witnessed your handfasting this was a love that would endure.'

'That it has. And what has happened to you since then?'

'I have been in Emden in Germany. Now I am come on a diplomatic commission to the Queen Regent here.'

'You have become a politician,' said John.

'No,' was the serious answer. 'I have had enough of society. Once I discharge my mission for the Duchess of Emden I will seek her leave to stay here. I see a change under way. The people of Scotland have a hunger for the new learning.'

'Yes,' said John. 'They have been starved too long.'

Lord James came frequently to the house, and he was often accompanied by other young men, the younger generation of nobility, waiting to come into their own. The town councillors of Edinburgh, most of whom were prosperous local merchants, came. Their wives came too and occasionally their daughters, and while the men talked with John, Marjorie and her mother made slow conversation with the women.

There were many evenings without the women, evenings when the men sat drinking and talking and arguing. They would start quietly enough, as they dined, but as the ale, and later the whisky, began to flow Marjorie, lying upstairs in bed, would hear the voices floating up to her, louder and louder.

Marjorie gradually understood that the people were passionate about the Protestant new learning. The young were impatient for change, but the older men advised caution. The Queen Regent allowed freedom of worship. Though her advisers were French, and she was heavily under the influence of the Catholic Church, she claimed to be relaxed about the change sweeping the country.

'She keeps the peace,' said William Maitland. 'That is what matters, surely. No one has been imprisoned, or burnt.'

'Not yet.'

'She's biding her time. Waiting for her daughter to grow up. If she has her way the child will be Queen of Scotland and France.'

'Our alliance with France has brought us nothing but trouble.'

'But we do like the benefits which it brings,' said William Maitland smoothly, raising his glass of claret.

William Maitland was one of the clever young men in the employment of the Queen Regent. He reminded Marjorie of William Cecil, able to weigh every side of an argument and consider what would be the best outcome. In other ways he was different. Where Master Cecil was dry and serious with an occasional flash of learned wit, Maitland blatantly used his charm. Even his flirtatiousness with the women, when he seemed to have drunk too much wine, was calculated. Where Master Cecil was kind and patient, Maitland could be snide and sarcastic. Marjorie did not much like him.

But though he came often, he didn't agree with John. He saw no harm in the mass, and many and loud were the arguments between them. One night he said to Marjorie as he was leaving, 'Arguing with your man is like arguing with

God at the Judgment Gate. Our opinions matter little beside his.'

'Surely,' she said to John when she had him to herself, in bed, 'Since he works for the Queen Regent all that is discussed in our house will find its way back to her?'

'It doesn't matter,' said John. 'We have nothing to hide. He can repeat all he wishes. Besides, I am done with politics. From now on I only preach the word of God. Lassie, we are far beneath the notice of the Regent.'

John Willock came regularly, and Lord James Stewart, who tended to silent listening, and rarely ventured his thoughts. One day he brought with him another grave quiet man but one whose eyes creased with pleasure when he was introduced to Marjorie.

'This is John Erskine, the Laird of Dun, north of the River Forth. He is wise beyond his years,' said Lord James.

'You knew Master Wishart,' said Knox.

'I did. He stayed with me that last time when he came here. I tried to persuade him not to go into Lothian, but he would, and we know what happened after that.'

John Knox clasped his hand. 'My friend,' he said. 'Anything I can do for you and yours I will do, in memory of my dear mentor.'

'I take you at your word. Come north,' said John Erskine. 'Come to Dun and talk to the people. We need preachers like you in Scotland.'

Please, thought Marjorie, no more separations. Let me have my husband to myself for a while.

He had his way. John was persuaded by go north with Erskine to stay with him for a month, and after that he set off on his travels round Scotland, staying with the nobility and gentry who did not come to Edinburgh, many of them families of the young men they already knew.

All that beautiful autumn and winter he travelled, preaching and teaching, while Marjorie and Elizabeth stayed in Edinburgh. He wrote regularly. Everywhere he went, he

222

told them, he left behind congregations of people reading their bibles and worshipping in the new way in groups in their own homes. The petty churches, he called them. He penetrated even as far as the south-west which had been, she was told, almost a country independent of Scotland for so long, cut off as it was by ranges of mountains. A prosperous country, he wrote, with good farmland and many busy sea routes over which they traded with Spain and the countries of the Mediterranean.

There is a centre of pilgrimage here, he wrote, *by name Whithorn, where they acclaim a dead saint. I did not go there. Where coinage flows, the ears are stopped.*

He spent time with the man who was fast becoming a close friend, the Earl of Glencairn, at his seat on the banks of the River Clyde. From there he travelled north and into the far west to Argyll, where he was welcomed by the great Duke, almost a king in his own country.

How much, Marjorie wondered, is it the new learning people welcome, and how much is it a dislike of the power of the Queen Regent? Why are all these powerful men so set on change? Scraps of memory came to her, memories of herself as a child, memories of being crushed in a crowd while a man with an eyepatch ranted. She shivered.

Lord James had never been known to say a word of criticism of his stepmother, and he was known to be fond of his little half-sister the Queen. But his father and his grandfather had both died fighting against England at the behest of France. And so had the fathers and grandfathers of these men who now welcomed John.

John was at home in Edinburgh during the darkest days of winter, and then in spring went once more to visit Erskine of Dun. And then without any warning, he was back in Edinburgh.

'Marjorie,' he called, bounding up the stairs to her room.

She hastened out. 'John, I had no warning!'

'I sent none. I had to get here quickly.' He pulled a paper from his jerkin.

'Look,' he said, beaming all over his face. 'What do you think this is?'

'What? Don't be daft, man. What have you there?'

'A summons from the bishops.' He was almost crowing with delight. 'A summons. To report to the Church of the Black Friars, on a charge of heresy.'

She felt her knees tremble. 'John. Not heresy. That's ....' She was speechless.

'Punishable by burning. Yes. Fools that they are. This is how they trapped Wishart. A summons, and then an arrest, and no chance to defend himself but burnt without trial. Well, they won't catch me the same way.'

'You must leave.'

'Havers. Listen.'

There was a tumult in the street outside.

'They're coming for you. They will burn you too.'

'Nay. They've chosen the wrong man.'

The door burst open. In the street stood a dozen armed men.

'Let's go,' growled the man at the head of them.

She pushed forward. 'How can you? How can you arrest a man you've broken bread with? You're his friend.'

The man gave a whoop of laughter. 'Arrest? No no, Mistress. We've not come to arrest him.' He gestured to his men. 'Bodyguard,' he announced triumphantly.

'Right, friends,' said John. 'Let's go.'

The whole troop of them, with John striding at their head, marched to the Calton. The people in the streets, seeing the to-do, joined in with cheering and laughter, and soon John had a great train of people at his back. From somewhere appeared a man with a drum and another with a penny whistle.

At the house of the Bishop of Dunkeld he knocked on the door with his stick.

'Open up,' he cried. 'John Knox is come to answer the summons.'

The door was opened cautiously and he was admitted, the crowd pressing forward, threatening to invade the house. They were pushed back by the Bishop's men, and the door slammed shut.

It was a fine May day and the weather was warm. Everyone settled down in the street to await events. In no time at all food pedlars and jugglers were at work among the crowd. Inside the house all was silent. The crowd had been waiting some two hours, and people were starting to drift away when an upper window was thrown open and John appeared at it.

'Good people,' he cried. 'The summons has been withdrawn. The bishops have changed their minds. But I've not. I have declined to leave. I've been invited to answer a charge of heresy and answer I will. I'll stay till I can persuade the Bishop of the truth of the gospel.'

And then impromptu, when he was always at his best, he talked and preached and argued with the crowd for the next two hours. From time to time, men appeared at his back and attempted to draw him inside, but he shook them off and continued to talk. When a particularly persistent servant tried to drag him away there were roars of disapproval from the crowd. The servant, looking scared, disappeared. Eventually he did stop, when his voice was hoarse and the day was wearing on. He bade the crowd goodnight and closed the window.

Back home they waited for word. It came eventually in a note. *Would you be so good as to send a change of linen? I have decided to remain here as the guest of the Bishop.*

He stayed in the house ten days. Every day a crowd would gather and he would talk to them from the window. Lord James told Marjorie the bishops were frantically trying to get rid of him, that the Queen Regent herself was furious, not so much with John as with the bishops for causing the trouble in the first place.

'But Marjorie,' said Lord James. 'It is not good to have this kind of confrontation. I do not think we are ready for it.'

When John eventually came home she repeated Lord James's words to him. 'What do you think he meant?' she asked.

He looked thoughtful. He said, 'I was thinking it is time we left.'

'Left?'

'I have had a letter from Geneva. There is an English congregation there, exiles from England. They want to elect me as their minister.'

'But John, this is your own country. I thought we were settled here.'

He stroked his beard, in the way he did when he was not willing to speak the truth, but did not wish to lie.

'I have no settled congregation here.'

'You could have one if you wanted.'

'The climate is better in Geneva.'

'What is it John? You are uneasy.'

'I am uneasy,' he admitted. 'Do you recall, Marjorie, how the Duke of Northumberland was attempting to use me for his own ends? Claiming his purpose was reform of the religion when in reality he wished to drive out all opposition to his family and his own greed for power?'

'There is no great duke here.'

'No. But there is the little Queen growing up and the day will come when she is old enough to wed the Dauphin. Who is to rule Scotland? These are questions I hear in the great houses late at night. There are many who are making plans. I fear a stramash and I don't want to be part of it. Lassie, I just wish to live peaceably with you and the bairn to come. I have a congregation waiting for me in Geneva. We will be happier there.'

At that there was no argument.

226

'Mother,' Marjorie broached the subject with care. 'Mother, do you want to return to England? It may not be easy in Geneva, in a foreign country. You could return to live with any one of my sisters.'

Her mother shook her head. 'No, I will stay with you and John. I will be needed for the birth of the baby.'

'Do you ever hear from my father?'

'Through your sisters.'

But she volunteered no more information.

Elizabeth wept into her pillow many a night after they left Edinburgh. From there, return to England was still possible, but Geneva was another country. From Scotland she could have slipped over the border to visit her sons and daughters. After they crossed the sea, that chance vanished. But it was her choice.

Marjorie was concerned for other reasons. It had not been easy for Elizabeth to adjust to Edinburgh. Moreover, she had little idea of how to live in the simple style that their very low income now demanded. She had never had to economise, or indeed to trouble herself overmuch with household finances, for in her life there had always been an abundance.

Now, they depended for their income on the generosity of the people among whom John preached. And Scotland was not a wealthy country. At least in Geneva with a settled congregation he would be paid a stipend, but it would still be a modest living.

'With a more settled way of life, I will write more, and perhaps there will be a market for my poor efforts at penmanship,' John said. Marjorie agreed, but she had already learned that her husband was indifferent about his comfort, and had little idea of the costs of a growing family.

Their small household, Marjorie and her mother and the servant, left early in June. John himself stayed in Scotland a few weeks longer to finish up his business matters and take his farewells of the lairds who had been kind to him.

They had been in Scotland less than nine months.

He had barely joined them in Dieppe when word came that the bishops had made an effigy in straw and rags of John Knox and burned it at the stake at the Mercat Cross in Edinburgh.

Chapter 39

Geneva was a peaceful city, kept so by the rigid control of Master Calvin, who had a vision of what a city should be. Clean, sober, hard working, educated, Godly. After London it seemed unnaturally quiet, and sedate.

Marjorie contentedly awaited the birth of her baby. John was happy as the pastor of a congregation which valued him, a congregation growing with refugees from England. He was studying Hebrew, for he was working on a new translation of the Bible with Miles Coverdale and the other scholars. He was also writing tracts which were published all over Europe.

Marjorie was a help to him in this, scribing to his dictation, for he thought best when he was on his feet and talking. She gave over the management of their small household wholly to her mother. As she had feared, Elizabeth grumbled almost constantly for their income was small, and her French was only a few remembered phrases from her girlhood. She was sure the tradesmen were cheating them. They had a succession of girls to help in the house. None stayed long, for Elizabeth's manner was imperious and girls with poor or no English could not be expected to see the fundamental kindness underneath.

Her trouble, Marjorie suspected, and this had been brewing for some time, was that she no longer had the constant attention of John which she had been accustomed to at Norham. He was no longer the shy man who had been glad to be kindly noticed by an important lady. She could no longer treat him as her personal confessor, as she had been inclined to do in the old days. Marjorie saw this clearly but did not say it. It would have distressed her mother further. Marjorie could see the little tricks Elizabeth used to gain and keep his attention.

She was constantly preparing small treats for him. When Marjorie tactfully suggested he did not need these, for the girls were generally competent cooks, she gave as her excuse that the food here did not agree with him, and the girl did not understand his sensitive stomach. This was nonsense. In fact the simple food here suited him fine, but her mother would not be told, and urged sweetmeats on him. She was wasting her time, for John was not interested in food, and would eat whatever was placed in front of him without noticing. His mind would be on whatever treatise he was writing at the time, or on his next sermon, or anywhere else. Elizabeth would attract his attention and he would swallow the last mouthful, and pat her hand in appreciation and return to his book. The excessive cream and sugar in the food, which they could ill afford anyway, caused him discomfort all night afterwards, and he would sit up in bed beside Marjorie, sighing and sleepless.

The religious persecutions wrought by Queen Mary in England were at their height. John wrote urging old friends to leave when they had the chance. Two of those who minded his advice were Mr and Mrs Locke. They left London and travelled to Frankfurt with their children. Mr Locke found Frankfurt congenial. The English congregation there were using the prayer book of Archbishop Cranmer, and he felt comfortable with that. He also found many opportunities for business. But Mrs Locke was restless. She had taken to heart John's strictures against the prayer book.

When spring came and the roads were clear of snow, she left her husband and travelled to Geneva with her two children. Warned of her coming, Elizabeth and Marjorie prepared to welcome the family. She came accompanied not only by her children but by three servants. She was effusive in her greetings. Marjorie had not met her before, and knew her only as a woman who had been a supporter of John in London. Now she had time to study the woman whom she knew John admired and often corresponded with.

She saw a small woman some ten years older than herself. She watched Anne Locke clasp John on the arm and look up laughingly into his face. She was flushed with the exertion of arrival and tendrils of blonde hair were escaping from her cap.

'My dear John, I am so happy to be here. And my dear Marjorie, if I may call you that. Mistress Knox! Does it not sound odd, we never thought he would marry. We did not know of course that he was hiding you away all the time. My dear Mistress Bowes, Elizabeth, it is good of you to welcome us into your house.'

She chattered on, holding fast to John's arm all the time.

They settled down for a while, the three women and the two children. But only two weeks after their arrival the youngest child, a girl, fell ill. No one knew what caused it, but there was comment among some unkind women in the town that while they acknowledged that there had not been much choice but to bring the children from England, to subject them to the extra journey to Geneva had not been wise. Perhaps the child always had been sickly.

John spent a great deal of his time with Anne Locke by the bedside of the sick child. Marjorie was in the final days of her own pregnancy, and they would not let her near. She shifted restlessly about her room, listening to the unusual silence in the rest of the house.

John came and told her the little girl had died. She wept then, for the child, and for her own child to come, and out of exhaustion.

John spent many hours closeted with Anne Locke. Why? Why? Occasionally the painful cry would echo through the house. And what about Marjorie? She waited. Eventually her baby was born safely, a fine healthy boy. They named him Nathaniel. Mrs Locke kept away from her after that, though she sent the conventional good wishes and little gifts, but she avoided being in the room with the baby, and

231

stayed out of the way when the women in the town came to visit.

As for Elizabeth Bowes, she disliked Mrs Locke from the start. When Mrs Locke was closeted with John in his study, Elizabeth would pace up and down and try and find an excuse to interrupt them.

'Mother, when you have troubles he will talk with you for hours. Would you grudge others the same?'

'Why did he invite her here?'

'He wrote to many people to leave England. I scribed the letters myself. She was not the only one who took that advice.'

'I am surprised you should stay so calm.'

'What have I to worry about?' But Elizabeth would not put her jealousy into words.

'They were in danger in London,' Marjorie said. 'You should not fret like this. The poor woman has lost her child.'

'I lost my children to follow him,' she replied. 'I did not weep for them.'

Marjorie nursed her baby and listened to the sharp words being exchanged, sharp words followed by tears from Anne Locke and remorse from Elizabeth, and the disappearance of John into his study, not to be disturbed.

And then two old friends from Edinburgh came and turned their little world upside down. Master Barron and Master Syme were travelling, looking at trading opportunities. That was the ostensible reason for their journey. The real reason was to carry a letter that could not be entrusted to any messenger. Of course, they were using the journey to investigate business opportunities too. John opened the letter and read it.

'You know what this contains, of course.'

They nodded. 'And we heartily agree with it. The Pope has authorised France to establish an Inquisition like that which Spain has. Exactly like. Scotland will be next.'

232

John rose. 'I will need to discuss this with my wife. And of course my congregation here. Meantime, stay with us and welcome.'

Come back to Scotland. Here you will find the faithful you left behind you ready to jeopardy all, lives and goods, for the forward setting of the glory of God.

'Fine words!' said a furious Marjorie. The letter was signed by a group on behalf of the Lords of the Congregation.

'The Congregation. Who are they?'

'They are the people in all the petty churches. They band together to form Congregations. People who will uphold the truth.'

'And these Lords of the Congregation? Who are they?' asked Marjorie.

'They have been appointed the leaders.'

'Or they appoint themselves.'

'It will be the wish of the Congregations that these lords speak for them.'

It was signed by Lord Glencairn, by Erskine of Dun, by Lord Lorne (he who was heir to the great Duke of Argyll), and of course, Lord James Stewart.

'Of course he has a hand in it,' Marjorie raged. 'What new plot does he have?'

'I thought you liked Jamie.'

'I do. As a man. But as a politician I distrust him. I always feel he has some scheme that only he knows about.'

'They want only the best for Scotland.'

'Best for themselves,' said Marjorie, and stamped off to attend to the baby, crying in another room. She bent her head over her son and wept herself.

*

Europe was in turmoil. England had declared war on France. France was mustering warships on her coast. Other

233

nations were aligning themselves on one side or the other. In Scotland the Queen Regent had broken off diplomatic relations with England.

Their visitors left, to return home, with no commitment from John. He was in an agony of indecision.

'I have consulted Master Calvin,' he told Marjorie. 'He thinks I should answer the call.'

'He thinks. He thinks. He does not think at all. What of the baby? Why should we be disrupted again? Give up our home here?'

'I would go alone.'

'Alone?'

'It will not be safe crossing France now. There is a new edict against heretics.'

'Alone? Travelling into danger? Leaving us here? We have had such a short time together. Are we to be separated again?'

She let him go, of course. No one could have stopped him. He didn't go immediately. Their son, growing bigger daily, entranced John enough to keep him at home. He had always had a fondness for children. It was teaching the children in St. Andrews that had first attracted attention to his abilities.

'When will he speak?' he asked anxiously.

'Not for a few months. And if you are in Scotland you will not hear his first words.'

He ignored that. 'Look, he smiles at me.'

It took time, too, to make the financial arrangements for his family to be looked after in his absence. He and his fellow ministers reorganised the services and ordained a young preacher to take John's place.

And how could he leave when Anne Locke was still in such distress at the loss of her child? That's the least of it, Elizabeth Bowes was heard to mutter, and was reproved by John for hard-heartedness.

He lingered. Marjorie lying in his arms after lovemaking desperately wanted to ask him if, deep in his heart, he did not want to go, but she did not. She knew that he would go, no matter what his heart said. With John Knox it was always duty that won over inclination.

Eventually, Anne Locke found other accommodation for herself and her household, and the house became peaceful again. John and Marjorie had the summer together. In the autumn, as the leaves were beginning to turn golden, they parted with heavy hearts.

His journey through France was hazardous but none paid much attention to a lone traveller, and he spoke the language fluently. In Dieppe he found two letters awaiting him. Marjorie never learned who sent those letters. He tore them up in a rage, he told her, and after that she knew better than to mention them.

Rage he might well. The Lords of the Congregation had changed their minds. Since they had first written the situation had been overturned. The Queen Regent had raised an army and sent it south to attack the English. They were instructed to take Norham Castle and thus to take the war into England itself. But at the border they mutinied. They refused to lead their men any further. They would defend Scotland with their very lives, but they would not venture into England. They saw no just cause. They had had enough of fighting England on behalf of France.

All trust between the Queen Regent and the nobility had broken down. She was now intent on subjugating Scotland to French rule, and to that end was pushing forward the marriage of her daughter to the Dauphin. Now was not the time to be thinking of establishing a new Church, said the Lords of the Congregation.

John raged. *I hazarded much to answer the call, and now those who called me find it inconvenient. That is the word they use, Marjorie. Inconvenient.*

He waited at Dieppe, hoping for more instructions, writing letter after letter to the pusillanimous Lords. They must not rebel against the Queen Regent; they did a disservice to their people who would suffer most. They received homage and tribute from the people not by reason of their birth, he told them, but because they had the duty to protect the people. They had no right to jeopardise their people by open revolt against the lawful ruler of the country.

Negotiate, negotiate. Negotiation with the Queen Regent, not confrontation; that was the way to peace and freedom of religion.

They did not reply. Despite Marjorie's urgings to return home, he stayed on at Dieppe for six months, preaching to the congregations of Protestants at great risk to himself. The persecution in France was increasing. Known Huguenots were being rounded up and imprisoned. Burnings had started and the Cardinal of Lorraine, who, John reminded the Lords in Scotland, was the very dear brother of their Queen Regent, was urging wholesale executions.

Would Scotland be next?

He waited for word that he would be welcome in Scotland, word that never came.

Then, one bitter day, he stood on the hillside above Dieppe and watched the glorious contingent of Scottish nobility land in France to negotiate the marriage settlement of their Queen with the Dauphin. Lord James Stewart was among them.

A relieved Marjorie welcomed John home. He was tired, melancholic, and with the scrappy meals and poor diet of travelling, his old kidney trouble was flaring up again. When he had slept himself out, and lay in her arms rested, he admitted to her that he was glad the adventure was over.

Scotland at war with itself would be no place to preach the word of Christ. The Lords were right. Never again would he leave his comfortable home to chase a will o' the wisp. Never again would he be at the beck of fickle power-hungry men. As the days passed and he slipped once more back into the comfortable routine he became overwhelmed with a sense of failure. He berated himself.

'It was common sense, John,' Marjorie attempted to reassure him.

'It was cowardice. I should have gone to Scotland, no matter whether I was welcome or not. I saw the French troops embarking from France, hundreds of them, Marjorie, a veritable army of occupation. I saw and did nothing, save to write to Scotland and warn them.'

'What else could you have done?'

'I don't know.'

'We are safe here.'

He turned on his side away from her.

'I was safe when my dear Master George Wishart went to the fire and I stayed at home.'

Chapter 40

In the time John had been away Nathaniel had grown sufficiently to be almost walking. John was fascinated watching him. Marjorie often had the child playing beside her while she scribed John's dictation. He would break off occasionally and gaze at the child.

'What kind of world will he grow up in?'

She waited patiently, the quill laden with ink, ready to go on writing.

'I am weary of this work,' he said.

'We will leave it for today then.'

'I think I might leave it forever.'

She waited. He had laboured at this particular tract, a justification of Master Calvin's thinking on predestination, for months. But his heart was not in it. He did not agree with it. He never argued too forcibly with Master Calvin. People didn't, now, in Geneva. John had little taste for theological argument and could be bested by scholars. He was a practical man; the twists and turns of philosophy were not for him. His faith was a simple one, based on the scriptures. He saw no need to overlay it with philosophy.

'Master Calvin is too harsh in his judgment of people. He does not allow for human frailty. And surely, Marjorie, if we are made in the image of God, it was God's choice that some human weaknesses be built into us. No, don't write that. Master Calvin would disagree.'

In any event he was rapidly losing interest in that particular tract. It looked as if it would never be finished and published.

He was silent and moody round the house. She had seen this before. When action was needed he was a whirlwind of activity and optimism. But cocooned in comfortable routine his spirit wilted. Elizabeth did her best to wheedle John out of his ill-humour, and ever courteous, he smiled and acted once more the cheerful man, and her mother would glance at Marjorie with a triumphant look on her face. See, I know him better than you. I can encourage him out of it.   And it took all of Marjorie's self-control to refrain from snapping at both of them.

She knew by his shortness of temper that he was frustrated with himself. When he was in these moods he did not seek out his friends to spend an evening in drinking a flagon of good wine and talk far into the night, voices raised sometimes in argument and sometimes in songs of Scotland. He had a fine tenor voice and could remember the ballads sung in his childhood. His closest friends were men in exile, on the one hand determined to make a good life for themselves and their families, on the other hand always looking yearningly back to the land they had left. But now there was none of that. He brooded.

In this brooding, isolated mood, John began a new tract.

There were too many queens.

'It was Mary Tudor killed Anne Locke's child as surely as if she had taken a knife to her. She is a murderer.'

And then there was the little Queen Mary of the Scots, she who had just been married in Paris to the Dauphin. News of that wedding brought back all the resentment he felt against the Scottish lords who, he felt, had betrayed him.

'Not just me, Marjorie. That matters little, though I was angry at the time, stuck there in Dieppe. No, they betray the people. They think they are important because of their birth. They are not. They abuse the trust the people place in them.'

Also that April came news that was the most distressing of all, because it showed the way the wind was blowing in Scotland too. With the new-found power of the alliance with France, the Queen Regent in Scotland ended her tolerance of the Protestants. Word came that the Bishop of St. Andrews had accused Walter Myln, a priest, of heresy.

239

The priest was put to death by fire. He was eighty-two years old.

'I knew him well. He was a gentle goodly old man, ready to meet his maker, deserving no more than to die quietly in his bed. Did he die on the same spot as my own dear friend Master Wishart? Oh, the cruelty of it!' John shut himself in his study all day and would see no one.

'Women should not have that kind of power,' he said. 'What is happening to the world? The English Queen marries a Spaniard, and England must become like Spain. The Scottish Queen marries a Frenchman and Scotland must become a colony of France. Men and women die because they cannot worship God quietly in their own way, but needs must be in thrall to a Church that practises hypocrisy and superstition. Women like our dear Anne Locke must flee their homes to the peril of their children.'

He called his new tract *The First Blast of the Trumpet against the Monstrous Regiment of Women.*

'Is there to be a second?'

'I don't know. Others may take up the matter.'

Marjorie wrote to his dictation.

To promote a woman to bear rule above any realm, nation or city is repugnant to nature and the subversion of all good order, equity and justice.

As the days passed and the tract grew she became increasingly uneasy.

'John,' she said, 'you will offend with this.'

'Does that matter?'

'It matters if we wish to return to Scotland. Or to England for that matter.'

He was instantly concerned. 'Do you wish to return to England, dearie?'

'No. My home is here with you,' she said. 'Except all my sisters and my brothers are there, and all their children, and it would be good for our son to know his cousins, do you not think? But he never will if we offend the Queen and she will not allow us to return.'

'She will not allow us to return anyway. I have been outlawed there.'

It is repugnant to nature that the blind shall lead those that cannot see, that the weak nourish the strong, that the sick heal the healthy. Such be all women that have authority over men.

'You overstate your case,' she said.

'There are perhaps exceptions. We will insert a passage that allows of exceptions. Make a note. You, my Marjorie, would make an admirable leader, but God has ordained you to be the wife of a poor preacher.'

A woman cannot be a judge in the court, not lead an army into battle, nor steer a ship, why then should she have the power of a sovereign over a nation, over the judge in his court, or the captain of the army, or an admiral on his ship? And so he built up his arguments.

'You are being too heavily swayed by the cruelties of Mary in England.'

'And Marie in Scotland.'

'She has only burnt one man.'

'How many will follow?'

The tract was published, and copies smuggled into England and Scotland. It caused uproar, though most scholars in Europe agreed with it. Master Calvin received a strongly worded letter from the English congregation in Strasbourg which he showed to John. No matter that Queen Mary Tudor had driven them from their homes, she was still Queen of England. He rounded on John for embarrassing him. The Geneva imprint made it look as if Master Calvin had approved of it, when he did not. He was kept busy protesting to everyone everywhere that he had nothing to do with it.

Relations between the two men were tense.

'I consulted him more than a year ago on the point,' complained John. 'He said then that queens were a punishment consequent on the Fall of Man.'

'Perhaps he was not thinking of real flesh and blood women. He doesn't, you know.' Marjorie tried to soothe his hurt feelings.

All that summer they had word of unrest in Scotland. The Queen Regent had promised freedom of worship to all if the Parliament would grant her new son-in-law the Dauphin the Crown Matrimonial of Scotland. But when that was achieved she reneged on her word. Protestants might worship quietly at home, but all public worship was to be in the Roman style. There were to be no exceptions.

As a result of this there were once more disturbances on the streets of Edinburgh. When the Black Friars there attempted to hold the annual St. Giles Day procession, the day descended into riot and bloodshed. The previous year the crowd had snatched the wooden image of St. Giles, which the Queen Regent had followed in procession, and thrown it into the Nor' Loch. This year, the friars borrowed another image, but that too was wrested from their hands by the mob and destroyed. The riots in the capital were the worst, they heard, but all over Scotland people were restless.

Then came the hardest blow of all. News arrived from Berwick that the congregation there, that congregation of the Church where they had worshipped together, that congregation who had been so staunch and loyal to John, had renounced all and gone back to worship in the Roman way.

'They perhaps had no choice, John,' Marjorie tried to tell him. 'The persecutions had grown so great.'

'It is true I would not ask any man to be a martyr,' he agreed, sadly. 'For I would not be a martyr myself.' And this reminded him once again of his own mentor Master Wishart, who had indeed been a martyr, and he slid once more into a depression.

242

Brooding, he began to change his mind about many things. He put pen to paper, and once more found he was in profound disagreement with Master Calvin. Master Calvin cleaved to the words of Jesus in the bible. Render unto Caesar the things that are Caesar's and unto God the things that are God's.

Not so, said John Knox. There is no reason why good Christian people should always obey the sovereign.

'The time for that is past,' he told Marjorie.

He reasoned thus: the sovereign and his advisers rule by consent of the people. God may have ordained society into kings, nobles and commoners but in heaven all are equal. All must follow Jesus equally. Kings are as subject to the will of God as is the poorest labourer.

'Why, oh why do the people of England not rise up against the wicked Queen?'

Their second son was born in November. John named him Eleazer, after that Eleazer in the bible who saw the promised land, while his father the priest did not.

'John,' Marjorie asked. 'Do you think our sons will see a Protestant Scotland?'

'Maybe. But I shall not. The cause is lost in my lifetime.'

Chapter 41

Word came from Aske that Captain Bowes was dead.

He had cut both Elizabeth and Marjorie out of his Will. Elizabeth now had her jointure, the trust fund set aside when she married, in preparation for her widowhood. This was small relief to her. She shut herself up in her room with the letter from her son and would not be comforted. She sorrowed for the husband she had wed as a young girl, to whom she had borne fifteen children.

'I was not there,' she wept. 'I should have been by his side, as a true wife must. I will never have his forgiveness.'

Even John could not comfort her. He was uncomfortable trying. 'I have no arguments,' he said. 'I was the cause of her leaving her husband. He was a good man who did me no harm. I have never been able to make amends, and now I cannot.'

Marjorie threw her eyes up to heaven and busied herself with the household duties, now neglected by the mourning Elizabeth.

John himself received a letter from Marjorie's brother George.

'Your father before he died repented of his refusal to give you a dowry. He left instructions that a small dowry could now be paid.'

'That's good, John. I hope it means that in his heart he understood. And you could use the money.'

'Lass, lass, I dinna want the money. You are precious to me without the siller. We'll put it aside for the boys when they are grown.'

He went about his duties to his congregation in a sober mood.

One day Marjorie was helping to clear away the breakfast dishes when she heard his hurrying footsteps returning to the house. She wiped her hands on her apron and opened the door.   John stood there, panting, flushed with excitement.

'The Queen is dead,' he said.

'What?' Elizabeth Bowes raised her head from the bible she was reading. She spent a great deal of time reading these days. Reading and brooding.

'The Queen is dead.' He seized Elizabeth's hands and pulled her to her feet and attempted to dance her round the room. But his feet were clumsy and she was now too heavy.

'What queen?' asked Marjorie.

'Queen Mary Tudor of England. Oh, bless us Lord for this day.' He sank onto the settle. 'Oh my Lord.'

The girl, hearing loud voices, came through from the kitchen, listened to their gabbling, shrugged and went back to her duties. A queen here or there, one more of less, what was it to her?

There were more footsteps and voices outside and soon the house was full of people.   Marjorie pictured the messengers hurrying from London and fanning out across Europe to bring this news. It was momentous, enough to turn the world on its head.

'Did she die in childbirth?' she asked.

'There never was any child.'

So there was no heir.

'Who will reign now?'

'Her sister Elizabeth of course.'

One of the men gave a short, sharp laugh. There was a murmur among the women. None there had forgotten that Elizabeth was the daughter of the Bullen who had been beheaded for adultery.

'Is there to be no end to these queens?' exclaimed John.

Marjorie remembered the pretty girl in white who had shared in her sister's ceremonial entry into London.

'But she is old King Harry's daughter, and that is what matters,' said someone, as if reading all their minds. There is no one else. That was the general agreement.

'Pray God there is no pretender,' said John. 'The last thing England needs is a civil war. If the lords and parliament accept Princess Elizabeth as their queen, then surely there will be peace. She is said to be a good Protestant.'

'Is she?' asked someone else. 'We do not hear of her suffering persecution for her beliefs.'

'Was the Queen supposed to burn her own sister?'

They set to with a rumbling undercurrent of argument about this while others hurried off to spread the news. The baby, disturbed by the racket round him, began to cry. Marjorie picked him up and rocked him in her arms to shush him.

The men gathered round the fire with their argument and John sent the girl for ale. The women clustered round Marjorie and cooed over the baby, but their minds were not on children at the moment.

'We can go home,' said one of them, and there was a general silence.

'Home,' said another. 'I suppose we can.' She burst out crying.

Across the next few days Marjorie heard this everywhere. We can go home. And sure enough, word came from England that the Princess Elizabeth was to be crowned queen, with no one to oppose, or at least any who did oppose kept silent for, it was said, the great majority of the people welcomed her. The Spaniards who had swaggered through London with King Philip had sickened them of foreigners. Elizabeth was the daughter of good King Henry and his English queen.

Now they heard that it was the Catholics who were leaving England, for they could not bear to stay in a country under the rule of a heretic. The Pope, it was said, was angry

246

and fulminating against Elizabeth, who had declared that the Church would be as it was in the last days of the reign of her father, but quite what she meant by that no one was sure. All the laws concerning religion which had been passed by the late Queen Mary were quietly dropped, and it became permissible once more to have a bible in English and to read it. Now Queen Elizabeth was head of the English Church. The Pope, who had enjoyed a brief reinstatement under Queen Mary, was once more only the Bishop of Rome.

John Knox's congregation in Geneva began to settle their affairs and make arrangements to leave. There was a constant stream of people to the house, making their farewells and promising to stay in touch wherever they found themselves. Gradually the gatherings in the church became thinner and thinner.

Some chose to stay. They had lost family and businesses and homes in England and had built up a new life. There was nothing to take them back. But hardly enough remained to justify so many preachers and John and Marjorie could see that soon he would not have enough people in his congregation to keep him busy, or to earn enough to feed his family.

'Would you like to go back to England?' he asked one day.

It was after they had eaten. A fire had been lit, for the evenings were becoming cold, and the girl had brought in candles. John sat with a book on his lap but he was not turning the pages. Marjorie was rocking the baby gently in his cradle to send him to sleep, and her mother was sewing a shirt for John.

'Would there by a position for you?'

'I'll write to William Cecil. He has been in the service of the new Queen this long while. He could find me a position. She heard me preach once.'

'At court?'

'The year before King Edward died, when they were still pretending all was well. He had been reconciled with both his sisters and they were present at one of the Christmas sermons I gave.'

'Five years ago. It is a long time.'

'She will remember me,' he said confidently.

And oh yes, remember him she undoubtedly did.

Before they had an answer from William Cecil they had another visitor.   Master John Grey came to them as a messenger from Scotland. He also was on his way to Rome on behalf of the Queen Regent and the Parliament in Scotland. The Queen Regent was asking formally for the Pope's approval of the appointment of a new bishop in Scotland.

'Do you hear this, Marjorie,' said John, slapping poor Master Grey on the back.   'The Queen Regent's messenger to the Pope also carries a message for me from the Lords of the Congregation. Was there ever greater economy, to use your enemy's messenger as your own? Tell me, Master Grey, do the Lords pay a rent to the Queen Regent for the use of her messengers? Which part of you belongs to them on this journey? Your right leg perhaps, is under lease to the Lords of the Congregation while the rest of you serves her.'

'I only do as I am bid,' said Master Grey, stiffly.

'Take no notice of my husband. He will have his jest. Come, there are refreshments ready, and a bed. Is your journey to Rome so urgent you cannot spend a few days with us?'

The message to John was simple enough, and it was the same as before. The political climate in Scotland had become relaxed, they said. They thought it was time for John to return and build a new Church. They were confident the new Queen Elizabeth would support a Protestant Church in Scotland. It would diminish the power of the French and make the border safer.

'William Cecil would certainly be willing,' said John to Marjorie in bed that night. 'He was always of the opinion that friendship between Scotland and England would serve better in the long run than any treaty with France or Spain. A great chance was missed when the betrothal of Edward and little Mary fell through.'

'So you are of a mind to go back to Scotland?'

'No,' he said. 'I will not go back. They made a fool of me before. Do they think they can do it again? If we leave Geneva we do it together and we go back to England. That's your country, Marjorie and I was happy there. I will have nothing to do with Scotland, or her quarrelsome Lords of the Congregation.'

Master Grey received his answer and continued his journey to Rome.

They found he had also brought a letter for Master Calvin, who sent for John. Wrapped up warmly in his cloak, he would frequently trudge to Master Calvin's house and spend hours there and return in a bad temper, his head aching and his stomach upset, not, he said, from the thin wine which Calvin gave him, but from the sour arguments they had. Master Calvin was pressing John to leave Geneva.

'He tells me I am hardly needed here,' he said, dismally. 'The congregations dwindle daily as people leave for England. He is right. There will soon be no one for me to minister to, except you and your mother.'

The letter which Master Calvin had received from Scotland was asking him to persuade John to return. It was clear he badly wanted rid of John and was seizing on this as an excuse. The row over *The First Blast* had not diminished. A letter of complaint had come from William Cecil on behalf of Queen Elizabeth. When the Lords of the Congregation in Scotland wrote to Master Calvin to persuade John to return to Scotland, he felt no hesitation in pushing this.

More messages came from Scotland, but still John refused ' We will go to England,' he said.

There came, eventually, a reply from William Cecil. There was a private note for John, full of brotherly affection and remembrances of times past, and his greetings to Marjorie. But the official letter, written on behalf of Queen Elizabeth, refused him leave to return to England.

The Queen has read your broadside against the rule of women, and takes deep offence. Her Majesty can see no reason why a woman should not rule as well as any man. Also, it would appear from your writings that you support armed revolt against an anointed ruler. The Queen considers that you would not be a suitable person to reside in England. Permission is refused.

'I am not wanted anywhere.'

Marjorie thought of cold foggy Edinburgh and sighed. 'You are wanted in Scotland.'

'I wonder, anyway,' he said, 'whether I could have fitted back into the English Church. Remember the arguments with Cranmer, dear dead Cranmer, about the prayer book? Queen Elizabeth has decreed its use in the churches. I could not use it.'

'Create a Church in Scotland that fits with what you think it ought to be.'

'A church without bishops.'

'No one to tell men what to think.'

'A church where all men are equal.'

'Do it, John.'

But still he dithered.

He wrote again to William Cecil. This letter was less courteous than before, as if he knew that there was no harm in letting his spleen show, for the answer would be negative, whatever he wrote. He did go so far as to suggest he would write another tract about the rule of women and make an exception for the new Queen Elizabeth. He was willing to be persuaded that perhaps in time she could prove herself worthy to rule almost like a man. Marjorie, scribing this, doubted if Master Cecil would show this letter to the Queen.

Master Cecil was always a man of tact. Some things he would keep to himself. But it was sent anyway.

'My *First Blast* has blown away all my friends in England, I think,' John mused. Marjorie kept quiet. It mattered little to her whether they returned to England or went to Scotland or stayed here in Geneva as long as they were together.

It became difficult to find people to carry John's letters to England. Some of the people leaving told him straight out they would not carry messages, for they now believed he was out of line with the general mood. It was known that he would not find favour in England and those that would associate with him might find themselves at a disadvantage.

In the end, with more letters coming to persuade him, and with reluctance, John made the decision to go to Scotland. Marjorie and her mother both wanted him to delay until the spring, but he set off in January for Dieppe.

'The sooner I am there the sooner I will find a ship,' he said. He had many friends in Dieppe and would find a good welcome there. He arrived safely, sending Marjorie immediately a message to say he was comfortable once more in his old lodgings. He had found Dieppe in a state of great excitement, for there had been a resurgence of the new Church in France, and many people had turned Protestant. In every town there were meetings in private houses and the Catholic churches were struggling to persuade people to attend mass. The preacher in Dieppe was taken ill, and John once more had a ready congregation.

Marjorie knew from the exuberance of his letters that he was enjoying this enormously. The time for action had come, and he was relishing it. The last few months in Geneva had been dismal for him, but now in France he had found his energy again. Dieppe, a vibrant port full of Scotsmen, was congenial to him and he could forget the miserable months he had spent there previously.

He wrote that he had sent another long letter to William Cecil accusing him of being a mere time-server and a

251

defector from the truth, and would suffer like all dissemblers. So would he issue John with a passport through England or not?

Marjorie groaned when she read this and took out her annoyance on some bread dough, which suffered so much from the battering she gave it that it refused to rise. Why were the cleverest men sometimes the most *stupid?* It was no surprise to her that Master Cecil did not reply and perhaps it was no surprise to John either.

And then, in late April, she had a letter from John to say he had found a ship and was leaving Dieppe early on the next morning's tide, to travel direct to Leith in Scotland.

Chapter 42

Dundee, 7th May 1559
Dearest Wife,

We landed at the port of Leith on the Second day of May. It was a balmy morning and Marjorie, if I were a sentimental man I would say that the countryside had bedecked itself to welcome me home, for on our short journey to Edinburgh we passed through lanes lined with may blossom of white and pink, like a bride welcoming her husband, and the air was scented with the may and with the yellow gorse which stretches out over the hill.

By the evening I was being welcomed to the house of Master Barron. Aye, Marjorie, I have forgiven him for being one of the bearers of the abortive summons that was before. He was right glad to see me, and I him. He and Mistress Barron are thriving and more eager than ever to see changes here. The Queen Regent has issued a decree that all must attend the mass, but the people resist this.

Word of my coming had spread and I barely had time to shake my stiff limbs back into life ere the people came to greet me. Your husband's reputation has gone before him Marjorie.

The Edinburgh streets are plagued with swaggering aggressive Frenchmen, acting as if they owned Scotland, which indeed in many cases they do. It is like the time when the Spanish came to London when the Tudor married her prince, and we all know what came of that match made in Hell.

But now Scotland is in thrall to the French. A Frenchman keeps the Great Seal, a Frenchman is Comptroller of the Mint, and the Regent's brother the Cardinal of Lorraine has the benefices of the abbeys of Melrose and Kelso. All the wealth of those great abbeys, pouring out of Scotland to keep him and his kin in luxury. Money that could feed the poor.

Word comes also that the Scottish merchants trading through Rouen are required to pay tolls, against all the rules of their ancient liberties.

Marjorie lowered the letter onto the table.

'Mother, it is worse than we thought in Scotland.'

'I give no thought to Scotland,' said Elizabeth. 'John should not have gone there. His place is with us.'

'I hope he can contain himself.' Marjorie picked up the letter and read on.

I learn that the Queen Regent has overstepped herself. She has had her daughter proclaimed Queen of Scotland and England. She believes, poor deluded woman, that it is only a matter of months before the English people drive Elizabeth out and proclaim her daughter Mary as the true Queen. She has the support of the Pope in this.

But Marjorie, I know the English. Since I persuaded one dear one to unite her life with mine I understand their thinking. They will not change again. They are tired of religious quarrelling. If their Queen says no pope then they will content themselves with that.

I had a few days' rest in Edinburgh and then travelled north. I crossed the river by the Queen's Ferry. Do you recall, my Marjorie, that day you and I went there to let the wind blow away the noise and troubles of the city and walked on the beach? We thought then our travels and our troubles were at an end but God willed otherwise. And then another crossing of the Tay into Dundee.

Marjorie, everywhere I go I find the petty churches thriving, those that I established when we were here before. The light is shining throughout Scotland. The Lords now truly do speak for the Congregations. Dundee has come completely over to the truth. The Regent has demanded of the Provost that he hand over the local preacher to be tried for heresy, but the Provost gave warning

254

to the preacher, who fled in time. I stood at the Mercat Cross with the Provost by my side.

'Good people,' he cried. 'Is it your wish that John Knox be granted the right to preach in Scotland?'

The crowd roared. Marjorie such a roar of welcome was never heard in the land. Aye, they cried, aye aye. And your man stood for two hours at the Mercat Cross preaching the gospel with tears running down his cheeks like a daft bairn.

I have come home, Marjorie.

I break off this letter, for I can no more write for the emotion that fills my heart.

Much has happened since I laid down my pen. I will make haste to finish this for I hear of a messenger that can take it.

The Regent has demanded again that the preachers (and she names me) appear before her to answer charges of sedition. Does she know what she does? This is the question all around me are asking, for surely she knows we have the support of the people and they will not allow their preachers to suffer. But some say knowing this only makes her more anxious to punish the men she calls heretics.

Word comes that St. John's town of Perth has declared for the Congregations. Well named is that town. The Regent has sent word there demanding that the Provost, who is Earl of Ruthven, I do not think you met him, hand over the preachers. The Provost is a brave man and has retorted he can command men's bodies to prostrate themselves before Her Grace, till she was satiate on their blood, but cannot command them to act against their consciences. Was that not well said, Marjorie?

The Regent has now repeated her order that all the preachers appear before her at Stirling. We have had great discussion amongst ourselves and have agreed that we will obey her summons and all of us will go, and the gentlemen of every county shall accompany us.

To this end we travel tomorrow as far as Perth.

Marjorie stopped reading. 'That is all he says. He sends his affection to you and the babies.'

The women sat silently. Marjorie thought, this letter has been some days coming. What happened when they met the Queen Regent. Did she order his imprisonment? How could she not? Will there be another letter, or will the silence tell me the worst. He is in peril, there, no matter how bravely they talk. The Lords of the Congregation deserted him before. They can do so again.

Her mother rose stiffly and lifted her candle. Marjorie listened to her make her slow way up the stairs to her room.

Marjorie pulled the remaining candle close.

I wish you were by my side. My head is full of words, but my bed and my arms are empty without you.
Kiss the bairns for me.
Your loving husband, John.

Chapter 43

When the next letter came she tore frantically at the seal. She glanced at the dates in the letter. He had still been alive on the twelfth of May, and free to write.

Perth 9th May
My dearest,

At last I have a few minutes peace to write this to you.

We are arrived in Perth and I have been made comfortable in the house of the Provost, that brave man who so defied the Queen Regent. We were a happy convoy of peaceable men, gathering support on the way. It was agreed that John Erskine, the Laird of Dun, (who asks to be remembered to you) would ride on ahead and acquaint the Regent with our intention. He has the tact to speak to her where I could not.

He has gone to Stirling to tell the Queen Regent that such a large force came only in peace. He was to assure her our people were unarmed. They come only to praise God. It was hoped that he would parlay her into withdrawing her demands.

You should have seen the crowds which joined us on the road with every passing mile. It is a holiday jaunt for them, and glad I am to see such high spirits. It is that lull time in the year, Marjorie, when the crops have been sown and little more can be done save to wait for them to grow, and the weather has been fine, and people are in festive mood.

You have not been this far north, I think, and the beauty of the country would astonish you. We travelled over a vast flat plain and I could see this was wealthy farming country. Beyond us rise range upon range of hills disappearing blue into the distance.

There's a different world up there, beyond those mountains. I travelled through that part before. It is a world of great beauty, a land of mountains raising their heads to the glory of God and water in abundance for man and beast. When you go there and you are all your lee lain in the wilderness you can believe it is as close to Eden as God could create on earth.

And Marjorie, I give you greetings from an old and dear friend, John Willock, who has joined us here. He wishes you joy. He came with some of his congregation all the way from Glasgow, and a hard journey they had of it, for they had to travel through the mountains to avoid the Queen Regent's men.

Man, man, he told me, just three days ago you and I were both denounced as outlaws at the Tron in Glasgow. We enjoyed much merriment, as you can imagine. We are outlaws many times over, but can be hanged only once.

We were preparing to travel on to Stirling, when a message came from Master Erskine. The Queen Regent had changed her mind, and asked that we remain at Perth. She will make better arrangements, came the message.

A cheer went up and people prepared to rest. Many have turned and headed for home. They are not needed. I have snatched a moment to begin this letter to you.

10th May

This morning comes Master Erskine himself, riding hard, and in a state of some distress. The Queen Regent has reneged on her first decision. We were supposed to have appeared at Stirling. Since we have paused at Perth, all are now denounced as outlaws.

She has put all to the horn, inhibiting all men under pain of high rebellion to assist, comfort, receive or maintain us in any sort. She has force of arms, French arms, to back it up if necessary. What are we to make of a woman who twists and turns like the very serpent itself?

Erskine took us aside and told us privately one of the reasons for his particular distress. Lord James Stewart was by the Queen Regent's side, apparently approving everything she does. Others of those that called themselves the Lords of the Congregation were there also. They now refuse to declare for us. They stand by, waiting to see what will happen.

'I knew it, I knew it,' raged Marjorie. She burst into tears. Eleazar began wailing as if he sensed her distress. She gathered him into her arms and hushed him. Nathaniel paused in his play and looked anxiously at her.

'If I was there he would not be so deluded,' she said aloud, but something in her voice only caused the child to cry more loudly.

I say nothing of my own hurt in this, but grieve for the people they have betrayed. It was aye thus with these Scottish lords, dither and delay, they never know their own minds.

I am to preach tomorrow in the Church of John the Baptist, which stands at the centre of Perth. The perfidy of the Regent has given me my subject for a sermon.

12th May
Beloved it is with a heavy heart I write this.

The Church of John the Baptist is large, but more people thronged to hear me than it can hold. I preached, as who could not after what had happened, of broken faith and lies. I talked of cowardice on the brink, and those who put self preservation before fidelity. I thought of those who had begged me to come to Scotland and build a new Church, and at the test were found wanting. I attacked the idolatry of Rome, for now that I am back here I am convinced that at the root of all the ills of Scotland and England lies the hand of the Pope.

I was heard with loud acclamations and agreement by the congregation. This is how it should be, I believe. I think back to the respectful way the King of England and his courtiers would listen to me in his chapel and it had no more effect than a passing shower, and I used to long for some honest heartfelt reaction. I had it in Perth.

Marjorie, it grieves me to tell what happened next.

I finished the sermon, and the service came to an end, and I left the church well satisfied. It was dinnertime and the congregation began to disperse. All would have been well, I think, but for a priest's folly and a forward child. I did not notice the Catholic priest. The first I knew of it was the Provost drew my attention.

'He is going to say the mass,' the Provost told me. 'He does it every day at this time. Shall we stop him?'

'Nay,' says I. 'My quarrel is not with one deluded man. Puir wee soul that puts his trust in gewgaws. Let him do his bobbing and bowing. There will be none to hear him.'

For you see Marjorie, all were leaving and going their ain gait, and I followed the Provost back to his house where we were to dine, and then there was screaming behind us at the church. When we ran back we found a lad on the ground groaning, with women kneeling and keening round him and blood everywhere. One of the women leapt to her feet and pointed a finger at the priest, who was cowering beside the altar.

'Ye have killed him.'

I saw that the priest had opened up the tabernacle on the high altar, and had spread out his altar cloth and on it stood the pyx and crucible.

'The boy protested,' sobbed a woman, whom I have since learned is his mother. 'He told the priest he shouldna do it.'

'He threw a stone at the tabernacle,' claimed the priest.

'Ye struck him. Ye have killed him.'

'You fool, man,' I said to the priest. 'Gather up your toys and come away.'

The boy was already struggling to his feet but the damage had been done. Word spread through the crowd who came surging back. They laid hands on the tabernacle and smashed it to the ground. I pushed the priest and his helper out the side door of the church as the rascal multitude came surging back in through the main door in a great roaring wave. As God is my witness, Marjorie, that was the cause of the trouble that followed.

From inside the church came the sound of breaking wood, and even as we stood there, one of their small statues came flying through the window, smashing the glass which scattered over the paving stones at our feet and splintered into a thousand glittering pieces. The image, a thing of plaster and paint, broke in two and lay there in the dust. I cried to the people to stop. Even as we spoke a stone flew through the air and just missed the retreating priest. And then a veritable rain of stones into and out of the church, and we had to save ourselves. I saw wildness in their faces. They were blind with anger, twisted and inflamed, people have claimed, by my sermon. I tried to calm them, Marjorie. I went among them and tried to talk to them, but they had their blood up, and there was no stopping them.

They smashed all the idols in the church, and broke the windows. Then they surged like a shoal of fish on to the monastery of the Grey Friars which stands down by the river. The mob rampaged through the buildings and looted everything they could lay their hands on, blankets, curtains, beds, stools, tapestries, silks, cooking vessels, and food.

Salt beef, great puncheons of it – consider the time of year – May, when every other cupboard is bare. So much food, they say, in the stores of the Friars as would feed every man, woman and child in all of Perth and the country around for a whole year. They are sworn to poverty and that is how they live. And cellars of beer, wine and ale, on which many in the mob got drunk.

There was no violence there. Some of the heat had gone. We went among them, I and my fellow preachers, and spoke harshly, threatening that no man should steal as much as a groat. They let the prior and his brothers leave with as much gold and silver as they could carry. There were only eight of them. The town guilds have distributed the food amongst the poor.

Soon the crowd had sated their anger, and the streets became quieter. I went round with John Willock and the Provost's men to see what could be done, to help with the injured still lying in the streets. The women were bandaging up many bloody heads, but none have died and for that we can be thankful.

When dawn came and all was quiet I left them and went out of the town alone and found a place by the fast-flowing river, and wished that my sorrow could be washed out to sea as easily as the scraps of broken timbers the water carried. I prayed to God that this day's work will not damage our cause.

261

I did not intend such destruction or spoliation. Should I stop preaching if it has that effect? My friends mouth platitudes at me to say the riot would have happened had I not been here, but that is not true. I know it is not. The priest would have said his mass to an empty church and no one would have cared. The boy who was injured would not have been there, save to hear me. He would not have challenged the priest, and the priest would not have struck him. It was my presence that caused it. I am the flint that caused the spark that set alight the tinder, which is dry and waiting.

The Queen Regent will already know of this. The battle will be great and I am come to the brunt of it.

Your loving, sad and lonely husband, John.

'Is he safe?' Elizabeth stood in the doorway.

'He was when he wrote this letter.'

'Is there fighting ?

'There will be, I think.'

'What banner do they march under?'

'None. I don't know. He doesn't say.'

Chapter 44

My Dear Beloved,

Scotland is in a state of civil war.

We heard how the Queen Regent expressed her rage. I will sow Perth with salt, says she. She ordered out her troops, thousands of them. They are under the command of a French general named D'Oysel. They marched within ten miles of the town. The Provost of Perth who up until then had been as brave as the people, began to lose heart. 'Who will defend us?' he cried. 'They will fire the town. We shall be destroyed.'

'The people can defend the town,' said Erskine. 'Be brave, man.'

But when word came that Lord James Stewart and others of the nobility had equally condemned the rioting in Perth, and would support the Queen Regent, the Provost asked me to leave the town. I refused to do so. I will not abandon my flock at the first sign of danger. I have moved to the inn where I am treated like royalty, and indeed the quality of the viands here makes me wonder when I recollect the puncheons of salt beef gone from those rogues the Grey Friars. The innkeeper brought word this morning that the Provost has taken his family and left the town. It is said he has gone to join the Queen Regent and sent his family into hiding. Word of this has travelled round the town and people are beginning to panic. They throng the streets carrying as much as they can and head for the forests where they believe they will be safe. Your husband makes a peaceful dinner for he has no possessions and no cart or mule onto which to load them.

Not all are going. There came John Erskine to join me in drinking a glass of ale. 'Well, John,' says Erskine. 'It's just you and me, looks like.'

Marjorie, you may know your man makes a poor figure with a sword and being near blind cannot wield bow nor musket, so he takes up the fight in the best way he knows how.

263

By the Word. And so while Erskine gathered up all the able-bodied in the town who were willing to fight, I gathered some brave women who can write, and dictate to them. We scribed and copied long into the night, and the letters have gone flying to all the airts and pairts of Scotland, aye and beyond in great abundance. We asked that the printing presses copy and distribute these letters. Some may already have reached you in Geneva.

Marjorie called to the girl.

'Run out and see if there are any pamphlets or tracts come from Scotland. Ask at the stationers' shops. At the printers.' She read on.

I have appealed to the Roman Catholics everywhere to hear our cause in peace, to understand us, not to do battle against innocent men, women and children who are not traitors but only wished to worship God in our own way. Letters to the Congregations of Scotland and all Protestants throughout the land, not to stand aside any longer, but to join in the fight, if fight there has to be.

I caused one to be distributed among the French troops in the Queen Regent's army. I begged them to go home. This is not their fight. They have no right to meddle in quarrels in a land that is not theirs. I make it clear I do not blame the Scotsmen fighting with the Regent. They are contracted to do what they do.

I composed a letter to the Queen Regent herself, assuring her of our loyalty to the Authority of Scotland, and we deplore all bloodshed, but all we ask is that we may be allowed to worship, as our consciences tell us, in peace and liberty, God and the Lord Jesus in all His simplicity. Better, we think, to expose our bodies to a thousand deaths than to hazard our souls to perpetual condemnation by denying Christ Jesus.

We caused that letter to be laid upon the cushion of the Regent in the Chapel Royal at Stirling, where her heart might be opened to it. We wait, Marjorie, and daily more people flee Perth and the Regent is gathering her forces. But so too are we. For this morning early came thousands of men towards the town. At first we thought it was the enemy, and the men and women stood ready to defend the town, and then they came closer and they hailed us, and they were our own.

They have come from all over, willing to fight, from near and far afield, for I am hearing accents in the town I cannot follow, for they are speaking the Celtic tongue of the north and west. Those that can have found lodgings, for there are empty houses enough for them left by the people who fled, but they are so many that they have camped in the fields round the town, to the despair of the farming people who but a few weeks ago sowed the fields. But they give their animals willingly to feed this army.

And so we wait. I stop this for I must sleep. More anon.

We waited for an assault on the town. Erskine as you know has been in warfare before, though modest man that he is he does not speak of it. He has been given charge of the defences.

It is my task to put hope into the hearts of the men, who begin to weaken, discouraged by the defection of the Provost. All the long day with Willock's aid I have rallied the men. Their hearts were uplifted and their arms strengthened because they knew that victory would be ours not by our own strength but by the will of He who created us. They know that the men they will have to fight are seasoned mercenaries and Frenchmen in the pay of the Regent. They know the fight will be hard.

Then came a message that Lord James Stewart and the Duke of Argyll were both on the outskirts of the town seeking to parlay. We bade them come, and gave them a guarantee of safe passage.

It was indeed Jamie and the Duke. They had ridden hard to reach here from Stirling and we welcomed them most heartily.

'You have come to join us?' I ask.

'I cannot do that' says Jamie Stewart. 'You are rebels.'

'We are not,' says I, and would have argued but Jamie grasped my arm and silenced me.

'We come at the Regent's bidding to ask the cause of the gathering of this multitude of people.'

'Why, she has been told often enough,' says I. 'It is to resist cruel tyranny devised against the town of Perth and its inhabitants. She shall sow the town with salt, did she not say so?' All the men within earshot roared at that. We repaired to my lodging and sat talking far into the night. My argument to them was twofold. First, I reminded them that the religion of the Queen Regent was not the true religion but a superstition devised by the brain of man. Second, that she would not prosper in her tyranny, for the hand of God was against her.

'Brave words from a man who has no army,' sneers the Duke. 'Only a rabble of farm workers and boys.' I do not like that man, Marjorie, and will not trust him. I believe him to be my enemy.

'We cannot support you,' says Jamie. 'Whatever the cause you persuade these men to fight for, it is rebellion. Would you loose the four horsemen on our land?'

'It is my land too,' says I.

'Disband your army,' says Jamie. 'The Frenchmen will not enter Perth. All will be pardoned for their actions. Let all be quiet and no one will suffer.'

'Is that the Regent's promise?'

'It is her promise.'

I do not trust the word of the Regent, but I trusted Jamie and told him so. So after consideration we accepted the terms. We would disband our army, and the Queen Regent would leave Perth alone.

I preached once more in the ravaged church, to persuade the people in Perth to accept the terms of the treaty. They are unhappy about it, but they trust me. The Regent's negotiators stood at the back of the church, watching. Lord James looked grim. I think he knew, as we all knew, that this was only a pause. Only the naive could believe that the fight was over. The Regent's party left, to go back to Stirling to report that we had accepted the terms of the truce.

A rider came to us, having spread his news on the way through the town. The Earl of Glencairn, our greatest supporter, was practically within sight of the town. He had come with thousands

266

of men from the west and south. We learned that the Regent's herald in Glasgow had ordered them to turn back under pain of treason, but they marched on regardless through the forests and mountains to reach us. I sent them word to wait. They are not needed. Not yet.

All is quiet now in the town. I am preparing to return to Edinburgh as I write this to you. I will finish this when I reach there for there will be an abundance of messengers.

Later

We are not to go to Edinburgh. None of us will. I had put this my letter to you in my pack with my books and was making ready to leave when we heard pistol shots. We all rushed out of the inn into the street in time to see soldiers riding through the town. The Regent's soldiers. People were screaming and I could make out the words. They had killed a boy. Women were hanging on my arms and trying to drag me this way and that.

I saw troops marching towards the church. They gathered there and paused, looking round them and then settled down on the ground, as if they intended to stay.

D'Oysel sat on his horse, talking to Erskine. He looked down on us disdainfully, as if we were no higher than the worms beneath his horse's hooves.

'Is this the worth of a Regent's promise?' roared Erskine.

'Not so,' said the French general. 'These soldiers are Scotsmen. There is no Frenchman among them, save myself. And I,' he raises a white gloved hand, 'I do not fight.'

'They are mercenaries in the pay of the Regent.'

'Just so,' agreed the general. 'But it was Frenchmen she promised not to send. She keeps her promise.'

'They kill innocent children.'

'One boy. It was an accident. A pistol discharged without intention. There will be no more bloodshed. The town is in our hands now.' And it very evidently is. There were soldiers everywhere. There was no siege, for, trusting the word of the Regent, the town had not been defended.

Soon also, Lord James Stewart and the Duke of Argyll were back. 'Which side, Jamie?' I asked. The Queen Regent claimed that a promise given to heretics was not a promise at all. This double-dealing has sickened Lord Jamie. 'We will join you,' he said. His heart was heavy, I could give him no comfort.

This is civil war and it is not of our doing. We have sent word to all the Congregations. All are to meet in St. Andrews on the first Sunday in June. St. Andrews is where it all began for me. It comes full circle.

I seal this with a heavy heart. My dear. I think of you daily.

Your loving husband, John.

Chapter 45

Saturday

We hear that the Regent has moved from Stirling to Falkland, thinking perhaps to block our road to St. Andrews, for that palace commands all the crossroads. This delays us, for we have had to travel round the coast. I travel with a small party, only Lord James and his household and the Earl of Argyll and his household.

Were we travelling for a more joyous purpose our hearts would be light, Marjorie, for the sky is blue and the land is lush with wild campion and roses. The coastline here is high out of the sea and birds nest on the cliffs below us. Our men climb down and gather the eggs. Wherever the cliffs break we descend to harbours round which shelter the houses of the fishermen.

Everywhere we are welcomed. The people here remember well that devil Cardinal Beaton and the hypocrisy of his rule. Wherever 'e go I preach and share communion with all, and at every village . . . people listen quietly and just as quietly remove all the artefacts Roman worship from their kirks. We leave behind heaps of ken wooden and plaster idols and the good women with buckets whitewash obliterate the paintings of saints on the walls.

In Dysart all the people flocked to welcome us. It was their priest, old Walter Myln, who was so grievously burnt, and they weep yet for him. They told us how he had been dragged from his bed and thrown in the dungeon of the castle in St. Andrews and would have died there had not he been instantly charged with treason and burnt with no chance for any rescue or argument. They that saw his arrest had gathered round the castle to protest and they saw him die.

They tell me he hardly knew what was happening. His wits deserted him in the end but he greatly suffered in his body. He should have died peacefully in his bed. They built a cairn at the place. The Archbishop ordered it taken down, but the people built it up again. And so in the end it was left alone. We mourned

*together, and watched the sun go down, until the cries of children
returning from their play stirred the women to their duties.*

*As we travelled, a messenger came from Archbishop Hamilton,
the most abandoned of all the scoundrels, warning that if I enter
St. Andrews I would be shot on sight. This has caused Lord James
and the Earl to pause, for they have only quiet households with us,
and have no wish for a fight. There is no way of knowing who the
town will choose to support.*

*But Marjorie, the threat by the Archbishop has been made
personally against me. So they leave it up to me whether or not I
go forward. Go forward I must. I have not come this far to turn
back now. It was in that town I first came to the dignity of a
preacher. It was there I found my voice. And it was from there I
was taken a prisoner. How long I continued prisoner, what
torment I sustained in the galleys, and what were the sobs in my
heart is not now the time to recite. This only I cannot conceal, that
when my body was far absent from Scotland, in my heart I knew
that one day I would return there and preach, in open audience, to
my people, though it were the last thing I did before the breath was
taken from my body.*

*Thus the Lord has brought me to this place and for this
purpose. I need no protection from man nor weapon. I will do it,
and none will prevent me.*

And so to rest. Tomorrow we enter the town of St. Andrews.

Friday.

*We entered the town quietly on Sunday. None tried to stop us.
The Church of the Holy Trinity was full to overflowing. The whole
town was there, the Provost with all the Magistrates and Bailies
and all the people. They were crushed together and men hoisted
the little children onto their shoulders the better to hear me.
Marjorie, I saw kent faces for these were the people I had
ministered to before I was rudely wrenched from their midst, and
the bairns I had taught are now young men with bairns of their
own.*

I preached on the cleansing of the temple. I likened the corruption in the temple of Jerusalem to the corruption of the Church in Scotland. They heard me in respectful silence. I left then and returned to the quiet of my room, where I sank down and wept. I stayed quietly indoors, for it was as if all the strength had drained out of me.

The people heeded my words. Under the direction of the magistrates they cleared the Holy Trinity and all the other kirks of the false idols of Rome. They stripped the priory and the monasteries. The monks did not come to any harm. They are known in the town, and people do not harm those who are familiar to them, only strangers.

They built a pyre on the place where Walter Myln died and threw on all the gewgaws and watched them burn. Then they began on the cathedral itself, while the Archbishop cowered in his house. Under cover of the distraction, the Archbishop fled to join the Queen Regent at Falkland. So much for his threats, eh Marjorie. Shoot me on sight, would he?

The Congregations have come to our aid. Over the river Tay from Dundee have been brought small cannon and also came men who know how to use them. All week it is as if men have rained from the clouds. All of Scotland is with us, noble, gentry and commons, united under one cause.

It was agreed that we would not wait for the French Army which was marching forward under Monsieur D'Oysel, but go out to meet them. We did not want to be trapped here once more, to await the arrival of a French fleet at our back. There has been some fighting, at Cupar. Many of the men who left their homes to join us little thought it would come to that, but when called on they set to with a will, and the Frenchmen had to plead for a truce. Encouraged, our army marches towards Perth, to relieve that suffering town. All are clear what they must do.

Written in haste on the road to Perth. Our cause is just and God is on our side.

Your loving husband, John

The letter smelled of the messenger's satchel leather. He sat at Marjorie's table and mopped up the last of the stew with his bread but could tell her nothing of consequence, only that he was the last of a relay of messengers who had ridden hard to bring letters from Scotland. His fellows were fanning out across Europe. He had letters for Master Calvin and Mistress Locke still to deliver. Mistress Locke? John had time to write to Mistress Locke?

After he'd gone, Marjorie folded the letter and tucked it into the bosom of her dress. Beside her the baby snuffled in his cradle and on the bed Nathaniel muttered in his sleep.

Outside the streets of Geneva were silent.

She blew out the candle and climbed into bed beside Nathaniel, curving her body protectively round him and pulling the quilt tight.

Chapter 46

We arrived on the outskirts of Perth and there was still light and time for the town to be surrounded. The cannon which had come from Dundee were now put to good use, and salvos fired from both the east and the west towards the town. None did any damage, and were not intended to. Scotsmen were not going to fire on their own kinsmen. These shots were to warn, and warn they did.

The next day the captain of the garrison sent out word that if the Queen Regent failed to relieve him by Sunday at noon, he would surrender the town, provided he and his men could leave unmolested, and flying their flags. This was agreed to. We settled down for the night, and waited. No help came from the Regent. The next day at noon, the mercenaries who had garrisoned Perth in the name of the Regent marched out under their commander. Many of them slipped free of the ranks and joined us.

We entered the town to the cheers of the townspeople. They had been under occupation for four weeks, four weeks of tension and anger. The men who had entered the kirk called me to them. 'Look at this,' said they and showed me the board that had been set up by the Queen Regent's priests to form a new altar. He turned it over and there on the other side were the marks of the gaming table. A gaming table used as an altar! It is appropriate.

I climbed once more into the pulpit and preached to the crowd a service of thanksgiving for a bloodless victory. We now intend to travel to Edinburgh, avoiding Stirling for of course that impregnable castle is still in the hands of the Queen Regent.

It is essential the capital be in our hands. More later.

Edinburgh.
Marjorie, I weep as I write this.

Marjorie paused in her reading and rose and drifted into the room where John's desk stood, left tidy now and clear of papers. She picked up the quill which still lay there, put down when he had drawn a line under the last tract he had been writing before he left. In his absence she had seen that document safely through the press.

She longed desperately to be with him. He needed her. She should have left the children in the care of her mother and insisted on going. But it was too late now. Now she only had his letters, and as long as they kept coming she knew that at least some days earlier he was still alive. Perhaps there would come a time when there would be no letters, and she would wait until at last one came from a stranger to tell her that her husband was dead.

For he was in the midst of a civil war, and in an emotional state, and she knew that when he was thus he was at his most reckless, and who knew what he would do?

We were near Scone Palace where the Bishop of Moray lives. He it was who was most blamed for the death of Walter Myln. Some of our men, those who had known the old man, were determined to be revenged for his death, and marched on Scone with the intention of destroying it.

'We must stop them,' said Lord James, agitated. 'It is the most ancient abbey, and the place where all our monarchs are crowned. It must not be destroyed.' He prepared to forestall the men, but before he could do so, word came that the Queen Regent was moving to block our way at the bridge of Stirling. Lord James and his men rode fast towards Stirling.

'Go to Scone,' he cried to me, 'Calm the men.' We arrived to find looting had begun. The Bishop was at the abbey pleading with the men to spare the ancient building. 'Spare it,' he pleaded. 'Spare it, and I and my sons will join your Scots Parliament against the Regent.'

I could see that it would be to our advantage to have the support of men such as this with us and not against us. The abbey was no longer used as a Roman chapel. It has been quietly mouldering with neglect and was no threat to the new religion.

274

As the men heard me they quietened down and it looked as if all would be saved. But some of the mob had found buried in the abbey a great number of idols hid on purpose to preserve them. The men of Dundee and Perth could not be satisfied till the whole ornaments of the place were destroyed.

I sent word to Jamie and he came back and we laboured diligently to save the buildings and eventually all was quietened. But the next day some poor people from round about in hopes of spoil came up to the abbey. They were threatened by the Bishop's servants and grew angry. One man spat at the Bishop. I still had my hand raised to stop the man's action when with an oath one of the Bishop's sons who was standing by drew his rapier and ran the man through.

The mob, that might peaceably have left, rampaged back into the chapel, and with nothing more to restrain them, they ran amok. The old, old abbey of Scone, once the crowning place of the kings of Scotland, burned to the ground. We tried hard to save it, but it was beyond human endeavouring. For that I am sorry.

And so we are come to Edinburgh. Today I stood in the pulpit of the High Kirk of St. Giles in Edinburgh and gave thanks. My sermon was a quiet one, of reconciliation, for that is what we strive for. Afterwards John Willock and I shared communion with the people.

I think back to when Master Wishart came to preach, and he was captured and burnt without trial. I come and I am treated as a saviour. But, oh Marjorie, my dear, I wish with all my heart that it were George Wishart here instead of me. He was the better man.

The only people in the kirk to hear me were our own followers. The people of Edinburgh stayed away. They wait, as we all wait. The fighting is over for now. The Queen Regent and her French troops have withdrawn to Dunbar and our men have gone home. There is hay to be gathered in and crops to be harvested.

Edinburgh Castle is for the Regent. The governor has dropped the portcullis and drawn up the drawbridge, but no matter. The people can live without the castle, and the castle will not fire on the town. But I know, we all know that it is only a matter of time

275

before the French come to support the Queen Regent and to recapture Scotland. And then there can be no reconciliation.

Chapter 47

John Knox left Pittenweem in the early morning. On a quiet shore some distance from the town a wherry was waiting to take him out to the ship. As the *Heron* weighed anchor and the wind caught her sails William Knox left his place on the bridge and took his brother below to his cabin.

'Man, man,' he said as he reached for the tray of bread and cheese which had been left for them. 'All Europe rings with your exploits.'

'The French. What of the French?'

'They're gathering together an army to ship north.'

'Do the English know this?'

William laughed at that. 'The French flaunt their intention. They will defend their own. Even in the Protestant countries the rulers are uneasy. They say you are overthrowing a queen to establish a republic like the one in Geneva. And if one ruler can be legitimately ousted, why not all?'

'We do nothing of the kind,' said John. 'It is no revolt against the Queen.'

'Don't tell me,' said William. 'Tell them.'

He put John ashore at night on a shingly beach and almost without breaking the rhythm of his strokes the oarsman skimmed the wherry back over the water to the *Heron* and soon she too had gone.

The path was well worn and he had no difficulty in following it by starlight. He had been on Lindisfarne before, preaching. When he could see the mainland in the distance he settled himself down in a hollow in the sand dunes. He was back once more on English soil, and still a fugitive. Smiling, he fell asleep to the soft shushing of the waves.

He woke to the sound of voices. He stretched and straightened his clothing, and joined the small group where they stood at the end of the path which disappeared into the water. They looked at him and then looked away again. One of the women carrying a basket of eggs gave him two, which he swallowed raw, cracking the shells in his hand and pouring the contents into his mouth. He offered her payment. She only glanced at the Scottish coinage which he offered and then back at him, and drooped one eyelid in a conspiratorial wink, and shook her head.

The sun rose. They stood quietly and waited as the faintly rippling water in front of them was turned pink and then golden by the sun. The water calmed and retreated to right and left of them and slowly, slowly, the path became visible. The seabirds on the surface were no longer afloat but standing on firm ground. The women did not wait till the causeway was clear but splashed through the shallow water, the men following.

At Berwick Castle he was expected and hustled immediately into the presence of Sir James Croft, captain of the garrison.

'I had expected to meet Sir Henry Percy,' said Knox. 'Who will speak for Queen Elizabeth?'

'Sir Henry is at Norham. He will not meet you. Why did not one of your Lords come himself, instead of sending a preacher?'

'I ask again, is there someone who will speak for the Queen?'

'No one.'

'Then I have had a wasted journey.'

'There is food and wine here. Let's eat.' John was hungry. They sat and ate. Presently a door opened and a man entered, closing the door carefully behind him.

'Well, John?'

John leapt to his feet. 'Cecil, man, I am pleased to see you here.'

Sir William Cecil held up a hand. 'I am not here. And neither are you.'

278

'Oh but he is,' said Sir James Croft. 'The whole country knows he is here.'

Cecil sank down in a chair by the fire and swore. 'So much for secrecy.'

Knox drank up the last of the wine and moved over beside his old friend.

'I am sick at my country house,' said Cecil. 'If it is known I am here, negotiating with a rebel, then all the treaties in Europe will be torn up.'

'I am not a rebel.'

'In the eyes of Queen Elizabeth you are.'

'Do you speak for her?'

'I speak for no one. Queen Elizabeth cannot help you. All England is horrified at the destruction wrought by your people. All the monasteries and abbeys and simple village churches destroyed at the hands of drunken mobs.'

'Intoxicated with the truth.'

'Incensed by your preaching.'

'Would you have us do it your way, hand out the wealth to crawling courtiers and slimy favourites. Thankfully we have none such in Scotland.'

'Gentlemen,' murmured Sir James.

'We are desperate. The French fleet may arrive at any time and overrun the whole country. We cannot fight them without help.'

'You seek the Queen's help now. Do you not recall your own words, that a woman is not fit to rule a kingdom? Unfortunately, if you have forgotten, Queen Elizabeth has not. When your name is mentioned in front of her, she can quote your notorious pamphlet word for word. Do not think that aid will come from her.'

'England's borders will never be safe as long as the French occupy Scotland. William, William, we talked about it often enough. Scotland and England in unity would be powerful in Europe. None could threaten us.'

279

'England has a treaty with France. We cannot aid France's enemies.'

'We are no enemy of France, we seek only freedom of worship.'

'Is that not a matter between you and your ruler?'

'She is not her own woman. Man, there is no office in the land but is held by a Frenchman, and the wealth leaves the country and pours into the coffers of absent Frenchmen who hold the posts as a sinecure and do nothing. We must rid ourselves of them.'

'Then Scotland must deal with it herself.'

'Can you send us men?'

'Send an army to invade a foreign country? To intervene in a civil war? That would be folly.'

'If you cannot give us men, will you give us arms?'

'England must keep what arms she has for her own protection.'

'You will need to protect yourselves when Scotland is used as a base for the invasion of England. Lend us money.'

'The English exchequer, alas, is empty. There is no money to spare.'

'Something, anything. We do not ask that your queen support our cause openly. If she prefers to tut and cry on the sidelines that is up to her. Send us some soldiers but say they came without permission. Your queen need know nothing about it. She can dismiss them. Call them renegades.'

Cecil looked shocked. 'That would be deceitful.'

'Aye. Is your queen above deceit?'

'She is a good Christian woman.'

A servant came in and whispered something to Sir James. Rising, he said. 'You will excuse me. I have word that our French visitors have arrived.'

John leapt to his feet. He looked accusingly at Cecil.

'Frenchmen? You are negotiating with Frenchmen? Or are they come to arrest me?'

'Neither,' said Cecil wearily.   'They are an envoy travelling to Scotland from Paris with letters calling on your Lords of the Congregation to desist from their rebellion. Your Queen and the Dauphin, who I would remind you is also now your King, have no doubt about the nature of the troubles.'

They could hear in the distance the ceremonial of the arrival and reception of the French envoy.

'He is welcome,' said John bitterly.

'A few trumpeters and banqueting costs little and ensures good humour.'

To the accompaniment of faint music from the great hall beneath them they talked on. Finally, William Cecil called a halt.

'We get nowhere,' he said. 'I must return early tomorrow morning.'

'One thing you could do for me, William, if you would be so good. My wife, Marjorie, she is still in Geneva. May she have a safe passage through England to join me?'

'You would expose her to a civil war?'

'She will be kept safe. It is her desire to be with me. And mine to have her here.'

Cecil's expression softened.

'She is a good girl. You are a lucky man.'

'Aye.'

John spent a restless night and rose early the next morning, weary. He took his leave of Sir James. William Cecil had already gone, leaving no record of his visit.

'A substantial wraith indeed.'

John left Berwick ahead of the French envoy. He would have to return to Edinburgh and report that his rhetoric for once had achieved nothing.

Save that soon Marjorie would join him, and for that he was grateful.

Chapter 48

The lodgings which the English ambassador found for Marjorie and her family in Dieppe were on a street parallel with the harbour and her window looked out over the rooftops to the sea.

In the bay there were two French warships. Soldiers were gathering in the town, billeted on everyone who had space to spare. They were mustering all along the coast, it was said, waiting for the signal to board ship and sail for Scotland.

In the taverns the mercenaries boasted of their past exploits and grumbled at the delay. If they were forced to wait much longer the fighting season would be over. Besides, who wanted to face the northern sea once the winter gales came? They liked to keep firm earth below their feet, as who doesn't? Some talked of the prospect of plunder, but the word was that Scotland was a bog of a country, full of stunted people in rags, and France got the worst of the deal when the Dauphin married their Queen. Some of them, older and mindful that half of Dieppe was settled by Scotsmen, sat in quiet corners with their ale, and they were the ones the tavern girls eyed sideways and served first with an extra flounce of their skirts.

Marjorie's landlady told her all this. She was from the south, and it took Marjorie and her mother several days to attune their ears to the accent, though young Nathaniel picked it up quickly. Madame was uneasy living in a town full of Protestants. Her husband had brought her here, but now she was a widow, she was saving to return to her beloved Marseilles.

The merchants were unhappy too. They hated change. The rising in Scotland was bad for trade. The cursed Scots have revolted against God himself, said the more devout of

282

the soldiers. The merchants raised their eyes to heaven, but it was more to assess the direction of the wind than to seek the mind of God. The new religion appealed to these pragmatic Scottish merchants, John had once mused to Marjorie. It removed the power from the priests and put it into their own hands. Those men who traded in wines, wool, spices, silk, fine porcelain and anything else that people desired could not control the tides, nor the desert sandstorms, but now they could decide for themselves how, and how much, to worship God.

Marjorie's mother went up to bed with the boys. Madame boiled milk with nutmeg and the two women sat in the quiet kitchen. They had much in common. Madame's husband had been a soldier at one time; Marjorie's grandfather and father had been soldiers in the service of their kings and her brothers still fought for the new Queen of England, Elizabeth. It's in the nature of men to fight. It is in the blood.

They finished their milk, and Marjorie went up to bed. She found her mother was still awake, sitting by the window looking out towards the harbour where a myriad of torches still flickered. The town was quieter, save for the occasional yowl of a cat and the screech of an owl.

'Marjorie, what will be waiting for us in Scotland?'

'We'll find somewhere pleasant to live.'

'But what of John?'

'What of him?'

'This rising, this rebellion, do you think it will succeed?'

'They have God on their side.'

'They always say that.'

A ghost had risen up in the room, a ghost with an eyepatch and an oath and a marching song.

'How many women have lost their husbands, their fathers, their sons? How many more will die? But I have lived my life wondering if there was something more,

283

something I could have if only I tried hard enough, if only I was good enough. Is there a way to keep men safe?'

Marjorie touched her mother's hand and felt it for heat in case her mother was feverish. The journey from Geneva had not been easy. Geneva had been warm; here in Dieppe it was colder. Her mother could not stand changes in temperature as easily as the young ones did.

'I am not ill. I am sick at heart. I have been a wicked woman, Marjorie. A woman should cleave to her husband. It is what the Holy Bible says. And now my husband is dead and I cannot seek his forgiveness until I meet him in Heaven. He lied to me.'

'Who lied to you?'

'He told me I did right to follow my conscience. But was it my conscience, Marjorie? Or was it the devil tempting me?'

Which *he* was she talking about?

'Marjorie, I will not come to Scotland with you.'

'Mother, you talk nonsense. Now, go to bed. Shall I bring you some hot milk?'

'I have been in the wilderness. It was my punishment. It was a false Heaven. You must make your home in Scotland without me.'

'I was depending on you to look after the boys.'

'Any sensible girl can do that.'

'The boys love their grandmother.'

'They must learn to do without. As we all must. That is what I have learned in life. We have to do without. I will travel with you as far as York. I have more than one daughter, more than one son-in-law, though none so dear.'

She wiped her eyes and rubbed her wet fingers into the lap of her nightshift. 'I will make my home with one of them.'

'You will always have a home with us.'

'No. It is not fitting. I have not been comfortable this long time past.'

284

'Why did you not tell me before?'

Her mother sighed. 'I will not see him again. There, I have said it. I will never see him again. Let me sleep now.'

They did not speak of the matter again, and true to her word, Elizabeth Bowes left them at York, and Marjorie and her sons travelled on into Scotland.

Chapter 49

Marjorie listened while John told her of his mission to England. A mission that had failed.

'I am pleased that Master Cecil is well. And I thank him for granting me the safe passage home.' That indeed he was grateful for, to have his own dear companion and bedfellow beside him again. He pulled her close and wrapped them both tightly in the quilt.

'But John,' she asked. 'Why did Lord James and the others send you?'

'Why should they not send me? I am no use on a battlefield.'

'But why did not one of *them* go? There are ties of blood are there not? Queen Elizabeth would have listened to them.'

'They did not want to make an official approach. It had to be kept secret.'

'But it was not, was it? You were easily recognised.'

'Yes,' he said. 'I am well known in those parts.'

'But of course such a plea could not have come from the Lords of the Congregation. Is it not treason to invite England to intervene in our cause?'

'How can it be treason?'

'To invite in a foreign power? At least William Cecil had the right of it there.'

'We only sought to borrow arms and money. We would have repaid.'

'The Lords will not hazard their families and lands, however great the cause. Lord Jamie, could he be seen to plead for an invasion into his own country, against his sister, the Queen? Of course none of them would go. They did not dare.'

'You wrong him, Marjorie.'

'Do I? But why should they not send a priest, known for his inflammatory ideas, known to have a renegade past, one who has advocated that a people have the right to rise up against a monarch?'

'That is not how it was.'

'And then when it all goes wrong, they can disown you. They can claim you went without their knowledge or consent.'

'There was no such underhand dealing.'

'You place too much trust in these men.'

They were silent then, lying side by side. Marjorie was angry with herself for speaking. She understood that he was a man of impulse, a man who saw his way clear and believed in what he was doing. But he was also a man with an agonising conscience who forever afterwards questioned his own actions.

Her husband's weapons were not swords or guns. His weapons were words. Angry words and soft words, words spoken and written, words in Scots and English and Latin, words to persuade, or frighten, or comfort, or rouse. He believed in the word of God, and in his own words, and too much in the words of others. Words could hurt. And now words had failed him.

She slipped her hand into his. 'I'm sorry.'

He pulled himself up in the bed, and kissed the top of her head.

'You are dearer to me that life itself.'

'I am glad to be home,' she said.

*

By now the harvest was in. Men were available once more for fighting. The six-month truce was due to end in December.

The Queen Regent left Holyrood Palace and retreated with her troops to Leith. The Lords of the Congregation

287

called on her to cease to fortify that town, to remove the foreign soldiers. Her reply came. The conquest of Scotland was not by force, considering it was already conquest by marriage, and Frenchmen were naturalised Scotsmen and not foreigners.

She was in a strong position. The port of Leith controlled the sea routes into the River Forth. She was able to interrupt the food convoys without any difficulty. She only had to wait, there on the coast, to welcome the French fleet which was due any day.

In Edinburgh they held a council.

'I must keep them to the point, Marjorie,' said John, as she brushed down his clothes. 'They have, all of them, been asking my opinion and I have given it. Some of them favour deposing the Queen Regent. It must not happen.'

The preachers counselled caution, John loudest of all.

'We have said all along we do not fight the Queen or the Regent, her mother, only her power over the religion of the people. You must have one aim, and one aim only and that is freedom of worship. Meddle in the government of the realm and you meddle at your peril. One aim, and one aim only, clear to all, else who is to believe our good intentions?'

He came home to tell Marjorie that once again his rhetoric had failed.

An Act of Suspension was written and signed and read out at the Mercat Cross to a silent crowd. John stood in the High Kirk of St. Giles with Marjorie by his side.

'Look at them,' he gestured to the workmen round him, who were using the long nave of the church to build scaling ladders. 'They intend to attack Leith. It is whistling in the dark. We have not the men, nor the money to pay them.'

With the Queen Regent deposed, they proclaimed the Duke of Chatelherault, he that was also Earl of Hamilton, as regent. Chatelherault, who was next in the line of succession should Queen Mary die without an heir, had to proclaim to the crowds that he had no wish to be King. He was without ambition. His only wish was that Scotland be ruled in a peaceable and prosperous way. John raged for most of the day.

'The man gave up the regency before for a French title and French lands. It was he who broke the siege of St. Andrews. Am I to serve under such a man?'

'He's on our side, John,' said Lord James mildly.

'Now perhaps. As long as it suits him. Who is to say he will not turn again? The man will change his coat when the pockets are empty. I say again, if the Queen Regent is willing to accept the wishes of the people in the matter of religion she should be appointed again.'

The Queen Regent refused to give up her title and Scotland now had two regents, with two armies who fought minor skirmishes whenever they met.

The Lords of the Congregation struggled to hold their people together. The men lost heart and melted away, back to their homes. The mercenaries among their troops rioted, for they had not been paid, and there was fighting among them. One of the Duke of Argyll's men was killed in an argument.

Marjorie acted as scribe for the countless letters John sent out to all the towns, begging for money. John himself was exhausted and never well. He lay on the couch with hot compresses on his belly to ease the pain in his gut, still the old complaint of the kidney stone begun when he was in the French galleys.

He would pause in his dictation as a spasm of pain hit him, his face white and beads of sweat standing out on his brow. He crushed her hand in his and she waited quietly for his pain to pass. She learned quickly to make sure it was her left hand he held, else she could not have continued writing. When the worst of the spasms passed he would sip the mixture the apothecary had prepared, and use all his energy to relax. Then he would begin dictating again and she would recommence her writing.

Funds came in. Anne Locke, now back in London with her family, bustled among her friends, and sent money. Their old congregations in Frankfurt and Geneva, though greatly diminished, sent money. But it was never enough. The Lords of the Congregation sent to their homes for silver to be melted down to make coins. This would have helped but the workers at the mint sneaked out at night, carrying as much of the silver coin as they could, and slipped away to join the Queen Mother, as she was now known.

Among the letters which John answered was one from Berwick. It was said that William Cecil was chasing a rumour that Queen Mary and King Francis had quartered the arms of England not only on their dinner plate and jousting scutcheons but also on their official seals. Had Knox any knowledge of this?

Yes, replied John, writing to James Croft. On the ship that had brought him from Dieppe to Scotland in May there had been just such a seal for use in Scotland. The captain of the ship had shown it to him. Did not Queen Elizabeth know this? And he pleaded once more for arms, or men, or money.

The French army attacked the cannon on the Crags and captured the guns. They chased the men right into Edinburgh itself, and slashing right and left with their swords and firing off their pistols haphazardly, killed several people and injured many more. The cobbles ran with blood.

On the 6th of November, a food convoy for Edinburgh was intercepted by the French, and although James Stewart and Chatelherault's heir, the Earl of Arran attempted to recover it, they were beaten back with heavy loss of men. There followed a wearisome, restless night.

'We cannot stay, Marjorie,' said John on his return from the desperate debate with the Lords. 'Can you pack up our few things and be ready to leave?'

'Are you in danger?'

290

He shrugged. 'The people resent us. They resent the constant danger of the Frenchmen at the very gates. They cannot live like this. I do not blame them.'

It was only a few days later that the last of the Congregation's troops straggled out of the city, with the Lords at their head. It was a sad day. John walked with the Lords while Marjorie and the other women for their own safety slipped quietly through the back streets carrying their bundles of clothes. The women and children hurrying to see the fun paid them little heed. One woman caught Marjorie's eye, and perhaps recognised her, for she spat in the gutter and passed on. They could hear the people jeering.

'I never thought I would see the day when our fellow countrymen would rejoice in our destruction,' was all John said to this when they were once more united on the road to Stirling.

The Lords set up a Council of State with Chatelherault as Regent at its head. On this council were all the great Lords, Arran, Argyll, Erskine of Dun, and Lord James Stewart himself. Included were the Provost of Dundee, and the Provost of Perth, forgiven for his earlier cowardice. Many of the lairds who had supplied men and arms were on the council.

John Knox was not invited to join.

'I am no further use to them,' he told Marjorie. 'I am to confine myself to preaching.'

He preached to packed congregations. He preached controversially. 'Success would have been ours,' he said. 'We trusted in God and God was with us. When no lords or earls were with us, we were strong. Then the great Duke joined us and we heard that we should put our faith in men and arms. Where was God in this? And who was the greatest enemy? He now has come over to our side. I am sure he repents of his deeds. But he has not suffered as we have suffered in the cause of the Lord. God has punished us as a result. We must once more put our trust in God and not in men and we will prevail.'

All knew that the Great Duke he spoke of was Chatelherault.

The Council finished their deliberations and dispersed.

John and Marjorie travelled to St. Andrews to be with their children. There they spent their days writing, always writing; letters to go out to all of Europe, pieces for the broadsheets which were avidly read all over the country. John's rousing words kept the printing presses busy. They wrote appeals to all the people of Scotland.

If ye will not be slaves to have your lives, your wives, your bairns, your substance, cast at their feet to be used and abused at the pleasure of strange soldiers - then, brethren let us join our forces and both with wit and manhood resist these beginnings, or else our liberties hereafter shall be dearer bought.

When they were worn out with writing, Marjorie and John often walked up to the clifftops and looked down on the town. In the wind came the constant sound of masons' tools, for the townspeople were working among the rubble of the cathedral, lifting and hauling away blocks of stone to build new houses.

Christmas came and went, with no cheer, for there was nothing to cheer about. The armies were bogged down in winter quarters. In truth what remained to the Congregations could hardly be called an army.

'It's true what Argyll said. We have only farm workers and boys. No match for seasoned soldiers.'

In January they heard that D'Oysel was advancing on St Andrews by way of Dunfermline. A French detachment, estimated at upwards of four hundred men, crossed the River Forth to join D'Oysel. The Congregation's men under Ruthven and the Earl of Sutherland hastened from Cupar. They met and the Congregation suffered heavy losses. The French rampaged across the countryside, looting and killing. John Knox rode hard to join the dejected men and try and put heart back into them. He accused Arran of failure as the leader, and all but accused him of cowardice. It did little good. The hired infantry failed them, and only the exhausted men of Fife fought to defend their homes, much of it in hand-to-hand combat with the French raiding parties. It began to look as if St. Andrews was not safe.

Marjorie found her husband one day sitting quietly in the garden looking out over the water with a letter in his hands.

'I am not wanted,' he said.

She took the letter from his unresisting hand. In it Lord James was suggesting that it would be better if John did not preach. His sermon at Stirling had offended the Duke of Chatelherault. The sermon at Cupar had offended the Earl of Arran. If he was going to offend the Hamilton family, suggested Lord James, it were better that he not preach at all.

Chapter 50

At the end of January they began to evacuate the town of St. Andrews. D'Oysel was moving along the coast towards the town. He was approaching Dysart. Soon he was within six miles of the town. The harbour was crowded with small ships taking on more people and their possessions than was wise, and preparing to sail north to safety.

But even as the evacuation began the outlooks posted on the cliffs gazing south saw on the horizon the sails they had dreaded.

'All is lost,' said John. 'It is the French fleet.'

They counted five ships, and no doubt there would be more out of sight. The townspeople watched as they tacked westwards towards the mouth of the River Forth.

And then there was a great shout of triumph which spread through the crowd and echoed down into the town below. For those among the crowd with sharper eyes than John could make out that the ships were not flying the flag of France.

They were sailing under the English cross of St. George.

Word came soon enough by messengers galloping into the town. The people learned that the ships, a small number but effective, had seized two French ships and an ammunition boat. They had cut off the supply lines of the French army in Fife. D'Oysel retreated. He marched his men back to Stirling and thence to Leith.

Later came news that there had indeed been a French fleet on its way, but it had been scattered by the winter gales. 'God looks after his own,' exulted John Knox.

The Queen Mother left her forces in Leith to make what they could of such fighting as remained and retreated to the safety of Edinburgh Castle. They said she was ill. Some said she was dying

After the English fleet came a large number of soldiers. The French troops now faced an army of united fresh English professional soldiers and newly heartened Scotsmen. The fighting was desultory and soon over.

John and Marjorie laid down their pens and rested.

The Queen Mother died in Edinburgh Castle. Valiant in her cause to the end, she had been sending out messages to her French commanders, written, it is said, in milk, to be invisible on the list of drugs which her letters ostensibly requested.

With her death came the end of the French resistance. In June, only one year and one month since he had landed in Scotland from Dieppe, John Knox was among the dignitaries who welcomed the English envoys, including Sir William Cecil, into Edinburgh to sign the treaty between England, France and Scotland. All troops, French and English, would withdraw. Scotland was once more master of her own fate, with her own government.

The last of the French sailed from Scotland in July. John Knox led the great public service of thanksgiving in St. Giles, where all the nobility, the Lords of the Congregation, the gentry of Edinburgh and English visitors and all the people celebrated the great deliverance.

'Well, John,' said William Cecil afterwards as they held a quiet dinner for him and for Lord James. 'What do you do now? Will you live quietly in the country somewhere to minister to your flock? It was always your dream.'

John glanced at Lord James, who answered for him.

'We have demanding work for John,' he said. 'And for Master Willock and all the other preachers. They will need to draw up a new constitution for our church.'

'We have to have a new kirk,' said John. 'The English model does not suit the Scots. We will not have bishops.'

'Then who will make the rules?'

'The people will. It will be a Kirk run by the people for the people. They shall elect their own minister. The elders will be chosen by them also.'

'What do the people know or understand?'

'We will educate them. Every kirk shall have a schoolmaster appointed. The kirk here on earth will be taught not by angels but by men, and since the days of revelation are long gone, the only answer is compulsory education for all. Our universities will be expanded so that they study medicine, and we will found new ones. None shall any longer depend on the goodwill of men who have power over them. Every kirk will be responsible for the care of orphans and widows and those who have fallen into penury through no fault of their own. None shall go hungry.'

William Cecil looked cynical.

'Even Master John Knox cannot order God to provide a good harvest.'

'God will provide. But men will share.'

James Stewart caught Marjorie's eye and smiled. He raised his glass in a toast to her. Her answering smile was cool. She did not trust him, and he knew that she did not.

Chapter 51

Soon the English troops too had gone.

William Cecil and his party returned south with many expressions of goodwill on both sides. Henceforward Protestant Scotland and England would be friends.

No one spoke of the Catholic Mary, Queen of Scots and of France, dancing at her court at St. Germaine, who showed no wish to return to her northern kingdom. She refused to ratify the Treaty of Edinburgh. She mourned the death of her mother, but it was said rejoiced in the election of the new Pope.

The new parliament of the three estates, the Lords, the Commons and the Kirk, began their work of governing Scotland, and John Knox, John Willock and their fellow preachers settled down to draw up the Book of Discipline for the new Church of Scotland.

There was hope in the air. And hope in Marjorie's heart too. She was pregnant again and she and John could give thanks for their own private joy.

The future was all before them, to be made fresh and new.

~~~~~

Author's Note

There was everything to be hopeful about then. No one could know that within a short time the King of France would die and Mary, Queen of Scots would return to wreak havoc.

Not much is known about Marjorie Bowes. The men of her family are well documented but women of that era are mentioned in the historical record only in relation to their fathers, husbands and sons. Her marriage to John Knox, opposed by her family, was known to be happy, but she died fairly young. After her death Elizabeth Bowes moved to Scotland to help look after the children.

There were, of course, many other preachers involved in the Scottish revolt of 1559/60. John Knox wrote the first history of the Reformation in Scotland and perhaps inevitably comes across as the most charismatic of them, and he and John Willock as the most influential.

The political situation in Scotland in the mid-sixteenth century was fast moving and complicated. Historians can make some sense of it now that they know all the outcomes, and can make a reasonable estimation of the actions and motivation of everyone involved. A novelist can only describe events as seen through the eyes of her characters. I have tried to be true to the historical record, but this is a novel and not a textbook.

Readers wishing a fuller picture are referred to the bibliography.

Bibliography

Cowan, I.B. (ed.) *Blast and Counterblast, Contemporary Writings on the Scottish Reformation,* (The Saltire Society, 1960)

HMSO, Department of the Environment Guide to Norham Castle, 1966.

Ives, Eric, *The Reformation Experience, Living through the turbulent 16th century* (Lion Hudson plc, 2012).

Knox, John, *The History of the Reformation in Scotland,* (1982 edition, The Banner of Truth Trust)

Lamont, Stewart, *The Swordbearer, John Knox and the European Reformation,* (Hodder & Stoughton, 1991)

MacCulloch, Diarmid, *Reformation, Europe's House Divided 1490 – 1700* (Penguin Books 2003)

Mapstone, Sally & Wood, Juliette (eds.) *The Rose and the Thistle, Essays on the Culture of late Medieval and Renaissance Scotland,* (Tuckwell Press, 1998)

Moorhouse, Geoffrey, *The Pilgrimage of Grace, The Rebellion that shook Henry VIII's Throne* (Weidenfeld & Nicolson 2002)

Picard, Liza, *Elizabeth's London,* (Phoenix 2003)

Reid, Harry, *Reformation, The Dangerous Birth of the Modern World* (Saint Andrew Press, 2009)

Skidmore, Chris, *Edward VI, the Lost King of England,* (Phoenix, 2007)

Vives, Juan Luis, *The Education of a Christian Woman,* ed. & trans. by Charles Fantazzi (The University of Chicago Press, 2000)

Whitley, Elizabeth, *Plain Mr. Knox,* (1972 edition, Scottish Reformation Society)

Youings, Joyce, *Sixteenth-Century England,* Allen Lane, Penguin Books, 1984).

CPSIA information can be obtained
at www.ICGtesting.com
Printed in the USA
FSOW01n0906081017
39661FS